Willow Tree Tears
Mandy Eve-Barnett

PRAISE FOR MANDY EVE-BARNETT:

"Well-written and a fun read."
-Book Hoarder
"An intriguing story."
-Author S. Bavey
"A fun romp."
-Author Nina Munteanu
"Masterful, captivating, and entertaining."
-Author Anthony Avina
"A spell-binding page-turner."
-Author Lisa Nikolits
"Mandy Eve-Barnett makes a damn good first impression on readers."
-Author Julio Carlos

Acknowledgments:

Thank you to Kendra Edey (barrel racer) for her kind and informative advice,
And to Nancy Bell for believing in my manuscript.

Chapter One

Madison rode toward the Calnash AG event Center's rodeo ground entrance. Her leather saddle creaked as she shifted to ensure Amber Fire's girth was tight. She weaved through the crowd of people and horses, attending the year's final rodeo in Ponoka, Alberta. The action eased her tight muscles a little, although her heart rate increased the closer she came to the center ground. Horse sweat, manure, dusty earth, and hot oil from the food vendor stands competed in the warm August air. Madison pulled her mount's reins to the right to avoid a child running to catch a balloon escaping into the expansive clear blue sky. Amber's head came up as the bright yellow globe blew across her ears.

"Steady, girl, it's just a balloon."

Bending down and giving a quick pat to the horse's neck, Madison gave a gentle kick to encourage Amber to walk on. As her head came up above the horse's mane, a brilliant white shirt blazed on her right. The shirt covered a broad-shouldered, dark-haired man walking away from her. Among the usual checkered shirts, Stetsons and suede jackets, the brilliant white was a startling contrast. Another time she might have lingered to watch, but the man disappeared into the crowd. She shrugged, she had more important things to attend to, primarily her biggest competition, Charity Deeks. *I have worked too hard to let it go now. I'll show her who's a winner.* As if on cue, Charity's high pitched, patronizing voice sounded just behind her.

"I've got it won, Madison, nobody can beat my time...including you."

She grimaced at Charity's shrill voice grating like a knife blade against slate. All the smart comeback comments she rehearsed in front of the mirror that morning vanished from her mind. She sat struck dumb as Charity laughed and turned to ride away. She managed a single sentence just before her enemy was out of earshot.

"Better not boast too loud, Charity. I'm taking this all the way to the podium. I'm the barrel racing champion, this year."

Charity swung around pulling her horse's mouth and making the poor animal whinny.

"No way, Madison the best girl will win, and you know it."

"You haven't won until we see my run time, so keep a close eye on us, and watch me win this final round."

Madison's nervous excitement transferred through her body to Amber Fire, and the horse's muscles tensed in anticipation as they walked to the starting line. Madison's attention broke for a split second as another flash of bright white caught her eye again. *Who wears white to a rodeo?*

With a shake of her head, she focused once again on the task in hand. She steadied herself and gave a good kick on Amber's sides, knowing they needed to blast out of the alley to pick up as much speed as possible before crossing the electric eye. Her horse's hooves thumped on the hardened earth as they flew into the area, throwing up dust. Her knuckles cramped as she gripped the reins and laid low over the horse's neck, heading for the first barrel, the money barrel. She encouraged Amber forward, and a hard sharp turn got them around the first barrel perfectly.

She kept her eye on the upcoming obstacle. On to the next barrel. Her horse's muscular body fully extended for the sprint. Hollers of encouragement sounded from the crowd. Clods of dirt flew up as Amber curved sharply to the right. Madison drew her knee up out of the way, her body tense, and her mouth dry. *Mustn't hit it, stay up, stay up.*

The finish was just ahead, and she leaned low and let Amber do her job. The crowd's shouting and clapping filled the hot air, rising to a crescendo as she passed the finish line. Madison brought Amber to a halt at the edge of the arena in a cloud of dust. As her horse blew through its nostrils, Madison held her breath and looked up for her displayed time. It would mean the difference between a cash prize, a saddle and buckle, or a long drive home in disappointment.

She had to beat Charity in this third and final run to cinch the championship. They had been neck and neck all season long at rodeos throughout Alberta, taking a point here and there from each other to make the top score. Charity had run her heat three riders before Madison, giving her the time she needed to beat. She'd practiced extra hard with Amber Fire over the previous weeks and had actually beaten the exact time Charity ran in her previous heat. Practice was one thing. Making that time in the arena was another. A championship win would further the success of Willow Sway Ranch, Madison and her father's quarter horse stud's popularity would increase and another trophy on the mantel was always welcome.

Madison's heart raced. Sweat ran down Amber's neck. The crowd murmured in anticipation of the display lighting up. She focused on the scoreboard and gave a whoop of delight when the numbers confirmed she ran the fastest time. The crowd cheered in unison with her. She patted Amber's neck and nodded at nearby spectators as they congratulated her. The announcer shouted above their roar, stating she was the year's champion. Madison twirled her hat in the air in acknowledgement before exiting the arena in triumph. Several riders rode up to congratulate them as they exited the ground.

Charity stood nearby surrounded by her family - all were dressed in the mandatory Stetsons and jeans of the rodeo crowd. Her mouth twisted into an angry snarl as she kicked up dust. It covered her red boots as she lashed out at anyone trying to console her. Her high-pitched squealing turned heads as she ranted.

Madison shook her head and turned away. Charity was always a challenging opponent, and a sore loser. She was in too good a mood to suffer a tirade from her foul temper though, so she soothed her young horse as it high stepped and moved sideways. She talked softly to ease the horse's anxiety. She found herself looking for the white shirt among the crowd, but instead saw Daniel striding towards Charity. Admonishing herself for letting a sudden pain burn in her chest, she turned her young horse toward the trailer unwilling to watch him comfort Charity. Her mount deserved a well-earned drink and brush down.

As Madison rode back to the trailer, she relived the moment she found Daniel and Charity together. The hurt nestled deep within her chest. She chided herself for not listening to her inner voice at the initial resistance she felt in going out with Daniel. In the end, it was her father, who persuaded her that one date would not hurt. The date was perfect - a surprise to Madison, who then doubted her instincts. Daniel's words echoed in her mind now as she rode back to the trailer.

"You need to be partying, Maddy. You're not an old woman. Why be stuck out here on the ranch all the time."

In all honesty, city life, with its crush and noise, was not her idea of fun. However, she resolved to bear it for Daniel. At the club, Madison's chest tightened, her ears rang, her heart pounded, and her palms grew clammy. She requested they leave.

"Don't be such a bore, Maddy. You're twenty-four, not seventy-four. I'm going to get a drink and find someone to dance with if you won't."

Before Madison could reply Daniel abandoned her, so she exited the club. Several pedestrians remarked on a commotion in the side alley drew her curiosity. She heard the words, "Yes, Daniel, oh yes, you're such a stud." Madison witnessed Charity and Daniel kissing, their passion obvious. Daniel's head turned at Madison's scream. He stumbled backwards, pulling at his unbuttoned shirt. He issued excuses, while Charity smirked and taunted her. Madison raced down the street, hot tears streaming down her face. Even through the hurt and pain, she expected him to run after her pleading for forgiveness, but there was no shouting of her name or hurried footsteps behind her. He hadn't called or texted her, and three months later, all she had left was anger and hurt.

Chapter Two

Lucio noticed the many appreciative glances that came his way, he knew he stood out from the crowd, not only because he did not don a Stetson, but also due to his white shirt rather than the usual plaid, or suede. His olive skin, dark hair and eyes were also different from the weather-beaten faces of aged cowboys and ranch workers.

With this being the final day of the rodeo, he focused on selling as much of the remaining boot stock as possible. While Angelo manned the stall, Lucio scouted around the other vendors noting their last day sales offers. There were a couple other cowboy boot sellers, but from American wholesalers and nothing close to his Italian leather line. With the sales percentages noted, he made his way back to his stall, listening the excited cheers of the audience. He enjoyed watching the horses, but only at a distance. He appreciated such magnificent animals, but a childhood accident made him wary.

He did not allow himself to be drawn into conversation with the many young women fluttering their eyes and laughing with their friends as he passed by. His experience with Mariella made him wary of opportunists. It would take time before he was willing to trust again.

He pushed his way past cowboys and cowgirls and children of various ages all kitted out in tasseled jackets, plaid shirts, ornately decorated boots, and Stetsons. Food vendors called out to passersby, the hot oil aroma mingling with body odor, horse sweat and dry earth.

Lucio enjoyed the rodeos, the rowdiness of the audiences, the grit and determination of the riders and the pageantry of the events. It was so unlike where he grew up in a small town in Italy, where life moved at a gentler pace for the most part, although religious celebrations did electrify the residents. His company followed the rodeo circuit from place to place offering exclusive and custom designed boots made with high quality Italian leather. He ran the company with integrity and respect for his suppliers, without them his boot line would not be so successful, or sort after.

He was startled by a hand clasping his arm. It was sticky with cotton candy leaving small fingerprints on the linen of his shirtsleeve. A woman looked up in horror at him as her son's hand grasped the fine cotton material.

"Oh no, Wayne, no you mustn't. I'm so sorry he wanted to see your cufflinks."

"Do not worry. He can look if he wants to. The design is my family crest."

Lucio bent down to the child's height as his mother held the boy's hands ensuring he did not spoil Lucio's white shirt again. Surrounded by young nephews and nieces at home, Lucio was comfortable with children and their exuberance. Family was the core of everything in Italy. It was a way of life. All generations of the family meeting together at gatherings and holidays. Wisdom passed down generation to generation.

The woman gave him a slow smile and said, "Well, thank you for being so kind. See, Wayne, it is a castle with a lion under a flag."

"Mom, can I have some of those?"

"Well, I don't think we have anything as fancy as a family crest, darling. Maybe when you grow up you can get shirts that need cufflinks. Now, come along let the nice man get on, we need to find your dad. Thank you again, and I'm sorry about the stain, I hope it comes out."

"It is nothing, I have many more shirts."

The mother and son disappeared into the crowd and Lucio turned toward the line of vendor stalls on the far side of the main arena. He glanced over to see a female rider run the barrel course. He appreciated her swift and precise actions and her obvious skill maneuvering the animal. Her auburn ponytail flapped at her neck as the animal galloped inside the arena, swerving this way and that.

When he returned to the stall, Angelo was juggling sales for three customers, so he ran to the other side of the display table to help. A loud cheer from the arena echoed through the building, he hoped the auburn-haired woman had won her heat. Once the rush ebbed, Lucio told Angelo to go grab some food and take a break. He made a cursory note of the inventory and rearranged the display. Totting up the figures, he was pleased with the day's sales. With a push for the rest of the afternoon, he hoped to have little to no inventory left to haul back to the warehouse. His cell phone rang, he looked at the display and took the call from the factory manager.

Upon Angelo's return, Lucio thought about his own hunger and sought out a hotdog stand.

Chapter Three

Colton's voice broke into Madison's thoughts as she arrived at the trailer. As the main ranch hand, he accompanied her to all the rodeos and looked after the horses and trailer on each trip.

"You beat that grumpy bitch then?"

"I sure did, and you would have laughed at her hissy fit. Making a face and stomping her feet like a three-year-old."

"Well done, I knew you would. Yep, she's certainly got a temper that one. You'd best keep your distance from her for a while. She was just the same in high school, if you remember?"

"Yeah, absolutely, I mean to keep away from her, don't need that kind of spite coming my way. My win was genuine. It sure felt good getting one up on her for once. Of course, I remember, she cornered me more than once by the school lockers. Without your protection it would have been harder for me to cope."

"And I was sure glad to be around to keep those school bullies in check. You deserved the win, Maddy, after her stunt with you know who."

"Yeh, well we won't mention that cheating lowlife, will we? And without your protection high school would have been more of a nightmare, that's for sure."

She led Amber Fire to the water bucket and removed her bridle so she could drink. Colton waved to a rancher approaching them. With the saddle off, she listened to Colton talk about Titan, the ranch's top stallion, as she wiped the horse's flanks.

She replayed her win and relished the feeling of accomplishment. A broad smile creased her face. *I won!* She waited on the announcements for each round ready to make her way to the winner's presentation platform later in the day. She had one more event to attend. With her horse groomed and watered, she had time to deal with her own hunger. She saw Colton shake the rancher's hand then turn back toward her.

"Jake wants to visit Titan in the next few weeks or so. He has a couple of mares coming into season."

"I guessed that was what he wanted when I heard Titan's name. He's a popular stallion, that's for sure. I'm going to get a hot dog. Do you want one, Colt?"

"No, I'm good thanks, had a couple earlier while you were in the arena."

"Thanks for thinking of me."

She laughed as Colt protested her hotdog would have been ice cold by the time she got back. "I'm only winding you up, Colt, can't you take a joke?"

"Yeh, whatever, Maddy. I'm going to muck out the trailer. No end of the glamorous life for some of us."

"You poor hard done by man."

Madison pretended to play a tiny violin between her thumb and index finger and ran as Colton turned to chase her. "You won't catch me today, Colt, I'm swift on my feet just like Amber."

"Get away with you, Maddy. Go and get yourself fed."

Madison left Colton preparing Pallo for the intermission procession. She sighed when she saw there was quite a line up at the stand. As her stomach growled, she tried to cover the sound with a cough. There was a stifled, deep toned chuckle behind her. Madison chose to ignore it. *Some people are so rude.*

At last, Madison was at the front of the line, and she ordered two hot dogs, the long wait and tempting aroma of frying onions and burgers had heightened her hunger. After squirting generous helpings of mustard and ketchup over the heaped onions on her dogs, Madison turned to leave. Her elbow caught the next customer's arm, smearing a yellow and red mess across a white tailored shirtfront. One plump hot dog hit the dust. As Madison bent to recover it, apologies flowing toward the shirt wearer, she noticed the most stunning leather boots on his feet. *They must have cost a fortune. If I had money I would get customized boots, I know just what I'd want too, a willow tree design to reflect our ranch's name.* The startling whiteness of the shirt flustered her...it was *that* white shirt. The one she glimpsed prior to her race. A rich Italian accent answered her apologies, as the scent of spiced cologne tantalized her nostrils.

"Ummm... Oops. I'm so sorry, damn it. Clumsy me. Let me get you a hotdog in apology and give you my info to send me the cleaning bill for that shirt."

"No matter, I'm sure the stain will come out, it is not the first one today. As you can see, sticky cotton candy fingers caught me earlier. However, if you are offering a free hotdog, I feel it is a good enough apology."

When he said 'good', he rolled out the 'o's in the word, sending a shiver down Madison's back. She stood up and raised her chin. Deep chocolate brown eyes met her gaze, a feeling of vulnerability washed over her, an unaccustomed and disconcerting feeling, but it felt great at the same time. *Your front is most certainly worth a look, white shirt man.*

She stammered, "Um... all right. How do you like it? Your hotdog, I mean." *Why am I so uncomfortable, I must look like a right idiot?*

He grinned at her, clearly amused by her embarrassment.

"By the looks of it, the same as you, with everything piled on top. You can never have enough...toppings."

Madison turned and discarded the spoiled hotdog into the trash to hide her face. *Is it his accent that makes everything he says sound suggestive? Or those gorgeous eyes undressing me? He is mesmerizing.*

She ordered a replacement hotdog for herself and another for the tall dark-haired man, who stood beside her with mustard and ketchup covering the front of his rather classy looking shirt. His eyes penetrated into her very soul, Madison was drawn to him like no other man. She tried to quash the feeling, disturbed at her susceptibility to a stranger.

"Are you sure I can't pay for your shirt to be cleaned, it looks expensive. I just won the barrel race championship today so take the offer while I'm in the money."

She passed him the hot dog, their fingers touched. An electrical tingle pulsed through her.

A connection washed over her, deep down in her soul. Again, warmth growing in her heart, it was thrilling and frightening at the same time. Someone brushed past her arm, breaking their gaze, and he spoke.

"I have plenty more shirts but thank you for the offer, and congratulations on your win. Please, do not worry yourself about the shirt, the hotdog is enough. I have come to quite like the taste." His eyes did not waver as he gazed at her.

Succumbing to an impulse not to have their meeting end, Madison said the first thing that crossed her mind. "Not something you have often then?"

"No, it is not. I eat them only when I attend the rodeos. My Mamma would be horrified to see me eat such food. She is very traditional in her cooking."

"What tradition would that be?" *What's wrong with you, he'll think you so nosy.*

"Italian. My parents were born and have lived there all their lives. Due to our business expansion, I have traveled far and wide. Tasted other cuisines, but my mother refuses to eat what she calls '*trippa*'. I soon learned to keep my outside life and home life separate. It makes life easier with my parents' strong traditional views."

They ambled past corrals occupied by cattle and horses, the distinct smell of animal pervading the air. They enjoyed the fair food, their pace easily matched. After a time, Madison realized they were walking toward the vendor's stalls in the exact opposite direction to her horse trailer and Colton. Captivated by his looks, accent, and that spicy cologne, she had not noticed how easily he led her.

"Sorry, I need to go. I'm at the opposite end of the center arena and have another event in thirty minutes. Nice to meet you...?"

"Of course, how rude of me. My name is Lucio Calligaris and your name, *bella*?"

Is he flirting with me? Or just being nice or being condescending, I can't tell. "Madison, my name is Madison Beauchamp. It was nice to meet you, Lucio. Do you ride?"

Lucio shook his head. "Horses and I do not get along. I have the scar to prove it. If I have time, I will come to watch your race. What race are you in next?"

"I barrel race but just finished my last run. My next event is to carry a flag and lead the children into the arena prior to their events."

"What is that?"

"We ride the horses around the ground carrying colored flags and the kids follow us in."

"So, to carry this flag you ride one handed? It is hard enough to stay on a horse with two hands on the reins."

"If you have a good seat, it's fun."

"Ah...a tight grip, but I would not call such a thing fun, Madison."

He looked down at her legs as he said *grip*. Madison grew hot. *Please, don't blush again, please. Be pleasant, but matter of fact.*

"So, what brings you to the rodeo, if you don't like horses?"

"I admire the beasts, but I would rather watch them from a distance. My company makes cowboy boots. In fact, the pair you are wearing are from an old line of ours, the *Garisa*."

"Really? These were a birthday gift from my father quite a while ago."

"Well, I would say he has very good taste. You wear them well."

Again, his eyes traveled up and down her body. Madison was shocked as her face flushed. *Am I really blushing? How old are you girl?* Even though she looked down trying to spare herself more embarrassment, she was thrilled by this man's attention. A small voice told her to be careful, but her rapid heartbeat told another story.

"Thank you, they are my favorite pair and after today's win perhaps my lucky pair. Well, it was nice to meet you, Lucio. I must be going. I mustn't miss the procession because it's an honor to be picked."

"I will not delay you then. *Ciao bella*. If I can get away from the stand again, I will come to watch you." His eyes held hers as he spoke.

He leaned forward as if to place a kiss on her cheek, but Madison drew back. She mumbled an embarrassed goodbye and turned away.

She walked away feeling his gaze. His eyes were all over her the whole time they were speaking. *Pull yourself together. He lives in another world without horses, manure, dust, and sweat.* She glanced into a truck's wing mirror, a self-conscious action. A large smear of dirt covered her right cheek. *Oh God, does he think I'm a small-town country cowgirl? Why worry, I'll never see him again.* She brushed at the smear and when it didn't disappear, she licked her palm and wiped it down her cheek. *Very elegant, he would be so impressed. He's probably laughing at me right this minute. Get a grip, Maddy, you have things to do.*

Chapter Four

C olt had his feet up, his Stetson pulled down, and was snoring when Madison got back to the trailer. Pallo's ears pricked up when she heard Madison call her name. A swift kick on the base of one of Colton's boots as she passed made him grunt but not move. Madison chuckled. This laid-back Colton was not the high-strung kid she knew in high school, some eight years earlier. He became her protector then and still was. She knew he wanted more from her than friendship, but she didn't think of him in that way. She valued his friendship too much to risk losing it to a failed romantic relationship.

Colton had offered to teach Daniel a lesson after he'd picked her up that fateful night from town. She'd cried all the way back to the ranch and he'd comforted her, saying she was better off. Although it was tempting, Madison told him Daniel wasn't worth getting arrested over. Since that night, Colton was extra attentive...shadowing her around the ranch, working beside her in the stables, and persuading her to go with him into town for supplies. They would sing along to the radio on the trip and joke around. It was comfortable but there was no spark for her. At first, it helped her get over Daniel, but now she felt Colton was getting too close. For some reason, that made her uncomfortable. Sometimes she even caught him watching her and she couldn't quite discern what those looks said.

Nervousness had Pallo stamping the ground. She was tired of standing and reacted to the sudden noise of the loudspeaker announcement for the children's events beginning in five minutes. Her young horse's reaction redirected her attention away from Colton.

After she checked Pallo's girth, she gave Colton's boot another kick as she led her horse past him on the way to the arena.

"Funny, is it?"

"Just can't resist. See you after the procession unless you're going to get off your lazy butt and come and watch?"

"Not interested in the flag waving and little kids on ponies, Maddy, you know that. And who got the trailer cleaned and ready at four this morning? You're an ungrateful wretch, you know that?"

"Hey, chill, I'm only joshing with you."

"Yeh, all right, sorry, I'm just real tired is all. Go and have fun."

"If I get to follow the lead, Charity will most likely go into orbit. Better have the getaway car ready."

"I'll do that, Maddy. Go outshine her. Don't give Dicey Deeks a second thought."

Madison laughed at the nickname they had come up with for Charity. Her temper tantrums were well known in high school and many students kept a safe distance when Charity exploded into a tirade. Madison swung herself up onto Pallo's saddle and walked unhurried through the bustling crowd. She encouraged the young horse as she guided her through the multitude of people, walking, chatting and consuming. It took time for a horse to become accustomed to the noise and smells of the rodeo and its crowds. She had worked hard with Pallo on the ranch, riding past noisy trucks and machinery to get her accustomed to sudden noises.

At the ground entrance, she and Pallo took their place in the line-up for the circuit and Madison took hold of a flag handed to her at the entrance. She scanned the crowd looking for the bright white shirt. *Really, what's with you? It was a chance meeting. With those looks, he's bound to be in a relationship or married. Forget the Italian, it would never work, he doesn't even like horses!*

A loudspeaker burst into life overhead. Madison tightened the reins.

"Our next flag bearers are Madison Beauchamp on Pallo, and Charity Deeks on Trojan. You may recall this particular pair of young riders competing all season long. They, without a doubt, gave us an exciting battle for the barrel racing championship this year. Make sure you stay for the winner's presentations later. Let's hear it for these girls, folks."

As the crowd roared, Madison heard Charity speak in a furious low voice right behind her.

"Watch yourself, Madison. You don't want to break a leg or arm today."

"No chance of that, Charity, I can grip darn tight when I need to."

"Didn't grip Daniel tight enough though, did you?"

They were signaled into the arena leaving Madison unable to react to Charity's sneering remark. Charity took off ahead of Madison, flaring her anger. *There's no way you're going to get the better of me here either, Charity.*

At the start, each rider gave the other a look of defiance then poised for the signal to begin their circuit. Madison could feel Pallo's muscles beneath her. She sensed the young horse's nervousness, spoke to her softly and stroked her neck. The lead horse trotted in front of the waiting riders and their horses and ponies. Madison and Charity followed with both horses breaking into a trot. Charity stayed a little ahead. Madison bent low over Pallo's neck. *Come on girl, you can do it.*

She drew even with Charity. A sharp pain made Madison gasp, and her left leg was suddenly numb. She started slipping off Pallo, who tried to break to the right into the stadium wall. *What the heck was that?* Taking a tighter grip with her left hand and right leg, Madison managed to get back up straight and not lose the flag. She could see Charity was ahead. Just as she urged Pallo to settle and ease her down to a walk, the announcer's voice filled the air.

"Please continue with the parade but we call Miss Deeks to the judge's tent immediately."

There was some heckling from the audience as Charity trotted through the exit. Her head held high and gesturing to the crowd with her middle finger. Madison rubbed her thigh as she sat to one side of the grounds, unsure what had happened. The children rode past her, and she guided Pallo to ride behind them, holding the flag up high. Once they had made a full circuit of the stadium, she passed the flag to an attendant and exited the arena. Her curiosity made her turn toward the judge's tent. She wanted to find out exactly what Charity had done. Her leg still throbbed. Charity was talking to a group of family members just outside the arena. Her shrill voice carried to passers-by, who turned to look in astonishment at her vulgar language. Charity looked up.

"Coming to gloat, are you?"

"Give it up, Charity. What the hell did you do in there, anyway? My leg is still throbbing."

Charity spat in Madison's direction then trotted away. *Oh, very nice, shows what sort of person you are, for sure.* Madison followed at a discrete distance leading Pallo by a lead rein. When she arrived at the main judge's tent, Charity was standing in front of three judges, with Trojan beside her and his reins held in one hand. A large grey cloud covered the sun, matching the storm of Charity temper. Her fervent shouting increased when she saw Madison and pointed in her direction. *What lies is she telling now?* When Madison was within hearing distance, she understood Charity's ranting.

"I didn't do anything. She's an inferior rider, she can't control her horse as we all witnessed just now. It's not my fault. She erroneously took my barrel championship from me. She must have cheated. She doesn't deserve the winner's saddle, it's mine."

The three adjudicators stood composed, as one voiced his reply to her rage.

"Miss Deeks, firstly each race is monitored with the utmost vigilance as you well know. There is no way anyone can cheat. However, your blatant interference of a fellow competitor will not be tolerated."

"This is so unfair! I'm the rightful champion. She doesn't deserve it. You can't let her take my saddle from me."

Charity's face contorted with anger as she looked at Madison, contempt and frustration seething on her face. She did not turn to face the judge's until she heard the next statement.

"Miss Deeks, you are suspended from competitions until further notice."

Charity's distraught squeal made members of the surrounding crowd turn in her direction as well as making a couple of horses flinch sideways at the sudden sound including Trojan. Charity nearly lost her grip on his reins but managed to pull his head back, swearing at the animal. She turned back to the judges, who shook their heads in unison. Madison looked on in amazement at the display of temper. *Oh, Charity when will you learn your actions alienate people?* In the meantime, Charity stormed away, tugging at poor Trojan's reins making the animal's mouth froth and swearing at the judges under her breath. She kicked up dust with her boots as she went dismissing the numerous comments from bystanders. Madison approached one judge.

"Can I ask what she hit me with, it happened so fast I didn't see?"

"It was a small electric prod. Miss Deeks hit your leg then hid it in her boot. Totally unprofessional behavior and not something we tolerate in the association. If it were not for an eagle-eyed event staff member, the matter may not have been reported."

"Oh wow, no wonder it hurt so much, my leg had no sensation in it. I had a hard time sitting upright."

"Miss Beauchamp, it was unforgivable behavior by Miss Deeks. We expect a high standard of professionalism from all our competitors. We pride ourselves on the integrity of our rodeo. We monitor every race and event with scrupulous detail, and we know you have adhered to every rule throughout the season. Your conduct has been exemplary."

"Thank you, Sir. I want to win fair and square."

"We will see you later at the winner's presentation, Miss Beauchamp. We can only apologize for such disgraceful behavior of a competitor and be assured we will be discussing her conduct at length."

As the three judges turned away, the now familiar white shirt caught Madison's eye, blazing in the bright sunlight as the clouds dispersed. In fact, it must have been a new white shirt, as it did not sport the pink, red and yellow stains from earlier. As Lucio walked straight toward her, she noticed he kept some distance from the horse. She returned his smile.

Lucio spoke first with that disarming smile after glancing at the departing crowd and the raging rider, kicking dust and swearing.

"I had no idea how competitive *ragazze* are with these rodeos."

"I think my reply is thank you, but what is *ragazze*?"

"*Scusi*, it means girls."

Madison wasn't quite sure how to take Lucio's comment. There seemed to be an underlining sarcasm in it. *Maybe it was just his accent.*

"Each championship is hard won, Lucio. I can assure you of that."

"I did not mean to upset you, *bella*. I marvel at the skill it must take to stay on a horse's back. Will you forgive me?"

Madison's heart jumped and a flush crept up her neck. *Don't be so lame.*

"I will consider forgiving you."

"If I take you for a coffee sometime, will that persuade you? I have a flight on Tuesday evening, so I do not have much time left."

"Where are you flying to?"

"I have to return to my factory in Italy. Our new line is still in the development stage, so I must oversee the progress."

"Are you staying in Edmonton? I know it's a bit of an imposition, but would you be open to driving to my small town? I have an aversion to the city."

"No, I am not staying in the city I find the city hotels are too noisy for me. Give me directions and I will be there and I'm no stranger to early mornings, I can assure you. Shall we meet at eleven?"

"That's not early, half the day's gone by then. I'll have the horses fed and out in the paddocks by then. So, you're not an early riser." She gave him directions, which he jotted down in a small pocketbook. *That's a thing we have in common, disliking noisy cities.*

He glanced at the address and smiled. "I have business to attend to much earlier not far from there and am booked into a motel in this place. It is a coincidence, yes?"

"It certainly is. Eleven it is, then. Why don't we meet at Tina's Coffee Shop? It's just off the main street on 51st Street. You should be able to find it easily enough."

"This sounds good, Madison, until tomorrow."

Lucio took hold of Madison's hand and kissed it. She was surprised by the old-fashioned gesture, but liked it. Although, she worried her hand tasted of dust, but hoped her natural scent came through. His hot breath on her skin made Madison inhale. The aroma of his spiced cologne was as sensual as his electrifying touch. Her flesh tingled.

As Lucio walked away Madison could not help noticing how well his jeans formed around his tight butt. He's without doubt, well put together and has real charm. *Unlike the usual rodeo and ranching crowd, that's for sure. Take it easy girl, once bitten, and all that.*

Chapter Five

In her absence, Colton packed the buckets, tack and grooming brushes. He was leading Amber Fire into the trailer when Madison returned.

"What was all the fuss about, Maddy?"

"Dicey Deeks, that's what. She played dirty. Used a small electric prod to hit my leg hoping to make me fall off, spook Pallo, and make me look like a fool. It was all I could do to stay upright and keep Pallo from crushing me into the arena wall."

"You're joking, right?"

"No, not a joke, she really is a piece of work that one. She got disqualified, though, and banned from future competitions until the judges deem fit."

"Serves her right, if you can't play fair, you shouldn't be competing or representing the rodeo. So, how's your leg? Are you okay?"

"Sporting a good bruise I would say, haven't had a chance to look."

"Why don't you come over here then, I can take a look for you."

"Colt, get out. Let's get Pallo tied and the trailer ready to go home. I'm exhausted and need a good long soak in the tub."

"I could make it better, you know. A gentle rub with ointment, maybe?"

"Thanks, but no thanks. I'm more than capable of dealing with a bruise on my own."

Colton smirked at her then bent to pick up a couple of ropes. With Pallo secured in the trailer, and the remainder of the tack and supplies stored away, they sat beside the truck.

"They should be announcing the winner's ceremony in half an hour or so. Let's take five?"

"Good idea, Colt. I'm feeling weary."

Seated beside each other on fold out chairs, the two friends were soon snoozing in the heat of the afternoon. A couple of soda cans glistened with condensation on the ground between them.

The loudspeakers burst into life with an announcement for competition winners to attend the ceremony making their bodies jump from their nap a short time later.

"I'll lock up while you get your winner's goodies, Madison."

"Be right back, unless I get accosted by Charity."

"I would think she is well gone, with a bit of luck with her head hanging in shame."

"We would hope that but with her temper you can never tell. She's doubtless complaining to anyone and everyone she can accost."

Madison approached the winner's tent and waited for the mention of her name before walking onto the podium. She shook the judge's hand as he presented her with a cheque, and the black based barrel-racing trophy topped with a golden barrel and black horse. It would look good on the mantelpiece in the living room at the ranch. He then handed her an exquisitely decorated dark leather saddle, she inhaled the aroma of new leather. Her gleaming award in hand and saddle over her shoulder, Madison made her way back through the crowd. She hoped to see a white shirt but there was none. *He must be busy with his stall.* She tried not to let disappointment cloud her mind. Many spectators congratulated her as she passed them on her way back to the trailer. *Today was a good day in many ways.*

As she approached the trailer, Colton emerged from the truck cab nodding with appreciation at the trophy and inspecting the saddle's workmanship. "Well, don't they look great?"

"Sure do, Colt. This trophy will have pride of place at home, and I can't wait to break in the new saddle. Now, let's get out of here. It's a long ride home." Madison laid the trophy on the back seat of the truck, hung the saddle on the hook in the rear, and then got into the passenger seat.

Colton turned the key and the engine roared. He eased the truck forward so the trailer didn't shudder too much and frighten the horses. As he maneuvered the vehicle, he noticed a smile and a slight flush to Madison's cheeks as they drove out of the rodeo grounds past the rear of a boot vendor stall. *That's odd, why did she blush like that. Isn't she telling me something? I'll find out sooner or later, I always do.*

He maneuvered the rig through other exiting trailers and vehicles until he joined the highway heading north. The gentle humming of the truck tires on the Highway 2 pavement and her exertions of the day, along with Colton's silence, soon had Madison's eyes closing. It would be over an hour's drive and as Madison's head rolled forward, Colton put his arm around her shoulders and pulled her toward him, resting her head on his shoulder. He smiled, satisfied his Maddy was beside him, exactly where she belonged. He slowed the truck down, enjoying the weight of Madison's body against his. He wanted her beside him forever. However, doubts clouded Colton's mind as clouds cast shadows on the landscape. *Whatever your little secret is, I will get it out of you, my girl. No way, you're escaping me. Your future is with me on Willow Sway Ranch.*

The sun disappeared beyond the horizon and headlights illuminated the dark roads. Colton stroked Madison's cheek continually. He was happy and he mimed to the soft country songs on the radio, ensuring Maddy remained asleep at his side. Her skin was soft under his work worn thumb, and she smelt of horse mixed with a pleasant citrus scent.

Colton watched the road ahead, aware deer, moose and other creatures could cross at any moment. He was alert and happy at the same time. He imagined driving Maddy home in the years to come, to their home, Willow Sway Ranch. He let his imagination loose as his fingers stroked her long auburn hair.

Eventually he turned off a backroad and into a long a gravel range road. The crunch of gravel made Madison adjust her position, but she still lay against his shoulder. As he turned down the tree-lined drive to the ranch, the truck's headlights caught the shining eyes of rabbits on the lawns. Colton approached the stables slowly, easing the truck and trailer to a stop. He laid a kiss on Madison's sun-kissed cheek. She stirred, blinked and then pulled away from his shoulder.

"Wow, I slept the whole way home?"

"You sure did. Do you want to go straight to the house? I can stable the horses."

Madison yawned and stretched, shaking away her drowsiness.

"No, I'm not going to shun my duties especially as you did all the driving. I'll get Amber and Pallo settled in their stables. You can sort out the trailer in the morning, Colt. Thanks. Good night."

"Well, if you're sure. I could do with some shut eye, I'm bushed. Night, Maddy."

He walked to the bunkhouse, stripped and collapsed into bed too tired to wash. He listened to the trailer side hitting the dirt and the horse's hooves on the dry earth as Maddy settled them into the stables. Familiar sounds of his daily life soothing him as he began to drift into a dream of Maddy in her bathroom. He imagined her turning on the ornate bath taps, pouring in a generous amount of bath salts. And then he pictured her undressed and looking at the large bruise on her thigh in the full-length mirror, as the heat rose in the small en-suite. He reached out to caress her discoloured skin. Another heat rising.

Chapter Six

With echoes of his dreams from the night before making him smile, Colton found Madison already in the stables shoveling manure and hay. She jumped as he spoke. "You've got a real rosy glow this morning, Maddy. What secrets are you keeping from me?"

"What are you talking about, Colt? Rosy glow, my butt, it's all this shoveling shit. I don't have any secrets, it's too small a town for that, you know that all too well. Come and help me and stop your nonsense."

He shrugged. "How's the leg this morning?"

"You could say it's a real trophy it covers the upper part of my thigh. It'll take a while to fade by the looks of it."

"Well, I'm at your service if you need a soothing hand."

"Oh, I'm sure I am more than capable of looking after a bruise, Colt." She turned away that smile creasing her lips again.

He frowned. He wasn't convinced the smile he witnessed the previous day and this morning was nothing, he let the matter rest as he began cleaning a neighboring stall. He did not press for an explanation, he knew to accomplish his plan he needed to proceed with care. *I need to find a way of making her love me. I'll make Madison and this ranch mine sooner rather than later.*

For another hour they completed a thorough cleaning of the stables, tack was rubbed with oil, raising the familiar earthy bold smell into the tack room, and feed buckets filled with pellets, issuing a molasses aroma. Colton checked on the pregnant mares, marking down any changes on the white boards while Madison toured the paddocks for any toxic or poisonous weeds on the outer edges.

After meeting with the other ranch hands in the bunkhouse, Colt listed tasks for each man to complete before day's end. The running of the day to day tasks and chores filled his early morning. Throughout his time at Willow Sway, he'd made changes increasing efficiency and ensuring the upkeep of the numerous barns and buildings. He was investing in his future, when the ranch would be his, alongside Maddy.

Later, when he joined Garner in mending several loose boards on the side of the oldest barn, Colt glanced over to see Maddy chatting with her father on the porch. He was surprised to then see Madison hop into her truck and head out without a word. *Where could she be going? We need to list our supplies then go into town, making two trips doesn't make sense. Why didn't she mention she was going out? It's not like her to do that.* Garner distracted him by dropping a stack of boards and yelling as pain shot through his foot when they landed on it.

"Be careful, Garner I don't need to be buying more boards if you break them."

"Oh, yeah, very funny. Thanks for the sympathy, Colt."

"Come on take one end, I'll take the other, butterfingers."

Chapter Seven

L ucio replayed his memories of his encounter with Madison Beauchamp as he got ready in his motel room to meet her at the café the following morning. In his mind's eye her auburn hair glinted in the afternoon sun above her slender figure. He imagined releasing those locks from their band and allowing them to flow down her back. An inner heat pulsated within him – he needed to stop these thoughts. He'd enjoyed the apparent ease in their conversation, and how comfortable he felt in her presence. Not a feeling he'd experienced in a long time.

She seemed naturally inquisitive, but underneath he sensed something hidden, a hurt of some kind. Maybe that was why they connected on a subconscious level. He'd been disappointed when she left, but enjoyed watching her determined stride and the slight sway of her hips as she did so. He'd ignored Angelo's inquisitive looks as they dealt with a final rush of customers, discussing designs, sizes and custom boots and the packing up of the boots into their respective boxes and collapsing the canopy. He'd also declined Angelo's invite to join him for a possible double date, using an early morning conference call as an excuse.

Mere minutes from leaving the motel room, he received a call from the factory. He debated leaving it to voicemail but took it anyway. He tried to cut the discussion short, anxiousness curling a tight grip in his stomach. *If I am late, will she leave thinking I stood her up?*

He repeated the sentence, "Okay I will later" several times rushing to end the call, frustrated with himself for answering it in the first place. The factory manager droned on and on reiterating the same information. With time pressing, Lucio shouted a final *ciao* and broke the connection. He rushed to his rental car and typed the cafe's address into the GPS.

He maneuvered the car into a tight parking space between two large trucks, discarding it thinking, *if they damage it, the rental company will use my deposit*. Turning to his right he stepped out into the road, a car horn blared making him jump backwards. The driver gestured with two fingers at Lucio before driving away. With his heart racing even faster, he strode towards the high street cafe, willing Madison to be there. He spotted her auburn curls and her tapping foot as she gazed into a store window.

He placed a hand on her shoulder making her jump.

"Apologies, *bella*, I took a call from the factory, which I regret."

"Its fine, I only just got here myself. Why the regret, did something happen?"

"No just my factory manager explaining the same thing over and over. I should have left it to voicemail. Shall we go in?"

Lucio opened the door for Madison. As she entered, Lucio circled her waist with his arm. An electric shiver ran through his hand. The aroma of warm pastries and brewing coffee wafted through the cafe. The clatter of cups and plates accompanied chatter from several locals, which became low whispers as soon as they turned in unison to watch the couple enter. Lucio led her to a table by the window. He pulled a chair out for her and held it until she sat.

"What can I get for you, *bella*?"

"Coffee with cream, no sugar, and an apple Danish, please. You can call me Madison, you know?"

"*Scusi*, it is habit, if my calling you *bella* is annoying I will stop, Madison."

"It's not annoying. I just thought maybe you had forgotten my name and used *bella* to play it safe."

Lucio laughed at her honesty. She has no pretense. "I can assure you that I remember your name and those sparkling blue eyes and auburn locks. I will be *uno momento*. Do you recommend the apple pastry?"

"Oh, yeah, it's my favourite."

He approached the counter and returned the friendly smile of the server. He dismissed her obvious flirting and kept his answers short as he ordered. The server bent over the counter as she handed over the cups and plates to reveal a deep full cleavage. Lucio smiled as his mother's words echoed in his head, *if they reveal too much, they are loose in their affections.* Lucio thanked the server and turned around careful to keep the plates and cups balanced. His progress was watched by the other inhabitants of the café before they returned to their own beverages, steaming into the warmth of the café interior.

He returned to the table, balancing two small plates on top of their coffee cups, then with care placed the cups and plates on the table before sitting down opposite Maddy.

"Impressive balance you have there, Lucio. I'm sure you would be perfectly at home on the back of a horse."

"The idea of getting onto a horse fills me with dread, Maddy. May I call you Maddy?"

"Sure, you can call me Maddy, most people do. What makes you dread horses so much?"

The unpleasant ripple of memory made Lucio hesitate before speaking. "I was thrown and then trampled by a horse when I was a young boy. Even now, the memory makes me uneasy, as it brings back the pain. My right leg was badly broken. The surgeon inserted a plate and pins to stabilize the bone. Although now, it makes for an interesting time through airport security…"

"It's very unusual for a broken horse to throw a rider. Did it get spooked by something?"

"I'm not sure. To be honest, I was so scared at the time, I can't remember much, apart from the pain."

"Would you ever try horse riding again? I would be happy to help you."

"I feel safer on my motorcycle, more control. Let me think about it."

"I would argue that, Lucio. A horse and rider become a team and work together. A motorcycle is just raw power and two handlebars."

"I love the power and the wind rushing past me without the confines of a car, Maddy. Leaning into the corners and passing the other vehicles. It is freedom."

"That's the reason I love to ride. Out in the open, feeling the wind through my hair."

They sipped their coffee savouring the heat and aroma of freshly ground coffee beans. Lucio looked into her eyes. "We have similar goals just different methods of achieving it. Have you always ridden?"

"Oh, yes, from a young age. My father would carry me as he rode his horse. The beauty of living on a ranch is I can ride at any time and get away from everything. Why don't you come for a visit next time you are in town? I'll show you horses are nothing to fear."

She does not judge or make fun or show disappointment in weakness. "Maybe I will visit. If such a fragile girl can master a horse, then I am sure I can?"

She is intriguing, exciting and a mystery rolled into one. I want to get to know this woman. "What is amusing, Maddy?"

"You think I'm fragile? I've broken many horses and been thrown more times than I can count."

"Is that not man's work?"

"Which century are you living in, Lucio? We have equality now, you know."

Lucio saw the flicker of ire in Madison's eyes. "*Scusi*, I feel protective of women, it is my upbringing. I do not want to offend you."

She laid a hand on the tabletop. "I'm sorry, Lucio, I've been working alongside men for most of my life and maybe some of their harshness has rubbed off on me. My offer to let you ride stands whenever you can make it. When are you back in town?"

He nodded and took another sip of his black coffee. "So, it seems we are both conditioned by our upbringing. Maybe we can meet in the middle of these opposing views? As to your question, I am back in two weeks from tomorrow. Shall I call you?"

"We do seem at opposing ends because of our childhoods and rearing but meeting in the middle appeals to me. Yes, call me when you are back. I'll give you my cell number as I'm often out on the ranch and it's easier than trying to leave a message as my father refuses to buy an answering machine."

With their coffee and pastries finished, Lucio reached for Madison's hand across the table. A static shock of electricity shot up his arm. He released her hand for a second, and then tried again.

I must see her again. "You have me *percusso*, Maddy, how you say? Smitten. You are unlike any other woman I have ever known. There is such life in your eyes and an attitude that intrigues me. If I could remain here and spend more time with you I would, but duty calls. So, until we meet again."

He caressed her hand before standing and holding the café door open for her. Their exit was followed by a sullen look from behind the counter by the server, Ginny. Outside on the sidewalk, facing each other and squinting in the bright sunlight, Madison spoke first.

"Have a good flight, Lucio. See you when you come back."

"You will certainly see me again, *bella*."

He kissed her hand before letting it slide out of his own, then smiled and walked down the street. He ignored the giggling and butt gripping gestures of several young women as he passed them on the way back to his car. His mind was full of beautiful eyes, auburn locks, and a gentle accented voice.

Within four hours, Lucio had checked out of the motel, driven to the airport, checked in, gone through customs and boarded a plane headed for Italy. However, his mind was distracted from the documents in front of him. Madison's light laughter, her sparkling eyes and the tingle he experienced every time he touched her. *These things must mean something, a connection. It is not just, how different she is from Italian women, it is more than that. A freshness, a strength within, she is tantalizing.*

His cell phone's dark screen drew him to it, wondering if she had sent a message. He dismissed the idea as foolish, ordered a glass of champagne and began reconciling the sales from the rodeo. The flight attendant gave him a broad smile as she handed him the champagne, he thanked her with disinterest. He was captivated by another.

Madison waited until he was out of sight before holding her hand up to her cheek. *He kissed my hand, it may seem old fashioned, but somehow, instead, it feels glorious. I feel like a teenager again, churlish and thrilled. How does he do that? This is going to be the longest two weeks of my life.*

She walked back towards her car a block away from the coffee shop and enjoyed the walk down the main street in the warm summer air, her earlier worry at not finding him at the café forgotten. Her shadow undulated over the storefronts as she passed by. She stopped enroute to buy fresh bread and sliced ham. The store clerk remarked on her happy smile as she bagged her purchases. She did feel happy and lighthearted, something she had not felt for some time. Well, since Daniel's betrayal, in fact. Now that hurt seemed far away, replaced with hopeful feelings, a lightness of spirit.

She sat in her car for several moments, her breathing hurried. *How could a man affect her this much?* She'd vowed to protect her heart after Daniel's betrayal and now all her thoughts were consumed with what was the cliché tall, dark, and handsome stranger of romances. She'd even felt a pang of jealousy when he spoke with Ginny at the café counter, which was just ridiculous. Ginny flirted with every able-bodied man, who crossed her path using her amble assets to full effect.

Was it the timber of his voice, his striking locks, that electrical pulse when he touched her, or his emphatic gaze with those mesmerizing dark chocolate brown eyes, or something deeper?

He's so open and unafraid to show a venerable side, not all forceful and full of male bravado like the men i know. Although, he irked me with that fragile comment, I'm glad he quantified it, but still, I'm not the barefoot and pregnant kind of gal.

There'd been no visible signs of a wedding ring–a huge relief–and his hands, although broad and strong, are softer than

Pop's, or any of the ranch workers' hands she'd known growing up.

Something draws me to him. Is it because he is so different from anyone I have known? I need to tread with care. He's from another world far from mine. Besides, if Colt gets wind that I'm seeing someone, he'll more than likely get all ugly and possessive about it. He was so great after the Daniel fiasco, but he needs to back off now. I love him, but more like a brother than a lover. I don't want to hurt him. He is a good friend.

Madison sang along to the tunes on the radio as she drove home. The sunlight glimpsed through the trees and swift moving clouds. Doc's car passed her but when she waved at the doctor, he turned his head away. *Strange, maybe he didn't realize it was me, must be the sunlight in his eyes.*

Chapter Eight

Colton met Madison as she drew up on the driveway, enquiring of her whereabouts.

"There's no mystery, Colt, I was in town with a friend for coffee. Don't be so melodramatic."

He looked taken aback by her vitriolic reply. "Which friend was it then?"

"Are you being serious? You're not my father and I'm not a kid. I can do as I damn well please." She stormed towards the ranch house the shopping bag's erratic swinging back and forth signaling her anger.

Once inside the house, Madison stood still, gasping for breath. *Who did Colton think he was? She was free to see whomever she liked.* Deep down, though, she knew Colt's friendly enquiry was that of a good friend locking out for her and certainly, after Daniel's humiliation, Colt was decidedly more protective. She would apologize later, but for now, she was going to make lunch for her father and sit with him for a while. She'd noticed his preoccupation the last few days and wanted to find out what was going on. She opened the wrapped ham slices and threw a slice to Bandit, who swallowed it whole. The old dog didn't have many teeth left after years of encounters with horse hooves, but until he got too arthritic to chase them around the paddocks, he kept going back. Pops said he'd had too many hits to his head to learn to avoid the larger animals.

With the sandwiches made, she ruffled Bandit's brown fur. The dog wagged his tail and then waddled his way in front of her to the back door. At the porch the dog sat, not following his mistress, Madison believed it was arthritis pain on the dog's hips, rather than laziness that kept Bandit homebound. She remembered him as a boisterous puppy, chasing her around the lawns and paddocks. And then, when he was older, running zigzag trails in front of her as she rode over the far pastures. He'd been full of energy and very fit. Now his joints were worn out, life was slower for the old dog.

She walked across the rear lawn into the yard. She found her father in one of the mare's stables. Dust from the straw bedding danced in the sunlight rays piercing the interior, the sweet grassy smell so familiar.

"Hey, Pops, come and have some lunch."

Her father's eyebrows rose as he turned to look at her. "You made me lunch? What's going on?"

"Can't a daughter make her father lunch once in a while?"

"Not without an ulterior motive. What's up?"

"Just wanted some time with you, that's all. With so much time away with all the rodeo events, I missed you."

Her father put an arm around her shoulders. She inhaled his unique scent, a mixture of fresh hay, manure and the soap brand he refused to change.

"I miss you too, girl. So, what's for lunch?"

She led him back to the house and onto the veranda, shaded from the summer sun's heat, where thick bread slices filled with ham, lettuce, and succulent tomatoes waited, covered with tea towels to protect them from flies. Two beers were also on the table. Bandit lay under the table ever hopeful for scraps. Sitting opposite each other, father and daughter ate in silence for several minutes, enjoying the sandwiches and the view across the ranch house lawn toward the paddocks. They could see the distinct line of willows in the distance, where they bordered the stream. The crack of the bottle caps broke the silence.

"Now that does feel good. We need to do this more often, sweetheart."

"Yes, we certainly do need to do this more regularly. Oh, and I need to show you my newest trophy. Wait a minute, I'll get it. My new saddle is in the tack room, you won't be able to miss it."

Madison entered the cool interior of the ranch house and took the trophy out of her shoulder bag lying on the hallway floor. She had discarded it the night before, too tired to think of anything but a hot bath and sleep. The gold plated trophy glinted in the sunlight as she returned to the wrap around porch. Her father was sipping his beer and gazing across the lawns towards the willow trees. She knew he still missed her mother even after so many years. *You need a good woman, Pops, just as I need a good man.*

"Are you all right, Pops? You seem a bit distant lately."

"Oh, Maddy, I ought not to burden you really but I'm worrying about the ranch's future. Will it manage to make enough money for you when I'm gone? Will you be able to cope with running it? I hate to think of you alone."

"Pops, there's no need to worry. Our breeding stock is the best in the area. And if I continue to win heats, it'll only make more people want their mares serviced here."

"Maybe you are right, Maddy. I just want to keep my promise to your Ma."

"I know you do, and you are, Pops. I am happy and the stud is doing well. It will stay in the family. Our blood line is longer than most of the horses."

"I feel older than two trees now-a-days, Maddy. Bandit and I, we're slowing down. Some days I'd be happy to join your Ma."

"Pops! Please, don't say things like that. You're my only family."

She took hold of his hand and squeezed it, feeling the rough, dry skin and battered knuckles.

"I'm sorry, Maddy. Sometimes I just get real weary. I would love to see you settled with a good man and walk you down the aisle."

"There are not many choices around here, Pops, but it will happen. And if Daniel is anything to go by it'll take some searching, but I will find someone who shares my passion for horses and the ranching life, there's no hurry yet."

"That boy is lucky I'm not twenty years younger, I'd have made his guts into reins."

"That's near enough what Colton offered to do to him."

"Well, there then, how about Colton? He's a good worker and it is obvious he is very fond of you. He'd be a good match. He knows the ranching life, it's in his blood too."

"Pops please don't go down that road again. Colt is a good friend, but I don't see him any other way. Besides..." Madison bit her lip. Now he'd want to know what was going on.

Her father's eyes widened in anticipation. "Besides what, exactly?"

"It's nothing. I met someone at the rodeo finals. We had coffee this morning, but he's not from ranch stock. In fact, he doesn't even ride. So, in truth I can't see it going anywhere."

"I see. How did you meet him then?"

"We sort of bumped into each other at the hotdog stand. In fact, I ruined his shirt and then we got to talking. He sells boots, actually the pair I'm wearing are one of his company's lines."

"They are superb Italian leather boots, Maddy. Cost a pretty penny, too, but so worth it when I saw your eyes light up when you opened the box. Does this man work for the company then?"

Madison's thoughts tumbled. *Do I tell Pops Lucio actually owns the company? Maybe not! I don't want him pushing me in any direction. If he thinks Lucio is wealthy, he might push for a relationship. I know he only wants the best for me, but I have to feel it is right regardless of wealth, or looks, for that matter.*

"Yes, he was working at their vendor stand. I accidentally smeared ketchup and mustard all over his nice white shirt when we were lining up at the hot dog stand."

"You must have made a great impression for him to want to meet you for coffee after that."

"I suppose, but he flew back to Italy, so I doubt I'll see him again."

"Italy? What's he doing there?"

With a sip of beer to soothe her drying throat, Madison answered. "It's where the boots are made. The company sets up for the rodeo season over here and follows the circuit."

"Not the sort to get mixed up with then, girl. Roaming all over the place like that, it's no life for a ranching girl. You keep to your roots and what you know."

"You're more than likely right, Pops." *But he is so damned gorgeous. It's hard not to want to see him again. There is something about him. I can feel it deep down, a connection.*

With their sandwiches eaten and the beer bottles emptied, Wynne stood up after giving Bandit a quick pat on his head. The old dog stood stiff legged, wagging his tail but stayed on the porch as his master took the steps.

"Well, this old man needs to get back to it. Thanks for lunch, sweetheart."

That was close. Madison reminded herself, she and Lucio came from vastly different worlds and any romance was doomed to failure. Still, she felt such a strong attraction to him. His eyes caressed her as he talked and his touch was electric, literally, but there was something more between them. Something she could not quite understand. *Put it down to a chance meeting and don't get your hopes up, you will probably never see him again.*

Chiding herself, Madison picked up the plates and went into the kitchen. After putting their plates in the kitchen sink, and leaving Bandit to enjoy the shady veranda, she walked into the warm dusty interior of the brood mares stable to find it empty. Thinking Colton must have taken all the horses to the paddocks, she looked around. Two stables required cleaning out, so she grabbed a wheelbarrow and shovel and began working. Lucio's smile stayed in her mind even when she tried to shake it away. The physical exertion did not diminish her daydreaming, but Colton's voice did.

"I'm going to town for the supplies, like to come with me?"

"I'm good, thanks, Colt. I'll finish up here then take Pallo out for a ride. See you later."

Madison was grateful Colton hadn't pushed her to go with him. She could relax and enjoy the afternoon without him following her around like the preverbal lovesick hound. The unkind thought made her feel guilty, without Colton's protection in high school and his thoughtfulness after Daniel dumped her, she would not be so happy now. She would make it up to him somehow.

Chapter Nine

C olt shrugged and reentered the tack store to begin tallying supplies puzzled by Madison's earlier over the top reaction to his innocent enquiry. As he jotted down a list, his mind conjured up possible scenarios. *It might be a friend, but what kind of friend exactly?* Maybe he could find out who Madison had been with by asking a few discreet questions when he went into town. He'd have to keep a closer eye on her. *Can't let the ranch slip through my hands now, I'm so close.*

Later, enroute to town the truck's fan did little to cool the truck's hot cab, so he undid his shirt in an attempt to cool down and hang one arm out of the window. The heat of the sun caressed his skin. At the brick facade livery store, he greeted Bill, the owner, and then walked back and forth along the aisles, grabbing essentials from his list, before piling up his purchases on or beside the counter. A strong wood and overlying scent of leather, fertilizer, and oils permeated the interior of the store.

He whispered several rude jokes to Bill, careful not to shock the elderly female customers browsing the nearby shelves. Their laughter attracted some attention but when both men winked, the women huffed and turned away. Once Colton paid, he took his purchases outside into the heat of the day. His open shirt was discoloured with sweat on his back and under his arms as he loaded the sacks into the back of the truck.

A familiar voice called from behind him. "Hi there, Colton, how's it going?"

Ginny approached him sporting extra tight jeans and a low-cut T-shirt, her eager eyes staring at his exposed chest.

"Not bad, Ginny. Did you have much of a hangover after Saturday?"

"It wasn't as bad as some. I so enjoyed our night together. Why did you sneak off so early? I could have made you breakfast in bed, and we could have enjoyed more loving."

"I had work at the ranch to see to, Ginny. Maybe next time, eh? By the way how's working in the coffee shop going?"

"Busy, but I like that, and the tips are good. In fact, I saw Madison there with a real honey, this morning."

"Really... local boy, was it?"

"Oh, no, not this one!" She gazed into Colton's eyes, inhaling to expand her voluminous chest. "Yeah, he had an incredible Italian accent, and those eyes...made me hot just looking at him."

His fists clenched until his nails dug into his palms. *Bitch is lying to me.*

"Is that right? She hasn't brought anyone up to the ranch, maybe he's a client."

"I don't think Madison would get quite that cozy with a client, Colt. She was all flushed and he was caressing her hand like that over the table. I found it hard to concentrate, to tell you the truth. He sure was fine, but not fine as you though, Colton." She traced a finger over his chest and down his stomach.

Colton gritted his teeth before answering. *Maddy is sure going be sorry if she tries to mess up my plan.*

"So, you think they're dating?"

"I have no idea, but if she passes him up, I'm sure he would have a line-up."

"You'd be pushing to be at front, no doubt, Ginny."

"He may be handsome, but you know I only have eyes for you, darling. We fit so well together in every way." She licked her upper lip.

He ignored Ginny's suggestion. He could not mistake the longing in her eyes. Ginny was great company and sure knew how to have a good time. If he hadn't had other plans, he might have hooked up with her on a more permanent basis.

"Is this man staying in town? Where do you think that would be?"

"I have no idea, Colton, maybe the motel? I don't really care, but will you drop by for a little loving later?"

"Don't have time today, Ginny, thanks. See you around." *I have to get back to Madison and sort her out.*

He dismissed the pout Ginny made and finished securing the supplies into the truck bed. She gave a wave as he pulled out of the parking space and drove back to the ranch, his anger seething, his knuckles turning white on the steering wheel. *Keep your temper. Just 'cause she was having coffee with him, doesn't mean there's something going on. But if there is, I'll be making sure he leaves town real quick. Madison is mine and so is the Willow Sway Ranch. I don't need anyone, especially outsiders sniffing around.*

There was no sign of Madison when he returned. She was possibly riding somewhere on the ranch. He busied himself stacking the oat sacks and putting the saddle soap onto the tack room shelves. He then saddled Titan. The black stallion was his favorite horse on the ranch. They had an understanding after months of gentle training. Colton headed for the stream, knowing Madison liked to sit under the willow trees and watch the water flow over the pebble covered bottom. When he spotted her just where he expected her to be, he slowed Titan to a walk. She didn't turn around at the soft hoof falls. He pulled Titan to a stop and watched her for a moment, taking in her profile and watching the breeze move her auburn curls to make them shine in the dappled sunlight of the willow branches. He loved her with a fierceness and determination that consumed his thoughts night and day. She was his and no one would take her away, no matter what it took. Taking a long breath, he spoke making her jump.

"Nice afternoon for a ride."

"Oh, Colt, you startled me. It is a lovely afternoon. I'm enjoying sitting here in the quiet with just the willow leaves rustling. I can daydream and relax without a care. Did you get everything we needed in town?"

"Yes, all stored away, too. Bill was in good form. I got a good deal after telling him several new jokes. He'll use them on poker night for sure. I also bumped into Ginny."

"Did you? She was busy serving this morning when I popped in, so I didn't get a chance to chat with her. How's she doing?"

"She's fine. She said she likes working at the cafe. She also told me you were with a real handsome man this morning. Who would that be?"

"Just someone I met at the rodeo when I ruined his nice shirt with my hotdog. He was curious about the ranch, is all."

"He's a horse breeder then?"

"No, he's not. It was just coffee, Colton. He flew back to Italy where the business is based. Now, I need to get back. Pops wants an early supper."

She mounted Pallo and trotted away without a backward glance. *I'll make you and this place mine, just wait and see. I'll be watching you.* He looked across the paddocks, toward the stables, and then the ranch house and smiled. This was home.

With Ginny tied to him with a brood of kids and a good income from the stud, it would be a perfect life.

Chapter Ten

The next day, Colton was attentive but not in her face. A fact Madison was grateful about. She kept her thoughts of Lucio to herself. They worked side by side in the stables and paddocks throughout the day. She began to relax around Colton again as the days passed. Life on the ranch was routine and normal. As they worked, Colton reminisced about their old school days. Reminding her of their former schoolmates and how their lives had turned out. Madison enjoyed remembering some of it but most of all she remembered how Colton protected her from the bullies. Without him, her life would have been hell. She did not conform to the preconceived ideas of the city's in-crowd with their designer clothes, fake tans, hair extensions, and gel nails. Her first mistake was remarking how stupid it was to go to a tanning salon when working outside gave you a natural tan. Jordon and her little followers, including Charity, overheard and swung round to scowl at Madison.

"You stupid little hick, it's an all over tan, not just your arms and neck like a farmer, not to mention your plain ugly face."

Madison recoiled from the viciousness of the words, at a loss as what to say. She stood and turned to leave the canteen, but a hand grabbed her hair and pulled hard. Madison cried out in pain and reached out to clasp the hand, but Jordon tugged even harder making her fall. She hit the hard floor. Jarring pain ran through her spine. She could not stop the tears falling. All of a sudden, a large shadow blocked the light and Jordon squealed.

"Ouch, Colt, that hurt!"

"I'll do more than that if you don't get your skinny arse out of here. You go near her again and you'll answer to me. Understand?"

Jordon swore under her breath and Madison heard her heels clip away across the canteen. A large hand appeared in front of Madison. She took it and he pulled her upwards the gentleness in his touch opposite to its size.

"I'm Colton, if you need help again just call, okay?"

"Thank you, Colton."

That was their first meeting and ever since, he'd been true to his word, always protecting her and being a great friend. Jordon kept a safe distance from Madison although she did make unkind remarks whenever the opportunity arose. Now, Colton's voice broke into her reminiscing.

"Do you remember Jordan?"

"Do I, the bleached blonde cheerleader? She always dressed as if she was on a catwalk, but with a tongue that could slice a person in two. My nemesis until you came along."

"I saw her a month or so ago. She doesn't look like that now."

"Really? Has she gone platinum? Got huge bejeweled long nails?"

"Nope, mousey brown hair, chewed nails, and put on more pounds than you can imagine. And she's trailing three kids behind her."

"No way! She always said she would marry a rich man and live in luxury."

"Her rich man turned out to be Jesse Donald, the coke head. His father cut him off so now he has to work to feed his habit and, by the looks of it, Jordan and those kids have it rough."

"Now, that is karma. She always gave me such a hard time 'cause I didn't fit into her idea of what a 'real' girl needed to look like. I wasn't sashaying in designer clothes and tottering on heels with makeup an inch thick. I don't remember Jesse, though."

"No, you wouldn't. He was three years older than us. Always flashing his fancy car and buying beers for everyone in the bars. He started doing coke once he got into the club scene in the city. His father cut off his allowance once he found out."

"Just goes to show life doesn't always turn out the way you expect."

"Yeh, that's right. Although some people do get their dream coming true, just takes some time."

"And who would that be then?"

"Now that would be telling. Come on, enough chatting, let's get that tack cleaned."

Madison thought about pushing Colton to tell her who he was talking about, then decided it might be best not to. She had an idea he was talking about the two of them getting together. She could see it in his eyes sometimes when he didn't think she was looking. It was a focused look with a steel edge to it. An odd look she could not define as either love, or passion, or something else.

Chapter Eleven

A sliver of sunlight pierced through the curtains and danced on Madison's eyelids. She pushed her bed sheets into a heap at the end of her bed, her naked body radiating heat and her mouth and lips dry. She yawned and stretched, the text messages she received from Lucio every night at eleven when she was lying in bed were much later than she was used to being awake. At first, he told her about his day's activities and how he missed her blue eyes and flaming auburn hair, then as the days passed, their texts became more and more intimate. He confessed he could not get her out of his mind. She replied that he occupied her thoughts as well and last night asked him if such a connection had happened to him before. There had been a long pause before his next text.

Only once. Years ago.

Madison stared at the words, unsure how to reply. As she was trying to think, another text came through.

Maddy, do not worry about it. Please.

Madison typed a reply.

Is it something you would rather not share?

The screen lit up again after another long pause with his reply.

It was a long time ago. It does not have anything to do with us.

Madison loved the word 'us,' but was also curious. She realized the best way to have a conversation about something that pained him was certainly not by texting.

That's okay, Lucio. I need to get some sleep. Have a good day.

His reply popped up.

You are angry.

Her answer was rapid to put him at ease.

No, of course not, I ought not to intrude. It is midnight here and I have to be up at six.

His reply came quickly.

Thank you. Goodnight, bella. X

The kiss at the end of his message made her smile. She put the cell phone screen to her lips and kissed it before shaking her head at her own foolishness.

Madison's mind had conjured up numerous scenarios as she slept. Lucio's true love dying a tragic death, or maybe disabled in a horrific accident, or she broke his heart being unfaithful. By the morning, she had made the unknown woman into an obstacle between them. He was waiting for her to return and would never see Madison again.

Now, she wrapped a light robe around her body, and made her way downstairs, her steps sluggish on the wooden flooring. She entered the kitchen, the aroma of freshly brewed coffee in the air. She yawned, then smiled bleary eyed at her father.

"You're looking rather worse for wear this morning, girl. Are you okay?"

"It got too hot to get a proper sleep, Pops. I'll be fine. Where's that miracle coffee of yours?"

"Right here, I poured you a cup when I heard you on the stairs. I can't stay, Clancy asked me to help with some repairs in the garage. There was a time he and I could do heavy lifting alone but as we get older..."

"Pops, don't say that, you're still a strong, hardworking man and so is Clancy. You work well together after all these years."

"You're right, Maddy, Clancy was my first ranch hand when we bought the place. Over the years, we have chores down to a fine art and can figure out what the other is thinking without words. He is a dear friend, not just an employee after so long. Well, enough chit chatting, I'll see you later."

"Sure will, Pops."

SHe picked up the mug, sipped the hot liquid, but her mouth clenched at the strength, so she put an extra spoonful of sugar into it. If her father's brew didn't wake her up, nothing would.

Revitalized by the strong coffee, she showered, dressed, and then went out to the brood mare stable. The pregnant mare's stables kept them separate from the other horses, and were fitted with larger paneled stalls, extra lighting and video observation cameras. She refreshed the straw in Sienna and Winter's stalls, the earthy, dusty and ammonia-laced aroma surrounding her and horses alike. Both mares were heavy with foals and the skin around their bellies stretched as small hooves pushed from the inside. Once she had spread out new straw, she entered the supply cupboard to find the supplements and make mash for both mares. With the chores completed, she wrote down the time on the whiteboard. It had been one of Colton's ideas soon after he started working at the ranch. It maintained and documented the horses' routine, ensuring they had regular visits, but were not overfed. Just as she finished writing, Colton appeared in the doorway.

"Morning, Maddy. See you saved me a job. Thanks."

"Hi, Colt, yep, these girls are done. What's next on the agenda?"

"I have to fix some fencing at the northeast paddock. Want to help?"

"Sure. Let me grab some gloves."

She jumped into Colton's truck, and they drove up to the paddock. At the gate, she got out to open it and then closed it once the truck was through. Just as she got to the passenger door, the truck moved forward. *Oh funny, Colt.* She walked forward again, and the truck crept forward, too.

"Cut it out, Colt."

The truck stopped. She stepped forward waiting for the truck to move again. It stayed still. As she climbed in, she scolded Colton.

"Think you're funny, do you? I'll get my own back."

"I'm trembling in my boots."

They laughed as he drove to the back fence, where Madison could see a section collapsed on the ground.

"I have all the new posts and railings in the back. Let's get to it."

Colton dug the post-holes first, then while Madison held the new posts erect, one by one, he filled the holes with concrete. They put in a dozen posts, and once the concrete was set, they began to fix the railings in place. Maddy held the rail while Colton nailed it into place. After a couple of hours, hot and thirsty, they sat in the truck to enjoy a lunch of sandwiches and pop.

"That didn't take long, Maddy, we are the top team. We work so well together. The ranch can only get better in time."

"I think it's because we've known each other so long. It's easier when you know how someone else works. Like Pops and Clancy, they have wordless communication most of the time."

"Sure is, but this sort of repair could be cut out all together. This type of fencing is so outdated. We spend so much time running around replacing rotten sections. I'll have all this old wood replaced with pipe fence. It's much more effective."

She glanced at Colton, puzzled at his comment.

"When are you expecting to do that? I thought it was very expensive."

"Not in the long run, Maddy. A good investment in my ranch, I would say."

"What was that? *My* ranch?"

Colton stuttered and back-pedaled. "It's just a saying, Maddy, working here so long it seems like mine, that's all." He gave her his most winning smile and turned to haul the tools into the truck bed.

She let the remark go. It was true, he had been working on the ranch for a long time. He had even come up with some good ideas, resulting in a smoother run ranch and its many chores.

She managed to keep the conversation light all morning, concealing her worry over the absence of texts from Lucio over the last four nights. She sent several messages but each time they came up as undelivered. *Maybe she was a passing fancy to him, after all.* The idea gave her a pang of hurt in her chest, she so wanted it not to be true. They seemed so at ease with each other, and the attraction was all too obvious but maybe she'd fooled herself into thinking he felt the same way, wishing it instead of being levelheaded. She needed to forget the gorgeous Italian and concentrate on the ranch and her father. Even so, deep down, her heart beat for him. For the man, whose very touch electrified her, both in a physical and emotional sense.

Chapter Twelve

T he same evening, over a supper of cold cuts, creamy potato salad, and crusty bread, her father surprised Madison with an idea. She could tell he was pondering something as his fork hovered in front of his mouth and his eyes glazed over during the meal. She knew he would speak when he was ready. After placing his knife and fork on his plate, he looked at her.

"I'm thinking of promoting Colton to ranch manager from foreman. He's a steady, reliable man, and a hard worker."

"Yes, he is, Pops, but Clancy is more experienced and has been here longer. Won't that make for some friction?"

"Well, that's the other thing. Clancy gave in his notice this morning."

"What! You can't let him go, Pops. He's been with you since before Ma died. He's more than an employee to the both of us."

"I know, Maddy, but his sister is real sick and he wants to go and look after her. She never married, and now lives alone. He's worried about her. She's out west somewhere, can't remember where Clancy said now. I can't refuse him, can I? She is his only family."

"That is so sad for Clancy and can understand his need to go. Family is important, I don't know what I would do if I lost you."

Her father looked down avoiding her eyes for a moment then nodded twice. "I'll be around for some time yet, my girl. So, what do you think of my idea for Colton?"

"Pops, maybe we need to think on this for a while. I can take over the job in the meantime."

"Why are you so set on not letting Colton have the position? What's going on with you two, anyway?"

"Nothing is going on, Pops. I just think he's a bit young for that kind of responsibility."

Her father burst out laughing. After a few deep breaths, he managed to continue. "He's the same age as you, Maddy. What you've aged faster than him all of a sudden?"

"No, Pops, but…"

"But what, Maddy?"

"I can't explain it. He just seems…so…full of himself at times. Like he's owed something, and other times, he's just…"

"Just what? You are not making sense."

"It's that I remember the old Colt in high school. Even though now he is a lot more laid back and easy going, there's something off about him. Call it a gut reaction."

"Well, I'll think on it and keep a close eye on him. See if I can find out what he's about if what I normally see isn't just him working hard and caring for the place."

"Sorry, Pops, I can't narrow it down to anything specific."

"He won't get the ranch, it's yours, you know that right?"

"Yes, I know, Pops."

Madison's cell phone trilled, interrupting their conversation. The number was unfamiliar but that didn't stop Madison's heart from skipping a beat. *It might be him.*

"I need to take this, Pops. I'll see to the dishes and clear up later."

She turned away to hide her flushed cheeks and sparkling eyes, but saw him shake his head. She tracked his movements by his footfalls as he grabbed a beer from the fridge and a packet of chips from the side cupboard. He gave a wave of his hand as he walked by with Bandit trotting behind him. She knew he would settle into his easy chair, and switch on the evening news. He liked to keep up with current affairs. The old dog would lie on Wynne's feet, his favorite place, and would soon be snoring quietly. She would join him for the family match game later in the evening.

Her heart did a double beat at the voice on the cell.

"Hello, Maddy. It's Lucio. I'm so sorry for not being in touch sooner."

"Lucio, I was so worried, it is so good to hear your voice." *I sure hope he can't hear my heartbeat through the phone. It's pounding like a drum.* "What happened? I tried to contact you, but the messages would not go through."

"I had an accident."

Her breath caught in her throat. "Oh, no. Are you hurt? Was it on your motorcycle? Are you injured?"

"No, *bella*, not that sort of accident. I dropped my cell phone into a vat of leather tanning solution."

"Oh wow, how did that happen?"

"I was inspecting the solution with my foreman and another employee tripped and bumped into me. The phone slipped out of my hand and in it went."

"So, how did you get it out?"

"It was a couple of days before the solution could be drained and by that time the phone was, of course, beyond repair. All my contacts were on it."

"Then how did you manage to get my cell number?"

"You do not know this about me yet, Madison but I am a bit obsessed with making notes."

"Notes? What on your computer?"

"Well no." Lucio paused. "Actually no, I keep notes the old fashioned way, on paper. My desk and briefcase are littered with them."

Madison stifled a giggle. What an odd thing for a jet setter to do with all the technology available.

"Well, it's different that's for sure. In this case, I must say I'm thankful, but why did it take you so long to call?"

"Another situation out of my control, I apologize. A supplier in the northern part of Italy summoned me. They suffered a warehouse fire, and leather stock we purchased suffered damage. I needed to go and assess if any of the goods were salvageable. I did not have time to purchase a replacement cell phone, just flew straight there. Did you miss me?"

Madison blushed. *Even thousands of miles away, he can affect me.*

"Yes, I missed our evening messages."

Madison bit her lip. Don't seem too eager, his absence could be for another reason. I shouldn't be so trusting. I need to remember the hurt Daniel created in me.

"Yes, I missed you, too, my *bella.*"

"Well, now that we have contact have you thought any more about coming to visit the ranch and trying your hand at riding?"

"I have given it a lot of thought. If you can master a horse, then I will let you help me conquer my childish fear. When can I come? I fly in tonight."

She wanted to say *now, come now,* but bit her lip and answered as composed as she could with a racing heart.

"Why not visit the day after tomorrow? It will give you time to adjust to the time difference. How does ten o'clock sound, or is that too early? I'll text you the directions."

"I will be there, Maddy, with my boots on. *Ciao.*"

There was silence on the line, but Madison continued to hold it to her ear, smiling. She didn't pay much attention to the shadow moving away from the window.

Chapter Thirteen

With the contents of her wardrobe spread across the bed, dressing table, and most of the floor, Madison fumed. *Oh hell, what am I going to wear? It has to look casual, but a little sexy.*

An hour later and several outfits discarded, she looked in the full-length mirror happy with her appearance. Tight dark jeans, a white camisole under a pink checked shirt open halfway and held around her waist by a leather belt with a silver buckle. Her freshly washed hair tumbled over her shoulders in soft amber curls. She kept her makeup natural and used an eyelash curler and mascara to make her eyelashes long and thick. Glancing at her watch, Madison gasped. Lucio would be arriving in less than an hour. After forcing her discarded clothes into the bottom of the wardrobe and throwing a quilt over her bed, she ran down the stairs. She needed Colton out of the way and hoped her ruse would work. Bandit opened one eye as she gave him a quick pat on her way out into the morning air, the heat of the day just beginning with the scent of dew rising off the grass blowing in the breeze. There was a time the old dog would have run after her and Pops all day long, now he spent most of his time sleeping.

Madison walked around the side of the barn in the glare of morning light. She peered inside, no sign of Colton there. Next, she tried the two stables, still no Colton. *Where could he be at this time?* Most of the horses were out already. Maybe he was down in one of the paddocks. The sound of tuneless whistling alerted her to his whereabouts. She approached the garage to find him lying on the ground underneath the old ranch truck, his worn boots stuck out the side. The truck's green paint was faded and rust nibbled at the wheel arches.

"What's wrong with the old rust bucket now?"

"She needs some TLC is all, like my girl, Madison."

Madison bit her lip. *Make nice now. You need him out of the way soon.* "We all need some TLC now and again, Colt. Is she running?"

"Sure, I'm giving her a quick once over, a little grease here, a bolt tightened there. She'll run for a few more years yet. I shouldn't be much longer. Do you fancy going for a ride in a bit?"

"In fact, I came over to see if you could do me a favor. Frank Parks asked if we could send someone over to help him with breaking a stallion. With your talents, I'm sure you are the best man for the job."

Madison couldn't see Colton's face contort in anger, but his reply through gritted teeth gave it away.

"Sure, I can go. Maybe later this afternoon."

"Frank really wanted someone this morning. I can finish up any chores for you."

Colton swung out from under the truck and gave Madison the once over. Wiping his greasy hands on a rag, he raised one eyebrow at her freshly washed hair and swanky outfit.

"Who can pass up the chance to get out of loading the manure spreader? I'll be on my way as soon as I've scrubbed up.

You'd better change those clothes and put on some coveralls, though."

Her nose scrunched up at the thought of filling up the manure spreader even though she knew she would not be completing that particular chore. *I'll have to make up a good excuse for not getting it done, that's for sure.*

"Good idea I've got some old clothes to change into. Thanks for helping Frank. See you later, and have fun with that stallion."

She walked away towards the ranch house, breathing a sigh of relief, aware of Colton's gaze at her retreating back. From her bedroom window, she watched Colton drive out of the ranch gates. Lucio would be arriving any minute. Her fingers tapped on the windowsill. *That was too close.* She turned away from the window with a quick glance at her reflection, and pulled at a few stray locks. Satisfied with her appearance, she headed down to the veranda and sat on the swing seat. She tipped her feet back and forth and bit at a hangnail. Shadows of the trees danced on the boards in front of her as the sunlight pierced through the clouds, heating up the morning. She could see the worn paint on the veranda posts. *Poor house, we have neglected you, Pops and I, maybe we can spruce you up now the rodeo circuit is finished for the year.*

She shook her head disbelieving her own dream. There was always so much to do with the horses and their upkeep and care that their own home came second best. When her mother was alive, the house was always bright and cheery with fresh flowers and the smell of baking. Madison brushed a single tear from her cheek. She missed her mother so much, even after fourteen years. She could not share much with her father. She knew he did his best, but a born and bred rancher had no reference on how to manage a young girl growing up. Madison had spoken to a couple of friends at school, but a mother was different, more understanding and wise. She was jealous of the easy relationships her friends had with their mothers. When Madison was younger, she daydreamed of Pops marrying the perfect woman, who would take her on picnics, make beautiful shirts and dresses for her, and brush her hair at night while telling her bedtime stories. As the years passed, Madison realized her father would not marry again. His love for his wife was absolute.

Soon after her mother passed away, her father began working extra long hours, exhausting himself into a deep sleep. In time, the hours lessened, and he would sit with Madison encircled under one arm in front of the television. Although, he'd smelt of horsehair, sweat and manure, Madison relished those times. She yearned for cuddles and love. Now, as an adult, she understood the pain her father had borne. How he tried to save her from his pain by keeping it from her, but she thought they needed to mourn together, comfort each other instead of being separated in their grief. Madison looked up to the sky, watching several clouds float across it. *I love you, Ma.*

The crunch of car tires on the gravel drive made Madison look up. Patting her cheeks and hoping she had not smudged her mascara, she stood up. There he was, gorgeous as ever. He held up a hand in greeting as he got out of the sleek black convertible. She walked to meet him halfway. Bandit actually ambled down the veranda steps with obvious effort, and stood at her side. Madison rubbed one of his ears and the dog leaned into her hand.

"Good morning, you managed to find us then?"

"Yes, it was easy with your directions. Nice setup you have here. Who's this?" Lucio bent down to scratch the dog's back. Bandit's rear leg quivered.

"Thanks, we are proud of our ranch. This is Bandit. My father bought him for me when I was twelve, a playmate of sorts. He's an old boy now. Would you like a drink or something?"

"The something sounds interesting." His eyes made their way down her body and then back up to her face.

Madison's flush rose up her neck. *Again? How does he do that?*

"Well, I meant a drink, hot or cold. Either is on offer, or we can go over to the paddock instead."

"Let us go to the paddock then, I'm not thirsty for a drink. Is Bandit coming?"

"No, he spends most of his time on the veranda or at my Pops' feet in the evenings. He used to be our shadow and run with the horses, but not nowadays."

"I'm sure he has earned a well-earned rest at his age."

"Go on, Bandit, off you go." The old dog lumbered back up the veranda steps, circled twice and then lay down. His nose pointed through a couple of struts. Lucio walked close to Madison, their arms swinging in unison as they crossed the lawn.

She noticed Lucio wore a pair of ebony boots with superb leatherwork. "They sure are fancy boots you are wearing. How many pairs have you got? Oh, sorry, that was rude of me!"

Madison's hand clasped her mouth at her impertinent question.

"It is okay, Maddy. I wear pairs of our new boot lines. It's good promotion. Which ones do you like best?"

"Well, they are all beautiful, it would be hard to choose. To tell you the truth I've always wanted to have a pair customized with willow tree details to reflect my home, Willow Sway Ranch, and maybe in soft green and tan leather."

"That's an interesting concept, Maddy. Would the willows look as though they were sprouting up from the heel? Or just branches and leaves as decoration?"

"Now you have me thinking. I hadn't thought in any detail about the actual design until now. The willows' growing upwards sounds perfect. That's why you are a boot maker and I'm not."

"We all have our areas of expertise. Riding horses is yours."

"That may be true, but it is no reason for us to stop trying new things."

"Riding is an aversion to me. All I have as reference is a painful encounter. I had not planned to experience again."

"We will see if I can convince you otherwise. Here we are."

At the paddock fence, Madison pointed out each horse naming them as they strolled together. As she turned toward Lucio, she realized he was looking at her and not the horses. *Play it cool.*

"Do you want to get closer or is this enough for a first visit?"

"They all look like young and powerful animals. I'm not sure I could manage to ride one of those. Don't you have an old, slow horse I could try first?"

"Old and slow horses don't stay around here long. I could try you on Mai Curl. She's a brood mare and very gentle."

"What is this brood?"

"Her principal use is for breeding instead of racing. Her lineage is exceptional. I used to ride her when I was younger."

"Then that is the horse for me, Maddy, quiet and gentle."

As they turned toward the next paddock, Lucio slipped his hand into hers. An electric tingle ran through Madison's hand and up her arm. She could not help a grin of satisfaction from spreading across her face. When she looked at Lucio, he was smiling too. Without losing Lucio's handhold, Madison lifted a lead rope from the fence and called to Mai Curl. The horse's ears pricked up and she trotted to Madison.

"You call her like a dog?"

"We have known each other a long time, she knows my voice. I'm sure you will get on well with her."

With the lead rope on, Madison placed Lucio's hand on the horse's nose.

"Let her smell you and don't tense up. She will sense it."

Lucio's shoulders pulled back but then he took a deep breath and relaxed them. Sunlight sliced through the branches, its beams making Lucio's dark hair shine. Madison glimpsed his olive skinned physique through his thin shirt.

"Her nose is so soft, like velvet. I like her being so quiet. My first experience was with an excitable horse. It was stomping and throwing its head up."

"They were irresponsible in putting you onto such a horse, Lucio. What were the instructors thinking?"

"There were no instructors. It was just a friend of my father's encouraging me to get on. The horse was in a field behind his home."

"It wasn't even his horse! That is so reckless. No wonder things went wrong. How old were you?"

"I was around eight, I think, and I wanted so much to impress my father and uncle."

"Well, Mai will not be throwing you off. Let's put a saddle on her and you can just sit on her for a while."

Lucio gripped her hand, his intense look piercing into her soul. His jaw tightened with anxiety. *His fear is indeed real. I need to make sure he trusts me.*

"I am confident you will be fine. If you feel unsafe at any time let me know and I'll get you off. All right?"

"You must think me a feeble man to be afraid."

"After you explained the circumstances, I think I would have been afraid too. We will take it slow. Come on, let's get you saddled up."

With Mai Curl saddled and standing beside the fence, Madison instructed Lucio on how to mount. Once he was sitting in the saddle, Madison let him just sit, patting the horse's neck for a few moments.

"I will lead her forward at a slow pace, if you want me to stop just say so. All right?"

Lucio's knuckles grew white on the reins, but he nodded his agreement. She gave the lead rope a gentle tug and encouraged Mai to walk forward, parallel to the fence. With frequent glances backward to determine how Lucio was doing, she watched him gradually relax.

The sound of leaves rustling in the soft breeze, bird song and the occasional neigh from the other horses were the only sounds accompanying their slow walk along the paddock's fence. After almost twenty minutes, Lucio spoke.

"I never thought I would ride a horse again. Maddy, you have done a lot to banish my fear."

Madison turned to smile at him, but the sound of angry yelling coming from the barn severed her joy.

"What the fuck, are you doing on that horse? Get off now."

Oh no, Colton. Why is he back so early? She walked to the other side of Mai and faced Colt as he stormed towards the mare and Lucio. When Colton saw her, his demeanor changed, although not to the extent of being civil. She could see he was still angry, but her appearance tempered it. She held up a hand to ward off his tirade.

"It's all right, Colt, I'm with them. I am walking Mai at an easy pace. We are not galloping her around the field."

"She might be in foal, Maddy. You know she had trouble last time. Get that idiot off her."

"Excuse me? I know what I'm doing, Colt. Haven't you got chores to do?"

"*Bella*, if I am causing this animal distress of course I shall not ride her."

"We are not causing any harm to Mai, Lucio. Colt is overre-acting." Her eyes narrowed as she glared at Colton.

"We have to be careful with the brood mares, you know that, Maddy. What were you thinking?"

Madison spoke through gritted teeth while staring straight into Colton's eyes. "Colt, best you go now. I am helping a friend, and don't need your permission or help."

The veins in Colton's neck stood out. Without a word of introduction or apology, he turned and walked away.

"Sorry about that, Lucio. Colton is the head ranch hand here and he gets a bit possessive of the horses sometimes. Mai is fine as long as we don't ride her hard."

"He is, how you say...volatile?"

"Yes, that's one word for it. Come on, let's get you down. How was your first experience on a calm horse anyway?"

"I enjoyed it very much, Maddy."

"Next time we will ride around the paddock. It will boost your confidence even more."

"Next time? You think I can return? Colton would not like that."

"It's not any of his business who I bring to my ranch, Lucio." She led the horse and rider back to the gate, waited for Lucio to dismount, took off the saddle, and then let Mai loose back into the field. They watched the horse trot to the far side under the shade of the willows. The sun was warm and the sky a pure blue without a cloud in sight. Madison turned to Lucio and met his deep brown eyes gazing at her. She looked down, fumbling with the lead rope. Heat radiated up from the dry earth.

"I could do with a cold drink now. How about you, Lucio? There are plenty of bottles in the fridge."

"A cold drink of any kind sounds great. Lead the way."

As Madison began to walk towards the house, Lucio again slipped his hand into hers. She ignored Colton's glares.

Beers in hand, they sat in comfortable companionship on the swing seat, watching the horses graze in the far paddocks. Bandit lay on Lucio's feet. *He never does that with anyone else but Pops. Bandit must feel quite relaxed with him, in fact exactly like me.*

Madison felt a deep satisfying happiness. This, she could get used to. They talked about their childhoods and drank a couple beers, she felt secure and content in Lucio's company. It was easy to be with him. He didn't seem to have a hidden agenda. She felt a connection she had not experienced before. When they got hungry, Madison went inside to make sandwiches for them both. Lucio followed her into the kitchen and smiled.

"I can feel this is a family kitchen, just like my mother's. I would watch her prepare meals when I was small. She flowed around the room from one task to another. It was like poetry in motion."

"What a wonderful memory. Unfortunately, my memories have dimmed over the years of when my mother was alive and cooking for Pops and I."

"Madison, I am so sorry. I did not mean to be so insensitive. Please forgive me."

"Not at all, I have fond memories of my father and me cooking and eating in here. We were not, however, floating around in expert finesse. More smash and grab."

Their laughter filled the room and echoed along the hallway. With the lunch made, Lucio took the plates while she carried a tray with soda cans and packets of chips out to the warmth of the veranda. Sitting back at the table, Madison smiled when Lucio gave Bandit a couple of pieces of meat. The rapid passing of the afternoon dismayed her. She would rather stay in this moment forever but in time Lucio put down his empty can and turned toward her.

"As much as I would like to stay, I have to go. My time is always limited no matter where I go. When can I come back for my next lesson?"

Could I cope with his absences? Would I travel back and forth with him? It sounds exhausting and rootless to me.

"You are welcome anytime. What days have you got free?"

"I have several business meetings in quick succession here, and then I fly to Italy for production and distribution matters, so it will not be for a week or more but then I am free. Shall I come in the morning again?"

"Yes, that would be perfect." *He's perfect.*

Lucio stood, and Bandit rolled off his feet. He took Madison's hand and kissed it, then descended the steps of the veranda. Bandit gave a short bark, and she waved as his convertible drove away, leaving a plume of dust in its wake. Footsteps from the far end of the veranda made her turn. Her father came and stood beside her.

"Was that the boot guy?"

"Yes, Pops. His name is Lucio. He's the Italian I mentioned before."

"Fancy car for a mere salesman, he must be doing well on commission to afford that kind of rental car."

Not wanting to outright lie Madison changed the subject. "Yes maybe. Bandit took a real shine to him, and lay on his feet."

"Did he? Well, that's a first." Wynne rubbed the dog's head, who sat next to him, leaning against his leg relishing the affection.

"I know. I've never seen him do that with anyone else. He doesn't even lie on my feet."

"That's true but animals tend to have a better sixth sense than us. If that young man has Bandit's trust, it's good enough for me. Will you be seeing him again?"

Madison wished with all her heart that she and Lucio would continue to see each other. "I hope so, Pops, I really do."

Wynne gave her a smile. "I can see happiness in your eyes, it makes my heart warm."

But his sudden frown made her question him. "So, why the worried brow?"

He shook his head and began to turn away, but Madison caught his arm. "Tell me, Pops, what are you thinking?"

"It's nothing, really." The intensity of her stare made him fess up. "Okay, a thought came into my head. What if you get on so well you give up the ranch for him, or take to traveling?"

She shook her head in disbelief. "Pops, I've only seen him a couple of times, aren't you getting ahead of yourself here? You know I love Willow Sway, it is home, and I can't ever see me giving it up."

He embraced her, a sigh of relief exhaling. She knew her next remark took him by surprise. "I meant to ask have you made any decisions about Colton yet?"

"To be honest, I can't see what your concerns are, Maddy. I've been keeping an eye on him and so far, all I see is his usual confident maintenance of the horses and buildings. He organizes and works well with the other ranch hands, but is always first to help out. Can you tell me what's got you worried?"

"As I said before it's a gut feeling, Pops. I've known him a long time, and yes, he is a hard worker. No argument there. Sometimes he acts as if this place is his and that he's entitled to it somehow. I could be reading him wrong. Wouldn't be the first time my instinct failed me."

"How about I ask him to work the manager's position for three months as a trial? That way if there are problems, I can tell him it didn't work out."

"That's a great idea, Pops. Thanks for humoring my concerns. Well, I need to help bring the pregnant mares in. See you later."

Not waiting for a reply or further questions about Lucio, she hurried down the steps. Colton was roping one mare and had two others on lead ropes when she found him at the paddock. Madison grabbed two more ropes and walked toward two mares standing under a tree on the far side of the paddock. She called to Colton as she passed him.

"I'll get those two, Colt. See you in the stable."

He did not reply. He walked past her, leading the three horses.

You have got to be kidding. He's sulking? Once she had roped the mares, Madison led them into their stable. The smell of fresh hay filled the air as the sun dropped below the horizon. A hand grasped her upper arm. Before she could react, Colton had her pressed against the wall. His body pressed against her, his hands clenching her arms to her sides with a vise like grip. The pain shocked her.

Instinct made her try to put her hands up to push him away. He was much too strong. The lead ropes fell to the ground and the mares wandered to the far end of the stable, where they found an opened bag of oats.

"Get off me now, Colt, or you'll regret it."

"Maddy, you know you are mine. Why waste time on losers like that flashy pretender? You need a real man, not a pathetic excuse for one."

The smell and taste of whiskey was strong as Colton's mouth covered hers. His tongue pushed against her lips. Madison bit down hard. He let out an agonizing cry, and his hands released her as he held his mouth. He looked at her with a puzzled expression, his body swaying.

"Are you drunk? What is wrong with you?"

Colton swayed. She pushed away from him, her mind reeling with shock.

"Maddy, I'm so sorry. I don't know what came over me. I would never hurt you. When I saw you with that foreign guy, jealousy filled me. The hurt I felt was physical. Please forgive me. You know I think the world of you. I love you."

The last three words shocked Madison. She knew Colton had feelings for her, but this was a whole new level.

"Colt, I'm fond of you, you know that. We've been friends for a long time, but I don't love you in that way. Your friendship is important to me and if we got involved and it didn't work out, I'd lose a good friend. I don't want that to happen."

To her astonishment, Colton began to cry. All she could do was hold him, feeling guilty for making him so miserable. With a loud sniff, Colton pressed closer into Madison's arms.

Thoughts bombarded Madison's mind. *What have I done? Colt has always looked after me and this is how I repay him? Am I blind because I've known him so long?*

Colton stood tall as he backed away from her. He wiped his nose on a shirtsleeve. "I'm pathetic, aren't I? Thinking I'm good enough for you. Loving you."

"Colt, please don't be like that."

He looked deep into her eyes then turned around in one swift movement. She watched as he ran to catch the two mares, as they exited the stables through the far door. She ran after him. Taking hold of a rope each, they led the horses back into their stalls.

"I'm going to sober up and do some thinking. I'm sorry for behaving that way. Sorry, Maddy."

"Later, Colt."

Deep in thought, she entered the kitchen. Her father was concentrating on frying bacon, watched by a mesmerized Bandit, whose nose twitched with the aroma of the rashers cooking in hot fat as he sat beside his master, ever hopeful for a scrap.

"You are just in time. Can you grab the toast?"

Thankful her father's back was turned, Madison wiped a single tear from her cheek. *I've got some thinking to do, too, Colt. Best not involve Pops just yet. Need to get a grip on my feelings. Do*

I settle with someone who has known me for decades or chance life with someone who jets around the world?

"Smells good, Pops, but do we need an evening snack of grease then?"

"Oh, stop your fussing, there's nothing like a bacon sandwich before bed."

With Maddy gone, Colton raged through the barn, kicking any object that came close. *How dare she have the foreigner ride Mai and then minimize my concern for a brood mare and make out like I'm in the wrong!*

He went to his office, opened a desk drawer, and retrieved a bottle of whiskey. With a determined stride, he entered the rear barn. The image of the two of them holding hands and sitting on the veranda all afternoon added fuel to his ire. *I need to get rid of that fucking stranger. I won't let her slip away now. She's my ticket to this ranch. If my act of spurred lover doesn't work, nothing will. I need to keep working the sympathy angle, our years of friendship. Madison was going to be mine, no matter what.*

A half bottle of whiskey later, Colton formulated the perfect plan. His loud snoring echoed through the barn, his body splayed across a couple of straw bales. The whiskey bottle's golden liquid emptied, leaving a darkening pool at its neck beside him in the dirt.

Chapter Fourteen

L ucio had fought with his conscience ever since shutting off his message after their last nightly exchange. *Should I have told her when I visited? Is it something I can explain over a text? She would not understand, and texts are always misunderstood, but...will she allow me time to explain?* He'd picked up his cell, and then put it down several times with incecision and frustration. And when he'd eventually decided to call, the time in Canada was 1:24 a.m. He resolved to tell her when the time was right.

Then life interrupted and his decisions were required elsewhere, beginning with the factory manager knocking on his office door. Soon, all his thoughts were on tanning solution stock, lower productivity of one production line, and a host of other decisions he had to make. He'd eaten a solitary supper that first night looking across the Tuscan countryside under starlight, imaging Madison beside him.

He kept busy, organizing deliveries of supplies and overseeing new designs. With templates for a new line of boots approved and the production crew versed in the procedure, he began to relax. The leather supplier, whose factory suffered fire damage, shipped the entire undamaged product they could salvage, but Lucio knew he would need several tonnes to make up the difference. Traveling to Arzignano, under the golden light of his home country, his mind wandered. *Madison would love this countryside. I will show it to her soon. She's used to flat plains and sparse vegetation. Here, it is valleys and hills, lush land full of trees, vineyards, and red-roofed houses.*

Turning into the leather factory's main car park, he switched his mind into business mode, again determined to make a good deal with this new supplier. A tall dark-haired man stood at the entrance to reception and gave Lucio's hand a firm handshake.

"Senor Calligaris, it is a pleasure to meet you. My name is Franco Pecorella."

"Please, call me Lucio. Your company was recommended to me, and I am looking forward to seeing your facility."

"*Per favore*, follow me. Would you like something to drink before the tour?"

"No, thank you, my time is limited. Can we get down to business?"

"Certainly, this way we have box leather stored in a building to the side of the office and away from the production areas."

Lucio was impressed with the factory set up and the quality of the product, but kept his expression bland. If Franco saw his enthusiasm, it could mean a higher price. Once the tour was completed, Franco led Lucio to his office on the third floor of the office building. One wall was glass and looked out over a deep valley abundant with undulating hills, Cyprus trees and sparsely dispersed terracotta roofed buildings.

"You approve of my view, Lucio?"

"I certainly do, my office is in the interior of my factory, so I have machinery and fumes as a constant. I would much rather have these kinds of views to enjoy." *Although, an office looking over Madison's ranch would be as beautiful as this.* He admonished himself. *Stop, no daydreaming. I must concentrate on business now.*

The two men sat opposite each other either side of Franco's large leather-topped desk and discussed quantities and pricing for an hour. Lucio realized Franco was a smart and astute businessman. Finally, they reached an agreement both men felt comfortable with, and they shook hands.

"I will have all the paperwork drawn up, Lucio, and sent to you in a day or two. It is a pleasure to do business."

"Thank you for your time, and I feel we have made a good arrangement today for both our companies. I trust we can deal with each other more in the future."

Franco shook Lucio's hand again and pressed a button on his desk. A slim, dark-haired woman appeared at the office door and led Lucio down to reception. Her eyes traveled up and down his body and she inhaled deeply in the elevator. Her classic Italian looks, and cool demeanor only made Lucio yearn for Madison and her vibrant locks and vivacious nature. On his drive back to his factory, he let his mind wander again to his meetings with Madison, recalling her voice, the touch of her skin, and her easy laughter.

Later, at his parents' home, he avoided any mention of his time in Canada and a certain young woman. He kept the conversation strictly business related. As usual, his mother mentioned several local women she thought he might like to invite for supper, but he used pressure of work as an excuse.

While his mother was busy in the kitchen, his father poured them a glass of red wine as they sat on the veranda. He sipped the aromatic wine and said, "I worry about you, *figlio*. I am sure it is difficult to trust again, but Lucio, you need to think about having a good woman in your life."

"Papa, has mother put you up to this?"

"I know she is more forceful about it, but I am concerned about you, as well. I was already married at your age, and your mother was expecting your elder brother."

Lucio nodded and adjusted his position in the lounge chair. He understood his parents' anxiousness, but knew not to mention Madison. At least, not until he was sure their relationship was on solid ground. He'd been tricked once before and was determined not to repeat it.

"Papa, I am happy with my life, and a woman, a good woman, will come into it when the time is right."

His mother's call for them to sit for supper broke their conversation. His father hugged his shoulders as they walked into the dining room where the aroma of osso bocco met them. Another full-bodied red wine accompanied the meal, and as Lucio enjoyed the delicious food, he thought about how Madison would enjoy it too.

After the meal, he excused himself and went to a local bar to meet a couple of old neighbourhood friends. It was a good evening of catching up and laughter. Several women approached their table but as his friends were married and he had no interest they soon left for easier prey. He found himself comparing these women to the flame-haired Madison, and found each one lacking her vibrancy, her openness—the two things he found so appealing.

Chapter Fifteen

Over the next couple of weeks either her father, Colton, or another of the ranch workers managed to startle Madison repeatedly, as she gazed into space. Each time she made up an excuse and hurried to resume whatever task her inattention had stopped. She couldn't help daydreaming about Lucio. Anticipating the day, she would see him again. She wished her days away, anxious for his late night texts. They made a perfect end to the day. Every night she fell asleep with his image in her mind. Her dreams filled with imagines of the two of them in hot embraces. She longed to feel his naked body against hers. One evening laying in a hot bath her hands had soothed her thighs gently, until her fingers rose to find the softness between her legs. With Lucio's face foremost in her mind, she'd moaned softly as her orgasm flowed through her body.

During the day, Madison told herself not to be so eager to fall in love. Not to be so desperate. Laying her heart on the line in the past had seen it broken. *Is my infatuation with Lucio, based merely on our differences? Is it the excitement of an unknown lifestyle? His exotic looks?*

As she entered the kitchen the next morning, her father turned to her. "Good morning, sweetheart, could you look after a couple clients for me today? I want to take my time with a particular client called Marshall. He is an east coast breeder and looking to increase his operation. It could be a great opportunity for our ranch, too."

"That is super news, Pops. No problem, I can manage the other clients. Are they for the tour, or the breeding program?"

"Ethan Abbots is here to have a mare serviced with Titan so that will not be a problem. He has been here enough times to know the routine. Colton can assist you with that. Then there is a Charlton Spires coming to take a look around. Said he was interested in the bloodline. Tread careful with him, Maddy. I'm not sure what he really wants."

"Why do you say that?"

"Just the way he was talking. He didn't give me a whole lot of information. In fact, he was rather evasive. See if you can use your charms to figure him out, okay?"

"I'll do my best. If I have any concerns I can get Garner, or Colton to join us."

"Sounds good. We'd better get breakfast over and done with before any of them arrive."

With the plates and mugs washed, Madison rushed to get dressed and went to the office. Her father had written down the appointments. Abbots would arrive first. Realizing she had some time, she thought about texting Lucio. She counted seven hours ahead, which would make it mid-afternoon in Italy. Madison hesitated.

What if he's engaged in an important meeting or maybe driving? Should I really bother him during the day? He has a business to run. Don't they have siestas in Italy? Her decision was made for her by a knock on the office door. Madison turned to see Ethan Abbots standing in the doorway. A middle-aged rancher, whose weather-beaten face made him seem older.

"Good morning, Ethan. How are you?"

"Good, thanks, Madison. Is your Pop about? I have my mare with me."

"In fact, I will be assisting you today. Let's find a couple of hands to get Titan ready then we can introduce your mare to him."

"Sounds good, I'd much rather have your pretty face to look at this morning. Titan sure is the best stud around these parts. You must have a stream of ranchers coming by."

"We're kept busy that's for sure."

She and Ethan walked to Titan's stable. Garner was busy mucking out the stalls.

"Hi, Garner."

"Morning, Miss Madison."

"Can you help get Titan to the breeding shed? Mr. Abbots has a girlfriend for him this morning."

"I'll finish up here and then we're good to go."

Garner shoveled a heap of straw and manure into a wheel-barrow and then wheeled it out of the stable. Titan snorted. Madison soothed him with soft words and gently blew into his nostrils.

"For a pure stallion he has a real good nature to him, that's for sure, Madison."

"He does have a great temperament, but a lot has to do with Colton's training. He has a way with the horses."

"Yes, I've seen him calm Titan down before. You are right about that, Colton does have a real gift when it comes to hors-es."

Garner picked up a lead rope and hooked it to Titan's har-ness. Madison and Ethan walked to one side, while Garner led the stallion to the shed. Titan's head came up as they neared the shed, uttering a loud neigh.

"He knows what's about to happen."

"Keep a tight hold on that lead rope, Garner. If he gets loose, he'll head straight for Ethan's trailer."

"And he won't stop at the doors either, I shouldn't wonder."

"You are right about that, Ethan."

"I have him, Miss Madison."

Madison opened the shed doors so Garner could lead Titan in. Once inside Titan snorted and reared up lifting Garner off his feet. Madison and Garner both grabbed the lead rope to hold the stallion down.

"I'll go get my mare. You two stay with him."

"Okay, Ethan, but on your way, call out for Colton or Clancy. Titan seems a bit more enthusiastic than usual."

Ethan laughed at Madison's joke as he exited the shed. Madison looped another lead rope over Titan's neck and stood to one side of the horse while Garner stood on the other. As Ethan led his mare into the building, Titan tried to rear up again but this time he was held down. Ethan turned the mare around so she was facing away from Titan. The stallion tugged at the ropes. Madison and Garner walked him up to the mare and then let the lead ropes slacken. Titan smelled the mare, whose tail was up.

Ethan commented. "Not going to need any coercing by the looks of it. She must like your magnificent boy. I can't blame her."

Titan performed his duty. Once Ethan was satisfied, his mare was impregnated he led her forward. Madison and Garner took hold of the lead ropes again around Titan's neck and held him still. He jerked his head up and down several times, as Ethan led his mare out of the shed.

"Let him rest here for a while, Garner and then he can go out into the high paddock."

"Yes, Miss Madison."

Madison followed Ethan back to his trailer.

"A good morning's work that, Madison, thank you."

"If you want to come into the office once your mare is settled in your trailer, we can do the paperwork."

With the papers signed and a check for stud fees handed over Madison said goodbye to Ethan. She'd just finished locking the safe when another knock on the door made her turn around. The whole doorway was blocked by the figure of a large man, dressed in black.

"Can I help you?"

"Looking for Wynne Beauchamp, he around?"

"That would be my father. I'm Madison Beauchamp. Can I help you?"

The man looked Madison up and down then tipped his Stetson at her. "Well, I'm sure you can, little missy. Charlton Spires. I've come for the tour. It'll be mighty nice to be shown around by such a pretty girl."

The leering made Madison uncomfortable, but she swallowed her revulsion and said, "Thank you, Mr. Spires. Do you have a particular interest with our ranch?"

"Well, I've got some good breeding stock, but my stallion is getting too old. Don't get me wrong he has given me strong stock, but I think it's time for new blood."

"We have three stallions. All of them have good lineage and have been bred here. Titan is favored by quite a few of our clients, but we also have Cosmic and Farrow."

"Is it possible I might I see all three?"

"Well, of course. Please follow me."

"Sure will be a pleasure following."

She cringed at the innuendo. *What was it with these old cowboys?* She walked Charlton over to Cosmic's stable. "As you can see, Cosmic is a blue roan and is fifteen hands."

"He has a sturdy frame and good legs, but I'm not keen on his head shape for my stock."

"Okay, let's go and see Farrow, then. His stable is around the back of the barn. You can see it from here." Madison pointed in the direction of Farrow's stable. Charlton looked across the yard and scanned the layout before walking toward the barn with Madison. The crunch of gravel made Madison look back towards the ranch house to see a long sleek Cadillac pull up in front of the ranch house. She watched her father walk down the steps to greet its occupant. The driver got out and opened the rear door. A tall thin man emerged and shook her father's hand.

"Someone you know, missy?"

"No, Mr. Spires. A new client, I believe."

"Is that so?" He smiled weirdly as they turned the corner of the barn.

"This is Farrow. He is a liver chestnut and also fifteen hands. Is he more what you were looking for?"

"He has some real good structure to him, Madison. He'd make some fine foals."

"Would you like to see our other stallion or are you happy with Farrow?"

"I might as well see them all, missy. Lead the way."

"Titan is grazing in the high paddock. I can take us up in my truck if you want."

"Sure. If it's no trouble."

"No trouble at all, Mr. Spires. I'll get the truck. Why don't you stay here and get acquainted with Farrow while I'm gone. I won't be long."

When Maddison returned, Charlton had his hand on the stable door latch, making her wonder what he was doing.

"Mighty fine animal you have here, Miss Beauchamp, good natured too."

"Thanks, Mr. Spires."

They drove past the line of trees which obscured the high paddock from the house. As she concentrated on the rutted track, the Charlton surveyed the terrain giving a slight nod of his head.

"Here we are. You can see Titan over to the east by that clump of bushes."

"Now that's a magnificent animal, even at this distance. How many hands is he?"

"Titan is superb, isn't he? He stands at seventeen hands, Mr. Spires. He is a big boy for sure."

"Any chance we can get a closer look?"

"I brought a couple apples. Titan will come for food." She called out to the stallion. His head came up from grazing. With an apple raised above her head, Madison called again. The horse threw his head up then began walking towards her. She saw the man's intense observation.

"Look at his stance. His coat is so dark."

Titan took the apple from her and chewed at it while Charlton inspected him. "Now, Farrow is a fine animal but compared to this, he is second best."

"I can assure you Cosmic and Farrow sire fine healthy foals, Mr. Spires."

"Don't get me wrong, missy, both are first-rate, and I have several mares I feel Farrow will do well with. However, it is obvious Titan can give me superior stock for other mares of mine."

"Well, that's the tour of the stallions. Is there anything else I can show you?"

"If it's not too much trouble, I would like to see the other stables. It is quite a set up you have here, but only if you have the time."

Although Madison would rather have returned to her chores, she knew every client was important. "Of course, I can drive you around, although not in the style of that fancy Cadillac."

"It is a nice car, isn't it? Your truck will do just fine. I'm sure the Caddy would be wallowing in the ruts around here in no time."

Madison drove Charlton around the ranch pointing out the breeding shed, barns, and stables as well as the numerous paddocks. She put his intense stare down to curiosity. After a full tour, she drove back to the office.

"Well, I'm more than impressed with your stock and the ranch, Madison. I'll be in touch."

"Glad you liked it, Mr. Spires. Do you have all our contact details? I do have some brochures if you would like one."

"A brochure would be fine, and yes I have the number." He shook her hand before making his way to a brand-new truck. It was black and white with a large solitary star on the side. Although the truck was jacked up, Charlton had no problem stepping into the driver's seat.

He is a big man. I wonder how Pops is making out with that Marshall client. Madison walked over to Cosmic's stable.

She could hear her father's voice inside. "Yes, Marshall, we are proud of our line. My great grandfather started it. He used stock from Spanish breeders."

"I had no idea your family had been in the business so long, Wynne. Your horses are without doubt top quality."

"May I ask how long you have been breeding horses, Marshall?"

"Ten years in which time I've been rigorous in my selection of stock, which has given me an excellent reputation back home. I can see you keep a tight ship around here."

"We aim to please all our clients and, of course, the animals' health and welfare are foremost."

"It shows, Wynne. The ranch is a credit to you."

Madison thought she had eavesdropped long enough so walked off to find Clancy. She knew her father would tell her all about his meeting at supper.

Chapter Sixteen

At the supper table, Madison smiled as she listened to her father relay his meeting with the wealthy ranch owner, Marshall.

"He's got more money than sense but it sure will do us some good, Maddy. He wants Titan, Farrow, and Cosmic on rotation for his five ranches."

"He has five ranches. Wow, Pops."

"We could just service his mares and not worry about any other clients. He has almost three hundred. Can you imagine?"

"I thought we were doing well with the twenty we have. He must be super rich, Pops."

"Did you see that car of his? Top of the line that and a chauffeur as well."

"I did see it. When is Marshall thinking of starting this breeding scheme?"

"He said he will have to get things organized and will call me in about a month or so. It would really turn things around here."

"We don't do so bad, Pops."

"Yes, I know but this would make us some real money. I could invest in new buildings and get that fencing Colton was talking about."

"Fencing? You mean the pipe fencing?"

"Yeh, he mentioned it a while back. I told him at the time it was just not viable."

"When we fixed the fencing in the northeast paddock, Colton mentioned he would swap out all the wooden railings for pipe. I told him it was too expensive. Maybe he will get his way with it now."

"He just might, Maddy. Well, it's been one hell of a day. I'm going to relax. Are you joining me?"

"I'll clear up first then be in, Pops."

Bandit trotted after Wynne into the living room. With her hands covered in suds, Madison gazed out into the night sky, her reflection staring back at her on the windowpane. *He'll be here tomorrow.* She shivered with anticipation.

Five miles away, a large jacked up truck and Cadillac parked side by side outside a motel. The two men sat inside the motel's bar facing each other smiling. Their whiskey-filled tumblers clinked together. A plan was formulating.

Chapter Seventeen

Madison's excitement kept her awake. Tomorrow, Lucio would be visiting again. She admonished herself, trying to sleep. *I will look awful tomorrow with great big bags under my eyes and sallow skin. Fall asleep, damn it.* In the end, she gave in and took half a sleeping tablet fearing a whole one would have her sleeping late.

The crash of a pan downstairs frightened her awake at seven o'clock. *Was that Pops?* She hurried to grab her robe and ran down the stairs into the kitchen. She found her father scooping scrambled eggs off the floor tiles and swearing under his breath.

"You frightened me half to death, Pops. What happened?"

"Damn thing slipped right out of my hand. Darndest thing."

"Sit down, I'll clean up the rest, Pops, if there's anything to clear up! Bandit seems to have managed most of it. Are you sure you're okay?"

"No need to fuss, girl. It just slipped."

She bent down to mop up the grease off the tiles. From the corner of her eye, she could see her father rub his left arm and then smack it as if it were numb. *He's keeping something from me. Maybe Doc wasn't out this way for someone else the day I passed him on the road. Did he avoid my gaze for a reason?*

With the floor clean, Madison made a new batch of scrambled eggs while her father began to make a pot of coffee. Bandit slumped down under the kitchen table satisfied with his unusual morning treat, keeping one eye on Madison just in case there was another spill.

"Pops, how about using only two scoops this morning?"

"It'll have no taste, girl."

"Of course, it will, Pops, and my heart won't be racing afterwards and neither will yours."

Her father didn't argue. She sighed, worry crossing her brow. *There is something wrong. He would have fought for the usual four scoops any other time. I'm going to talk to Doc the first chance I get, patient confidentially or not. I need to know what's going on.*

She served breakfast and it was eaten almost in silence apart from the scraping of cutlery on plates, as father and daughter were lost in their own thoughts. Madison took time to watch her father ascend the stairs. He was leaning to his left and favoring his right arm. *Have I been so caught up in my own life to have missed this? I haven't noticed that until now.*

On her way to her room, Madison peered into her father's room. He was sitting on the bed rubbing his arm again. *Does it hurt? I need to say something soon. I'll talk to Doc first then I'll know what I need to do. In the meantime, I need to take more notice of what he's doing.*

Chapter Eighteen

L ucio's flight was on time. He took deep breaths to keep calm as a couple in front of him struggled with their hand luggage and two small children. The constant whining and fidgeting during the flight meant the passengers closest to them now showed their displeasure by pushing past them and huffing deep sighs. Lucio's own urge to disembark made his foot tap on the floor as he sat in his seat waiting for the initial rush of passengers to pass. He wanted to get out of the plane and be on his way to Madison's ranch, to touch her face and kiss those luscious lips. He glanced out of the window and saw the luggage carrier pull up alongside the plane's hold. He realized that even if he did push past the agitated couple and their offspring, he would still have to wait to clear customs and pick up his luggage, so he took another deep breath and relaxed. Within minutes, the young family walked out, and the stream of tired passengers lessened. Lucio grabbed his hand luggage and made his way to the exit, where a slender blonde flight attendant fluttered her eyes at him.

'Enjoy your stay, Sir.'

He nodded and smiled politely then walked into the airport building. As a frequent traveler, he knew airport protocol all too well and made his way through the corridors and elevators, then checked the display for the number of the luggage carousel and strode toward it. With his luggage collected he proceeded through to the customs check in. He would then make one more stop to check on confirmation of the safe arrival of his stock with all the accompanying customs checks and legal documentation stamped. Then at last, he would be on his way to the ranch.

Keys jingling on his fingers Lucio found the rental car and started the engine. Turning left out of the parking lot, he received a blast of a vehicle's horn and realized he'd not looked to the right before pulling out. He gave the irate van driver a wave and a smile but only received a two-figured salute in return. *Concentrate, Lucio, you are driving on the other side of the road now!*

After checking into the motel and leaving his luggage unpacked, he tucked his shirt into his jeans and left two shirt buttons unbuttoned at the neck, then grabbed the rental car keys and locked his room door. The uneasiness of what was to come made him jiggle the keys as he walked across the parking lot.

Can I do this again? Sit on a horse. Will fear paralyze me and make me look like a fool in front of Madison? He sat in the driver's seat taking deep breaths, the air conditioning cooling the interior of the vehicle as his body grew hot with trepidation. *How will Madison react if I refuse to try again? Is it possible to rid myself of this fear with her help? Was it a onetime thing?*

With the directions to the ranch lying on his lap he typed the address into the GPS, the screen flickered then highlighted options none of which were the address Madison had given him. He tried again but the screen flickered then went dark. *So, I'll have to find the route the old-fashioned way by memory.* With a shake of his head, Lucio drove away from the motel and out into the sparsely populated countryside. He could see for miles ahead of him, long low flat lands with outbuildings. The land was so different from his home in Tuscany with its undulating hills, tall Cyprus trees and golden light.

He kept his mind on driving and the road signs around him peering at range road numbers and counting up to the one leading to Willow Sway ranch. There laid the charm of this place, this country. Turning into the long range road he saw the willow trees swaying in the breeze marking his destination.

Lucio's car crunched the gravel as he braked in front of the ranch house. He smiled as he walked towards Madison, but the smile left his face when he saw her expression.

"What is wrong, *bella*?"

"We can't talk here. Come over to Mai's stable with me."

Lucio's warm hand slipped into hers. Feeling her cold hand, he rubbed it between his as they walked. In the stable, he turned her to face him and gazed into her eyes.

"What is so serious?"

"I think my father is ill and hiding it from me. Lucio, I am so worried about him. What if it is serious?"

"Now, come, *bella*, sit down. Tell me what has happened."

"He dropped a pan this morning and told me it just slipped but then he was rubbing his arm and when I saw him go up the stairs he leaned to the left. That's not normal, is it?"

"Has he dropped other things? Has he fallen off a horse?"

"Now that you mention it, he has dropped a few things lately. The ranch hands would have told me if he had taken a fall. So, I'm sure that isn't it. I'm a bad daughter, aren't I? Why did I not notice sooner?"

"Calm, Maddy. If he has been hiding this from you, of course you would not know. Could you get him to see a doctor?"

"Well, that's just it. I saw Doc Cummings out this way the day we met for coffee. I didn't think much of it. He has a few patients out here, but he seemed startled to see me and turned his head when I waved, like he was trying to avoid me."

"Your father may not want to worry you, Maddy. If he is seeing the doctor already, it is good, no?"

"Yes, I suppose but I need to know what is wrong with him."

"I am sure he will tell you in time, Maddy. You must not worry so. Come closer to your Lucio."

He embraced and comforted her. He enjoyed how she buried her face into his chest and saw a few tears fall. He raised her chin upwards. When their eyes met, he could not resist and pressed his lips to hers, a soft and long kiss.

Madison's hands cupped his face and kissed him again. Her shoulders relaxed against him. A cough broke into their intimacy.

"Sorry, Miss Madison, I was going to clean Mai out. Shall I come back later?"

Madison shook her head and stood up, keeping her hand in his. "No that's fine, Garner. I'm taking her out so you will have the stable to yourself."

The young stable hand walked to the end of the stable, head down, and concentrated on untying a hay bale, his embarrassment showing in his flushed face. Madison took a lead rope, looped it around Mai's neck and led her out of the stable. Lucio smiled and followed her.

"This is no place for privacy, Maddy. I will have to take you away to make sure I have you to myself."

"And where would you take me?"

"To my home, of course, Italy, where else? The land of lovers. There are many places we can sit undisturbed to enjoy each other." Her eyes glazed. "Where is my *bella*? Are you thinking of Lucio in his homeland, making love to you?"

Her cheeks blushed. "Just daydreaming, Lucio. Let's get you saddled up, shall we?"

"I would rather know where you had me in your daydream."

"That's for me to know and you to wonder. Come on, its horse riding time."

He shrugged and followed Madison to the tack room. He watched and listened as she told him the name of each piece of tack. Mai Curl stood relaxed at the familiar procedure as Madison put on her bridle and saddle.

"There is so much more to know than I imagined, Maddy. You are at such ease with her."

"I have known Mai a long time. We are old friends, she and I. Being raised on a ranch, even if some things are not taught to you, there's a lot to say about experience. I'm sure you have the same sort of knowledge in manufacturing boots."

"Yes, you are right I learned from my father and my grandfather. The skills are passed down generation to generation. I will pass it down to my sons when the time comes."

Her head tilted. "How many sons do you see in your future?"

"As many as my wife will allow me to father, Maddy. Sons are important for the family line."

"So, are you saying daughters are not important?"

"Daughters are a joy to any family, but the lineage follows the men. Don't you think?"

She looked up at him, he could not hold his smile.

"Without the daughters there would be no line at all, Lucio. Aren't both sexes are as important as each other?"

"You can see through me, Madison. Of course, I want daughters as well as sons, but the eldest son has always run the company. It is tradition."

"You puzzle me, Lucio. You have an old-fashioned side to your personality but spend your life jet setting around the world. How do you balance that?"

"As I explained before, I realized at a young age, there were two different parts to my life. The one inside my parents' home with all its old traditions, and the one outside, full of fast paced business and modern technology. I have come to enjoy both."

"So, if I said I was the heir to this ranch. What would you think?"

"You are the only child?"

"Yes, I am. My mother passed away when I was young, and my father never remarried. It has been Pops and me for a long time, but you are avoiding the question, Lucio."

"It is different in the more modern western culture. Roles are merged but many Italian families live a more traditional way, where we have centuries of convention and religious doctrine. That is the way I was brought up - right or wrong it is how I view the world now."

"Come on don't make excuses. What do you truly think?"

"From what I have seen, I think you would be more than capable of overseeing the ranch but..."

Her hand went onto her hip. "Oh, here it comes. But what exactly?"

"It is hard physical work, and you would need men to work for you, would you not?"

"Yes, I would. But would you think me capable of running the ranch, not just overseeing it?"

"It is not for me to say, Maddy. Your father has to make such a decision."

"There you go again with the male thing. I need to drag you into this century."

"You are upset, now? Madison I am not trying to be difficult. I am a product of my upbringing the same as you. Can we meet in the middle? If we understand each other's view, we can make this work."

Madison pulled at Mai's girth and then turned toward him. "You're different to anyone I have ever met, Lucio. All my life, ranching men and women have surrounded me. We work together a lot, as equals. Would you expect a wife to stay at home waiting for you to return?"

"You have the wrong idea about me, Maddy. Women are seen as an integral part of the family. They are important and many rule their families more than the men do. I have met women like you, who have left that way of life and become independent." His voice hitched at the last word.

"We all have to find our way in life, Lucio. Sometimes we hurt those around us when we do that. I do agree it is best to be open and understanding. It's the basis of a good relationship."

Lucio looked into Madison's eyes but knew he did not want to continue the discussion. It was too close to a deep hidden hurt. Instead, he asked, "Shall I get up on this animal now?"

"Yes, if you are ready. We can take her across to the lower track. Would you feel more comfortable if I lead her walking, or can I get another horse to ride beside you and hold onto the rope?"

"I would like you to ride beside me, Maddy."

"Okay, I'll saddle up Amber Fire. If Mai tries to walk out just pull a bit on her reins."

His heartbeat rose, and his mouth became dry. "You will leave me here with her?"

His sharp rise in tone alerted her to his worry, she turned to face him. "I'm just at the other end of the stable. Don't worry."

Madison went to prepare Amber Fire and rode up to him after a few moments. His knuckles were white on the reins and his shoulders tense.

"Easy, Lucio, you need to relax."

"She moved."

"Well, horses do move, Lucio. They are living creatures unlike the rigid metal of a motorcycle." She giggled and a small grin turned up her mouth.

"Lucio, relax your grip on the reins and loosen your shoulders. Take deep breaths."

He did as she asked and saw Mai's ears perk up. She blew through her nostrils and Madison shook her head, as Lucio's eyes grew wide.

"There now, you and Mai are both relaxed and can enjoy the ride together." Madison took hold of the lead rope and led Mai out of the stable.

He gripped tightly his knuckles becoming white again but loosened his hands when he saw Madison shake her head. Once they were out of the stable, she turned them towards the west and the low track headed into the woodland. As they walked at a gentle pace along the track, enjoying the sunshine, Madison's encouragement eased his worry.

"Relax and enjoy what is around you. Move with Mai's gentle gait. That's it."

"It feels rhythmic, the way she walks." He looked around. "There is a lot of land here, Maddy."

"Yes, we have forty-two acres. It allows us to rotate the pastures for grazing and the horses have enough space. Now as we go into this tree line, pull Mai's reins to the left, don't jerk them just a gradual pull. The track to the right is too overgrown."

The riders walked their mounts into the shade. As the horses turned to the left, Lucio looked to his right. "I thought you said the other track was overgrown, Maddy."

He saw the surprise on her face. "It is...well it has been for a long time. I don't remember anyone mentioning clearing it like that. There is no reason to. It used to be the main entrance, but Pops changed it as it has a steep drop just before the main highway. He worried the horse trailers would get stuck or damaged."

"Maybe we need to investigate to see how far it has been cleared, Madison?"

"Yes, I think we should. It is certainly odd. I'm sure Pops would have mentioned working in here. I can't see a reason for it though."

The two riders changed direction and walked their mounts along the cleared track. Branches showed evidence of being chain sawed, and the undergrowth cut. Vehicle tracks were evident in the soft earth.

"I need to tell Pops about this."

He heard the concern in her voice. "How long has it been since you used this track?"

"Years, in fact I was still at junior school."

The led the horses further into the newly cut track.

"Is this the drop you were talking about?"

"Yes, but it never had a planked walkway like this. Someone has been very busy. Why haven't any of us noticed it going on?"

"That might be the reason."

She looked up following the direction of Lucio's pointing finger to see a road crew's warning signs and earthmover beside the highway.

"I've driven past those road workers for the last three days, I never thought anything of it. There's something going on here, Lucio. We need to get back to the house." She pulled at Mai's lead rope to turn her around.

Her next words made him inhale. "Do you think you can risk a soft trot, Lucio?"

Tension gripped his shoulders. "I will try."

"Grip with your thighs and hold the reins at the horn of the saddle. There, that's right. Mai will follow Amber so don't worry about trying to make her turn, okay?"

"*Si*, Maddy."

Madison gave Amber Fire a kick and the horse began to trot. As the rope tugged, Mai changed her gait to a trot as well, Lucio concentrated on the horse's movement and holding on tight. Worry creased Madison's features. A snapping of branches made him turn and then he felt a sideways motion. He was falling. Images of his childhood fall burst into his mind. Panic flowed through him as he called out.

"Madison, help I'm falling."

She turned, and without hesitation jumped off Amber Fire shouting instructions to him. "Hold on, pull yourself up on the horn. Push on the stirrup."

Her hands were pushing his thigh upwards as hard as she could. With some effort, he was back upright.

"Are you okay?"

"Sorry, it was my fault. I turned around because I thought I heard something and slipped. Thank you for helping me."

The concern in her voice made him appreciate her patient even more. "Are you going to be able to ride her back to the house? Did it spook you? What did you hear?"

"Maddy please one question at a time. *Uno momento*." He took several deep breaths, and then relaxed his shoulders. He kept his head down for a while before looking up. A bead of sweat ran down the side of his face.

"I am okay now. When I was sliding, memories flashed in my mind, but your confident instructions stopped my fear. I knew I could save myself if I did not panic. I can ride back."

"Well done. You hung on and that helped. You may not have noticed but Mai did not move at all. She knew you were slipping."

"Such an intelligent horse, Maddy, she is well behaved too."

"Let's get you back to the house. I can get Garner to see to the horses. I don't want this to be your last ride. By the way, what did make you turn around?"

"I think I will be able to ride again, my *bella*, with your help. I thought I heard branches breaking as if something or someone was running through the bush."

"It might have been someone from the road crew I suppose. Best we make sure though. Come on, let's get back."

Madison mounted Amber Fire after taking hold of Mai's lead rope and walked the horses back to the stables. At the stable, she called out to the young stable hand. He appeared at the door.

"Garner, can you take care of these two? Lucio and I need to find my father."

"Of course, Miss Madison, I saw your Pops go to the rear barn just a moment ago."

"Great, thanks. Come on Lucio."

Lucio took hold of Madison's hand and pulled her to him. Without hesitation, he kissed her on the mouth, cupping his hands around her face. As they parted, Madison looked into his eyes.

"Are you sure you are all right?"

"Now I feel calm, Maddy. I needed to feel something other than alarmed."

"Glad I could be of help."

Madison smiled, kissed his cheek, and grabbed his hand. They ran towards the barn and found Pops hammering a plank into place on the wall of the barn's side door.

"Pops, have you asked anyone to clear the old track up to the highway?"

"Why on earth would I do such a thing? You know we stopped using it ages back."

"Well, someone has cleared it, Pops. If you didn't, we need to find out who did and why."

"We sure do. That track is well hidden from the main house and most of the buildings. It would be good cover for anyone up to no good. I'll call the sheriff."

"Tell him there are road work signs where it meets the highway, too. It seems to be planned real well."

Wynne tilted his head and looked Lucio up and down. "Are you introducing this chap then?"

"Sorry, Pops, I was so worried about the track. Pops meet Lucio Calligaris. Lucio, this is my father, Wynne Beauchamp."

Wynne held out his hand and the two men shook hands. Lucio felt her father size him up. *What does he think, I wonder? I'm physically fit but my soft hands will be a giveaway. His are callused and weathered.*

"Maddy tells me you sell boots, Lucio. Do you make a good living from that?"

"Pops! Please don't be so rude." Lucio grinned at Maddy's exclamation.

"If my daughter is seeing someone, I have a right to know how he's fixed. Don't I?"

"It is all right, Madison. Your father is right. He needs to know what kind of man you are seeing. I do make a very good living, Mr. Beauchamp. In fact, our company's boots are sold across Europe and Canada."

Wynne looked at Maddy a frown creasing his brow. Both men watched her cringe under their gaze as Wynne asked, "Our company?"

"Yes, it is a family business started by my great grandfather. Did Madison not tell you?"

Both men looked at Madison.

She lowered her head, trying to think of an excuse. "I didn't get into specific details. I didn't see much point."

The men turned to each other and smiled, then chorused "Really?"

Then Wynne gave her shoulder a pat and said, "Come on, let's go up to the house. I'll call Sheriff Gordon and Maddy can get the beers, Lucio."

"A good idea, Wynne, thank you."

At the house, while Wynne picked up the telephone, Madison took him into the kitchen. Bandit leaned on his leg as he rubbed the old dog's ears. They were new friends but acted like old companions. With three beers set on the table, they sat side-by-side, holding hands waiting for Pops to finish his conversation.

Lucio kept his voice low as he turned to face Madison. "Why did you keep my position in the company a secret?"

"I had my reasons, but can we talk about them later, please?" She gave him a puppy-eyed look.

"You are a puzzle at times, *bella*. A real puzzle. I will wait if that is what you want."

"Wait for what, Lucio?" Pop's voice made them turn around.

"I'm just waiting to drink this cold beer, Wynne. What did the sheriff say?"

Madison squeezed his hand.

"He is going to check on the road working schedule and if that site is not on the list, he will take a closer look. He agrees there is no reason for a road crew to clear the track though." Wynne nodded toward Lucio. "You seem to have made a friend in Bandit I see."

"I had dogs growing up, their faithfulness is such a comfort."

"Yes, Pops, Bandit has taken an instant liking to Lucio."

Pops lifted his beer bottle cap off and took a long drink. Madison and Lucio did the same. After several sips, Wynne stood up. "Although I would love to sit and chew the fat with you two, I have to get back to fixing that hole in the barn door. It was nice to meet you, Lucio."

Lucio stood, shook her father's hand, and then looked between father and daughter. "It was good to meet you, too, Wynne. I would like to stay as well but duty calls. Thank you for the riding lesson, Maddy. I will call you later."

"I'll walk you out."

Pops left by the back door while they went through the front door, down the veranda steps and stopped on the gravel driveway. He turned as they stood beside his convertible and placed a gentle kiss on her cheek.

"I will text you later, *bella. Ciao.*"

He watched her wave goodbye with one hand and ruffle Bandit's ears with the other in the rearview mirror as he drove the black car away. He also caught sight of Colton leaning against a stable door his glare focused on the car's dust trail.

Chapter Nineteen

The deafening sounds of multiple sirens woke the whole household and everyone in the bunkhouse at three am the following morning. Madison and her father met on the hallway landing, blurry eyed. Bandit was barking at the front door anxious to get out.

"What the hell is going on?"

"I don't know, Pops. It sounds like the whole police force is out there."

As they walked out onto the veranda, they saw the glow of flashing red and blue lights of numerous police vehicles along their driveway and through the trees along the main road. Bandit stood at the top of the veranda steps his bark furious. Wynne took his collar to stop him running out. A large horse trailer fishtailed onto the main driveway pursued by three police cars. Its exit blocked by another four. As they watched, three men were apprehended, handcuffed and put into separate police vehicles.

One car drove up to the house and Sheriff Gordon got out.

"What's going on, Sheriff?"

"Looks like horse thieves, Wynne. There was no schedule for work on that strip of road. I had a couple of deputy's stake out the road works. At midnight, I received a call from them. They witnessed a large trailer being driven down that old track."

"Horse thieves! Are you sure?"

"It happens more often than you know, Wynne. Got three men in custody but it's the main man I want to get. One man has given us a couple of names hoping to lighten his charges. Do you know anyone called Marshall or Spires?"

"Yes, we do. Both were visiting the ranch only a few weeks ago but separately. You think one or both are involved in this?"

"It could be both of them, Wynne. Do you have any contact details for either of them?"

"Their details will be in my appointment book. Come into the office, Sheriff. I will give you all I have."

Madison stayed on the veranda holding Bandit while several police vehicles drive away with the arrested men. *If we hadn't gone down that track, we could have lost horses tonight.* She saw Colton was organizing the ranch workers to check on the horses. His yelling made everyone turn around.

"Titan's missing. Check that trailer!"

Madison pulled a resistant Bandit back into the house, shut the door, and then ran toward the horse trailer, wrapping her robe tight against the cool night air. She met several deputies, Colton, and Garner in front of the trailer.

Colton's voice was fearful. "They broadsided that damn thing. If he's in there he's bound to be hurt. Call the vet, Garner, now!"

She raced to help Colton in his frantic pulling at the latches. The ramp slammed to the ground. Faces peered into the trailer's interior. Titan stood to one side, his right foreleg held up and his eyes wide with fear. Colton raised one hand up.

"No one move or say anything. I'll go to him. Take my flashlight, Maddy."

Madison motioned the deputies to move back, out of sight.

Colton trod onto the ramp with care and precision, talking in a quiet gentle voice to the frightened stallion.

"There you are, boy. I'm coming to get you out. Stay calm. Good boy."

With utmost care, Colton crept to the front of the horse, as it watched him approach wide-eyed and snorting. Colton held out his hand to let the animal smell him. "Okay, Titan, it's me. Let's get you out of here and see what damage those bastards have done."

Titan let out a long breath and then nuzzled his nose into Colton's hand. Colton untied the rope restricting Titan's movement, inch by inch. Tensing the rope with a gradual pull, he eased the stallion around and walked him out of the trailer. Titan limped on his foreleg.

"I'll stand here with him, Maddy. Can you get a blanket?"

"Sure, Colt. You did good."

Before Madison left Colton soothing the stallion, she told the deputies they would have to wait before moving the trailer. They agreed, tipping their hats before returning to their vehicles. Flashlights threw beams of faint white lines across the grass, driveway, and fences. The night air filled with dust floating on a cold breeze. Madison made her way to the nearest stable and flicked on the lights. After grabbing a couple blankets, she ran back to Colton and Titan.

"How bad is it, Colt?"

"He has a cut from his knee to his cannon, but it doesn't seem too deep. He's calming down now so I can take a more thorough look. Can you take the rope?"

Madison held the lead rope and stroked Titan's nose, issuing soft words of comfort and reassurance. Colton covered Titan with the blankets and then ran his hands over the horse's legs and body. Titan flinched when Colton began running his hands down his shoulder.

"I think he was slammed against the trailer side when they slid around, Maddy. As far as I can make out, he is bruised from his shoulder all the way down to this foreleg. If I get anywhere near those bastards, I'm going to kill them."

"The police caught the ones using the trailer, but the Sheriff wants to catch the organizer. Thanks, Colt without you Titan would have been a lot more scared and would not be out of that trailer so fast."

"He and I have an understanding, Maddy. He's my boy."

Colton looked past Madison. As she turned, she saw the approaching vet. "Hi, Cody, glad you could get here so fast. Titan needs help."

"Hello, Madison, Colton. What went on here? Garner was frantic when he called. Luckily, I was just up the road with a mare breach birth."

"Looks like horse thieves. Can you believe that? Sheriff Gordon and his men found out about the scheme first and put a plan into action. Come and look at Titan. He was in the trailer when it was broadsided. I've calmed him down, but he's hurt."

Colton illuminated Titan's wound while the vet took a closer look. Madison shivered and wrapped her robe tighter around herself. Colton looked up.

"Go on in, Maddy. Once Cody is done, I'll settle Titan and then come and let you know how he's doing. You'll catch cold in this damp pre-dawn air."

Madison shook her head at Colton's suggestion. "Absolutely not I'll put on some clothes and be right back."

She walked into the house to find the kitchen light on and the aroma of fresh coffee hanging in the air. Her father and Sheriff Gordon were sitting at the table with the large appointment book between them and the Sheriff's notepad open with scribbled notes on the pages.

"There you are, Maddy, you look frozen. I'll pour you a mug of coffee. That'll warm you up. I'm giving Sheriff Gordon a list of our last visitors, before going back out there."

"Thanks, Pops, the dampness sure gets into your bones quick at this time of the morning. I'll take a sip when I come back downstairs. I'm going to get dressed then check on the horses in the barns. Colton is taking good care of Titan. He was in the trailer."

"Good God, is he all right? I'll be there in a few minutes."

She saw her father's worried expression, his eagerness to check the horses himself. "Cody is looking over him now. He did a great job of getting him out of the trailer without him going into a complete panic."

"How did Cody know to come over here?"

"Colton got Garner to call him while he calmed Titan down. Turns out he was at the Michael's farm with a mare."

"Luck was with us then for that. Colt sure does take control of a situation and he's great with the horses. We're lucky to have him."

"Yes, we are Pops. I could see the whites of Titan's eyes. It was amazing how easily Colton calmed him down."

The sheriff stood up, picked his hat off the table, and turned to her father. "Well, I'll get out of your way, Wynne. Thanks for this information. With a bit of luck, we can find these other two men."

"Thanks, Sheriff for your quick response, I'll walk out with you. We might have been less several horses without your intervention."

"Let me know how that fine horse of yours is doing, Wynne. I'll be in touch."

Sheriff Gordon nodded a farewell to Madison as she raced up the stairs to dress. When she came back down Pops was standing at the door waiting, and took her hand.

"We need to check on all the horses. All that commotion and noise will have affected them. Also, I want to make sure my boy, Titan isn't severely hurt."

As Madison picked a jacket out of the hall closet, her cell beeped. She looked at the display, it was Lucio. With a quick tap of her fingers, she returned his text.

Emergency here. Call you later.

With the message sent, she joined her father. They walked to Titan's stable and trod carefully so as not to spook the stallion to find Colton sitting on a hay bale in Titan's stall.

"Heh, Colt, my boy. Have you been here the whole time?"

"I had to keep him calm, Wynne. Vet's orders and he settles better if I'm here."

"What was Cody's verdict?'

"Deep bruising and Cody put a few stitches in the cut, but it's not as bad as it could have been. If I find them, Wynne they won't need a jail cell!"

"I'm right with you there, Colt. You've shown me your commitment to this ranch tonight without a doubt."

Pops looked toward Madison. She knew what he was thinking, and she nodded her head in resignation. *How could she doubt Colton after tonight? He would make a great manager.* To Madison's surprise, her father did not announce his decision but gave Titan a good pat on his flank and turned to leave.

"Best see how the others are doing. Well done, Colton, you are an asset to Willow Sway Ranch. Come on, Madison, Titan is in excellent hands."

Her father's arm around her shoulder, Madison walked out into the early morning light with him. When they were out of earshot, Madison turned to her father.

"Why didn't you offer him the manager's position, there and then, Pops?"

"Thought it would be nicer to have him over for supper sometime and announce it. We are all tired and need some time to regroup."

"You're right. It would be a better way to do it. Let's get to the mares and see how they are coping after all that commotion."

Every horse was checked over, and by mid-afternoon, under Cody's advice all the horses were settled in their stalls, brushed down and fed. It was earlier than usual, but Wynne told the ranch hands they could all go into town and have a few drinks on him for their extra time after the police raid. Colton said he didn't need the time, but Wynne insisted.

"Without your skill with Titan and calm instructions, Colt, we might have had a much less fortunate end to last night's events. You deserve it."

"Well, all right, Wynne, I'll go. Maybe Maddy would like to come too? What do you say?"

Before Madison could answer, her father patted her back and said, "That is a fine idea. Go and have some fun. Relieve some of the night's tension. It will be good for you to relax a little."

"If I'm going, you're going to have to come too, Pops?"

"I'd rather have a couple of beers in the comfort of my own home, Maddy. Bars are too noisy for me nowadays. You two young' uns go and have fun."

She resigned herself to accompanying Colton. It would make her father happy, and she knew Colton would be as well.

"I'll change and be with you in forty minutes, Colt."

"Great. I'd better wash up, too. Meet you out front soon."

She walked back to the house with her father. They mused over the events of the night and day as well as the confidence Colton had shown throughout. She acknowledged her father's statement.

"He'll make an excellent manger, Maddy. You mark my words."

She nodded before running upstairs to have a quick shower and change.

Chapter Twenty

Colton was sitting in his truck in front of the ranch house when Madison came down the stairs. Giving her father a quick peck on the cheek, she waved and jumped into the vehicle. She could smell alcohol on Colt's breath, but didn't want to start the evening off on a sour note.

"So which bar are we going to, Colt?"

"Do you really want to go to a bar?"

"I thought that was the plan. Where else would we go?"

"Well, I was thinking maybe a restaurant to have a nice meal. You haven't eaten yet, have you?"

"No, I didn't have time. I am hungry though."

"That's settled then. Leave it to me."

Colton put the truck into gear and drove down the driveway, turning towards town at the highway. Madison tapped her fingers to the tunes on the radio while they talked about the horse thieves and Titan. Colton drove to the west side of town and pulled up in front of a bistro.

"Will this be all right?"

"Sure, it looks nice, Colt."

They got out of the truck at the same time and entered the bistro to the aroma of garlic ribs and an herb infused dish she couldn't name. A server met them at the counter and pointed to a table at the back of the room.

"I'll be over to take your drink orders in a minute."

As they sat down, Madison thought about the way Lucio opened doors for her, pulled out her chair, and generally how different Colton and other cowboys acted around her and women in general. *Well, you can't have both. Independence comes at a price. It is so nice though.*

The waitress appeared and took their orders, giving Colt an appreciative glance. She returned with two bottles of beer. He raised his bottle at her.

"Here's to successfully averting a catastrophe at home."

"Cheers to that. Without your careful handling of Titan, we could have lost him. You sure have a way with the horses, Colt."

"I would rather have a way with a particular woman." His gaze fixed on her, sincerity in his blue eyes.

How do I feel about him, deep down? I've known him so long. I'm just comfortable with him. I would never have to worry about the ranch with him running it with me. Is that enough?

"Don't have an answer for me, then?"

"Colt, we are best friends. I just don't know if I want to change that."

"It won't change, Maddy. We could be so good together. I've tried so hard to be that good friend, but my heart needs more. A good friendship is the best basis for a relationship, or so I've been told. We will make an awesome couple, Maddy."

She didn't know how to reply and fortunately, the waitress arrived to serve their meals. Colton thanked her and cut into his steak. Madison toyed with her vegetables as they ate in silence - an uncomfortable strained silence. Her mind reeled - *I'm sorry I can't commit to you, Colton. Lucio has me electrified with feelings whenever he is near me. Lucio is new, exciting, and fascinating. How do I let Colton down without hurting him?*

Colton raised his bottle and tapped it against hers. "Here's to new beginnings, whatever they may be. I will wait for you, Maddy."

"Colt, please don't. I can't commit to a relationship with you right now."

"That Italian is turning your head with a fancy accent and an expensive car. I can sort of understand that it's exciting to go out with someone different, but if he gets too close, Maddy, then I'll have to make him back off. We both remember how much Daniel hurt you. I won't let anyone do that to you again."

"Do you think that's what it is - a passing fancy? He may not hurt me."

"Yes, I think he is just a whim but what do you actually know about him?" He took a deep breath and eased his shoulders down. "I'm going to put my cards on the table, it's time. Madison, my heart tells me, you and I are meant to be together. We've known each other for a long time through good times and bad, and we work well together. We can make Willow Sway so much more. I can be patient for a while longer, but don't take too long. Having you near but unable to touch is, I admit, agony. I held my feelings for you inside for long enough and now you know how I feel I hope you will see a future for us together."

He eased back into his chair his shoulders relaxing. "There I've said my piece, it's up to you now." He didn't wait for a reply. "Now let's change the subject and finish off with a dessert and something a little stronger."

Before Madison could react, he raised his hand to the waitress, who walked over to their table.

"We will both have the mud pie. I'll have a double whiskey, and my girl will have a rye."

Madison began to protest, but Colton shook his head. "I might as well make the most of a date with you. I have no idea when the next one will be. It's all on me."

The waitress looked from one to the other, wrote down the order, and left. Madison looked up at him. *I feel so guilty. Colton doesn't deserve such pain. He's always been so good to me.* Madison nodded. *He's right we need to change the subject.*

"How is Titan?"

"Good. I'll sleep with him for a couple nights just in case he gets spooked with any noises at night, but I think he will be all right."

"Do you think that's necessary? Cody could give him something."

"I don't want him full of medications if we can avoid it. No idea what effect they might have on his...well you know what."

"He's a strong horse, Colt, and I don't think his performance is at risk any time soon."

The waitress returned with the desserts and tumblers of amber fluid. "This looks delicious, thanks."

"You're welcome."

As she was about to turn away, Colton said, "And bring another round for the road, eh, Maddy?"

"I'm good, thanks, Colt. I take it I'm driving home."

"It's fine, Maddy. I'll take the back roads. We can use the track past the cow palace."

She smiled at the memory. "I'd forgotten about that nickname for the cattle auction site. Look, I can drive."

Colton threw back his drink, shaking his head at her suggestion. The waitress brought the next one and he took a sip.

"Thanks. Can you make up the bill please?"

"Sure, honey." Her eyes sparkled at Colton.

You could have your choice of any girl around here, why stick to me? Maddy sipped her rye and while Colton was paying the bill, managed to get the truck keys off the table. She was sitting in the driver's seat when he exited the bistro, after his visit to the washroom.

"I take it you don't feel safe with me driving, then? By the way, you left your second glass of rye, so I finished it off. Smooth."

"It certainly was a good rye. Now jump up and no arguments, I'm driving back."

On the ride home, he sat in the middle of the bench seat as close as he could get to Madison. By the time, they were half way home his head was on her shoulder. He must have fallen asleep.

Madison concentrated on the road and sung along to a favorite tune. The moon was full, and shadows danced on the road. As she parked the truck outside the garage, she nudged him with her shoulder.

"Okay, we're here. Wake up, Colt."

He stretched and surprised Madison with a peck on her cheek before she could protest. "Thanks for such a great evening. Next time we should try fine dining. See you in the morning. I'll dream of you."

"Night, Colt."

She watched Colton swagger into his bunkhouse. *What do I do about you, Colt?* Her cell beeped at that precise moment interrupting her thoughts. The screen displayed a message.

Is everything okay? Let me know. I'm worried. Are you naked under those covers?

Madison flushed.

Yes, all good now, I'll explain. But need to wash up first. I'll soon will be. X

Warmed by her shower and naked under her bedclothes Madison picked up her cell phone and sent another text to Lucio. His response was immediate. Their messages became more and more suggestive. She imagined his breath on her neck, his hands caressing her breasts, the taste of his skin, nibbling his ear lobes. Madison threw the sheet aside to ease the heat coming off her body. By the time, he said goodnight all Madison could do was satisfy herself. *Soon Lucio you can do this in person.*

The following afternoon felt like eons away. She needed to breathe in his cologne and feel his touch. Madison fell asleep planning a ride into the woodland with Lucio and enjoying more than a hot passionate kiss on a grassy knoll. She imagined the breeze flowing across their skin and the smell of crushed grass underneath them. Her dreams were explicit, and her fingers again satisfied her as she slept.

Chapter
Twenty-One

Colton sat on his bunk drinking the last of a bottle of whiskey and thinking over the evening. Fine performance that. *That will get her thinking and feeling guilty - with any luck. I'll show her it's better to be with someone you know than a fly-by-night stranger with no idea of ranching, or life around here. She's going to be mine whatever it takes.* He waited for an hour, and then, drove down the back road into town. He noticed Madison's bedroom light switch off just as he was leaving.

A perfectly timed text message from Ginny had Colton keen to start his plan. She'd found out where the Italian was staying and if everything went to plan, she would be in the Italian's bed in no time at all. A photograph would show Madison what kind of lowlife her stranger was. He coasted the truck behind the motel. A light was on in the room Ginny had indicted. *Great, the light will be better for a photo. Thanks for that.*

Leaving the truck door open, he trod with care on the gravel, and then crouched beneath the window. He listened intently but couldn't hear voices. *Maybe they are already at it.* Standing

up he peered into the room through a gap in the thin curtains. The Italian was sitting in a chair all alone. *What the hell?
Where's Ginny?*

"Pssst, I'm over here, Colt."

Ginny leaned against the motel wall. He walked up to her.

"You're supposed to be in there, you dumb bitch."

"Heh, less of the name calling, Colt, remember I'm doing
this as a favor. I tried everything and I mean everything. He just
wouldn't give. I've never known any man say no to these."

She opened her shirt to reveal generous breasts cupped in a
bra too small to contain them.

Colton felt himself harden. *No time. We need a plan B.*

"We need to get you in that room, Ginny, somehow."

As Colton continued to feast his eyes on her breasts, an idea
began to form. As if noticing the looks Colt was giving her,
Ginny left her shirt open, as if enjoying the effect her attributes
were having on him.

"I know how we can get you in there and looking attacked."

"How's that then?"

"You're going to go back pleading for help."

"Help from what, Colt?"

"You tell him you got attacked when he deserted you. He'll
feel responsible and you play it up. Lots of tears and snuggle into
him real close."

"And how do you expect me to be convincing enough?"

"Come here and I'll show you."

Ginny giggled as Colton grabbed her arms hard, sucking on
her neck, while thrusting her against the wall.

"We need to mess you up a bit, make it look a bit more real."

"How will we do that?"

"Let's rip your shirt and smudge dirt into your jeans and on
your back. Maybe slap yourself to make some red marks, too."

"I'm not sure I can do that Colton. How about you do it? It'll be more convincing with a man size mark."

Colton looked at Ginny realizing she liked it a bit rough. He gripped her and pushed her body against the wall, thumping her head on the stucco. Bringing his knee up, he raised her body upwards scraping a little skin off her back. Ginny gasped. Her breath was hot, her eyes excited.

"Oh, Colt! Yes! You're the one I want, the one I need."

Colton took a handful of hair and pulled Ginny's head back, and then bit into her neck. *If Maddy is half as good as Ginny I'll be happy, but damn she's good. If Ginny were Wynne's daughter there would be no problem getting the ranch that's for sure.*

"You're real good, Colt. You can do that to me again any time you want, darling."

"You sure are full of surprises, Ginny. Best we get you into that room before we forget why we're here."

"How do I look? Will he be convinced I've been attacked?"

"Without a doubt. Just don't look so pleased about it."

They laughed together and then he pushed her towards the corner of the building.

"Make it convincing. Get him holding you and keep those tits out."

Colton adjusted his jeans, and crept back to the window, picked up the camera that he'd abandoned earlier and waited for Ginny to knock on the door. A rapid pounding announced her arrival at the Italian's door. Colton stood and placed the camera lens on the windowsill ready to take rapid photos.

Chapter Twenty-Two

L ucio shifted uncomfortably on the motel room's one accent chair once the cell phone's display darkened. Images of Madison's mouth, the idea of her lips on his body burned desire through him. His heightened state was obvious, so he remained on the chair and gazed out across the illuminated parking lot to the outskirts of the town and a couple of trees swaying in the breeze. He vainly attempted to refocus his mind. Madison's affect on him was overwhelming and exciting all at the same time. No one, not even his last girlfriend affected him in such a way. He took a hot shower, then wrapped a towel around his waist and sat on the edge of the bed channel surfing.

A frantic knocking on the door startled him. He opened it to find Ginny, sobbing, dirty, and disheveled.

"*Mamma mia*! What happened, *bella*? Come in."

"Please help me, Lucio, I was attacked."

Lucio wrapped his arms around the young distraught woman's shoulder and guided her to the bed. She sat facing the rear window, clasping at his naked chest and letting her shirt fall off her shoulders. He stroked Ginny's hair and talked slowly in an attempt to sooth her distress. As she turned, her shirt fell open exposing a bugling breast. He turned away, pulling away and gripping the damp towel around his waist.

"We need to call the police."

Ginny hiccupped back her sobs. "Oh, I don't know about that. I've heard female victims are made out to be worse than their attackers in the courts. I can't go through that again, I just can't."

"Maybe think it over. Look I can call you a taxi to make sure you get home safely."

"I couldn't stay here, could I?"

"No, that's not going to happen. I have an early meeting and will feel uncomfortable with you here."

Ginny's eyes flicker to the rear window then she nodded. He picked up his cell, and then asked her for a number of a local taxi company. While they waited, he tried to distance himself from her, but she clung to his naked chest. Her eyes pooled with tears, and he kept his eyes averted from the rise and fall of her exposed breasts. Within twenty minutes she was in the vehicle and after locking the door, he slipped under the covers, exhaustion bringing sleep almost instantly.

Chapter Twenty-Three

awn was breaking as Colton woke up. His first task was to place the camera in a strategic place. where Madison would find it, but also where visitors had access. He needed to pull off another convincing act. He needed to be believable when he professed he had no idea of the camera's owner, but suggested looking at the images for clues that might help locate them. Once Madison saw the photographs, Colton could again be the ever-faithful friend - consoling and loving. Her infatuation with the outsider would vanish, leaving Colton as the hero. He smiled, relishing the thought and the certainty his plan would work.

From his hiding place, Colton watched as Madison sauntered into the stable, then looked down and picked up the camera.

"Good morning, Madison. You are earlier than normal. Have a bad dream, or were you busy dreaming about me?"

"Very funny, no I didn't on both counts. You must have been up extra early yourself to have all those mares out already."

"Just a quick worker, can't let the day get away from me."

"Yeah, sure. Look what I found, a camera. Do you have any idea who it belongs to?"

"Not a clue. Where was it?"

"On the floor beside this hay bale. There's no case and no markings on the strap. How do we find the owner? Maybe they will realize where they left it and come back."

"They might do. How about looking through a few photos? The owner could have taken pictures of themselves as well as the horses."

Colton made himself relax, inhaling deeply. In just a moment, Madison would see that no good foreigner with a half-naked woman.

Madison hesitated. "There might be private photos on it. Do I look?"

"It's the most obvious way to find the owner." Colton held his breath as he watched Madison's finger hover over the button. *Just open it!*

"Your right it's the simplest idea to find the owner, we only need to see a couple of photos anyway." Madison pushed the on button and waited. The camera did not spark into life.

Colton's clenched his jaw. *Work you damned thing, work.* He tensed as Madison tried again, but there was no whirring sound.

"The batteries must be dead. Maybe it's been here a long time. I'll put it on the office desk with a note so anyone answering a call about it will see it."

"Let me have a go. It must work."

He took the camera and shook it and then pushed the button. Still no response. He took out the batteries and then reinserted them. There was no whirring, and no light. Nothing happened. Teeth grinding and veins pumping in his neck, he just about controlled his temper. He wanted to throw the damn thing across the stable, but Madison had to see the photographs.

"The batteries must be dead, or the dampness has gotten into them. I'll get some new ones. Wait here."

"It's not that important, Colt, I'll take Sierra out to the paddock. I have to take Pops into town. We can look later."

He resisted the urge to grab her by the arms and shake her. Get it to work and then show her. Later, will work just as well as now.

"Sure, I can take Sierra, if you need to get to town. See you later."

"Thanks, Colt. We won't be too long."

He managed a smile, took the rope from her, and opened the stall door. As he hooked up Sierra's halter, he took several deep breaths, listening to Madison's footsteps fade. Once he'd released the last mare into the field, he returned to the stable and picked up the camera. *Useless thing, I'll get you working somehow.* In the bunkhouse, he searched several drawers, opening and slamming them shut in frustration until he found a new package of batteries. Discarding the ones out of the camera, he dropped the new ones in and flicked the on/off button. A green light flickered on.

Why couldn't you have done that earlier, and saved me the hassle of convincing Maddy to look at the images again? He busied himself around the barn and instructed the ranch hands on what chores needed doing, all the while trying to think up a plausible excuse to look at the camera images again with Madison.

Later, the sound of a vehicle coming up the main drive enticed Colton's curiosity. He stood up and looked out the office window. She was back with Wynne. Walking quickly, Colton met Maddy and her father at the veranda steps.

"Heh, Maddy. It was the batteries. It works now."

"What works, Colt?"

"Maddy found a camera in the stable, Wynne. I think the damp got into the batteries. We couldn't make it work earlier."

"I don't remember seeing anyone with a camera this week on the stud tours. Did you have any riding clients with cameras, Maddy?"

"Not that I can remember but it doesn't mean someone didn't have one."

"Are there any photos on it that might give us a clue as to who it belongs to, Colt?"

"I haven't looked yet. I've only just put the batteries in when I heard your truck, Wynne. Here, take a look. I need to get back to Clancy. He needs a hand."

Thank you, Wynne. You made my plan work even better. You'll be the one who makes her look now not me. I'm free and clear. I'll be the shoulder to cry on again in no time at all.

He smiled as he strode away, the mowed lawn crushing under his feet releasing a summer scent. He waited for Maddy's cry of anguish. He didn't have to wait long. Her scream filled the afternoon air, followed by a thud a yard or so away from him. Concern on his face, he turned around and raced back to find Wynne hugging his daughter as her tears flowed down her cheeks.

"What the hell happened?"

Wynne looked at his daughter and then shook his head from side to side an angry expression in his eyes. "Damned Italian's been playing her like a fool, that's what. There were pictures of him with another girl in a motel room. Need I say more, Colt?"

"No, of course not, I can make sure he doesn't show his face here again, Maddy."

Maddy wiped tears from her face and looked up at him her jaw set and anger blazing in her eyes.

"You don't need worry, Colt, if I see him on this property again, I'll shoot him as a trespasser. I'm going in, Pops, I need a drink."

The two men watched her angry stride as she walked into the house and then faced each other.

"You would take care of her proper, wouldn't you, Colt? She needs a steady, hardworking, honest man. Not these good-for-nothings she seems to get hooked up with. It looks like that Italian does more roaming than just around the globe."

There it is, the old man's sanction, the thing that will make Maddy see sense.

"You know I would, Wynne. Maddy means the world to me. She needs to be settled in one place, this place."

"I'm asking you to take care of her and keep that Romeo away. You hear me?"

"Yes, Sir, I do."

Wynne shook his hand and then turned to follow his daughter, saying, "She might need a drink but so do I. It was quite a shock seeing those photos and the devastating affect they had on her."

Colton suppressed his smile until he turned around. *She's mine now. I've even got the old man's permission to look after her and the ranch. You did good, boy.* His cell beeped just then. He looked at the display to find a text from Ginny.

Where did you go, handsome? Lucio wanted to take me to the police station! Told him my brother's taxi was coming for me. LOL. He didn't even try to fuck me. You'd better see me tonight. I want more. G. XXX

Thoughts of Ginny's soft flesh and appetite stirred Colton. *Maybe one more time and then I have to get her out of my life. I need to be seen as a loving and loyal man for Maddy and Wynne.* He typed a short reply.

You'll get a real man tonight. Meet me at Clarke's at 9 p.m.

Chapter Twenty-Four

A day later, Lucio drove through the Swaying Willow Ranch gateway, singing along to a song on the radio. The heat of the day, the blue sky and the daring swoops across the road by tiny birds added to his happiness. He could not contain his elation at seeing Madison again. The business meetings had dragged on and he'd lost concentration several times, a new experience for him and his suppliers. In the hot morning air, a heat haze shimmered on the horizon. Pulling up in front of the green tiled house, he looked around for Maddy. He'd expected to find her eager to meet him. After shutting off the engine, he got out of the convertible and ascended the veranda steps.

"One more step and I'll blow that pretty face into oblivion." Maddy's words were pure venom.

Lucio stood still as the shotgun pointed at his face. "Maddy, what are you doing?"

"Get out of here before I let you have both barrels, you son of a bitch. How many girls have you bedded in this town?"

Before Lucio could answer her the sound of thundering footsteps approaching made them both turn. Bandit barked then growled and only just made it out of the way, as Colton ran straight at Lucio, throwing a punch at his right cheek. The impact propelled Lucio onto the veranda slats. Lucio's breath whooshed out as his chest was crushed under Colton's weight as the ranch hand fell on top of him. Colton's knees had him pinned to the wooden planks, his face furious and focused, while his fists hit flesh again and again. Colton swore as each punch found its target. Lucio felt his nose spray blood under the impact of furious knuckles. He gasped with pain and saw Madison flinch shock on her face. She reached out to tug at Colton's arm, but he was moving so fast her hand grasped nothing but air.

She screamed, "Colton, stop, stop now!"

Colton's punches continued without hesitation. Lucio put his forearms up to fend off the attack but being pinned down his attempts at punching back were ineffective. He tried to rock his body back and forth to get his attacker off him, but Colton's weight was too much. At Colton's repeated strikes red marks appeared on Lucio's face and his exposed chest as his shirt ripped apart. Bandit was snarling now. Madison pulled at the old dog's collar. Lucio heard her frantic pleading.

"No, Colt, no, you have to get off him! Colton, no more, you have to stop. Stop now."

Lucio saw Madison's frustration spill over as she swung her boot at Colton's side. The steel tip hit his ribs and Colton gasped in pain then looked at her, his eyes dazed. Blood dripped from his knuckles. He got up and looked down at Lucio, then stood in front of Madison, shielding her. Bandit twisted in Madison's grip and snarled at Colton. He dodged Colton's boot heel.

"You get out of here before I use that gun. You hurt my Maddy real bad and that is unforgivable. She's my girl and don't you forget it. Now get."

Madison looked at Colton in astonishment. "Now wait a minute, Colt. Firstly, I'm not your girl. We are good friends, but that's it. Second and most importantly, Lucio has the right to explain those photos. It is up to me whether I believe him or not. You'd better leave now. Lucio has every right to press charges, but I'll try to persuade him not to. Now go."

It was Colton's turn to stare in amazement. "You are not seriously going to believe this scum. He cheated on you just like Daniel. He might try to swing it with his fancy accent, but pictures don't lie. He was naked and so was she."

"Colton, I need you to go. Get those knuckles patched up. I'll see to Lucio. God only knows what damage you have done. The last thing Pops and me need is an employee on charges for battery."

Fists still clinched, Colton turned to leave, venom in his words. "Come to your senses Madison he's just a pasta-faced charmer, he played you and probably many others."

Lucio eased his battered body up to sit on the top step cradling his face in both hands. Bandit was sitting at his feet. Maddy placed her hands over his and lowered them to reveal his battered face.

"Oh my, what a mess. Come inside, I'll get you cleaned up. We might need a trip to the hospital. You may need stitches in your lip."

He pulled his arm away from her touch. "I want him charged, Madison. It was an unprovoked attack. With that sort of temper, he needs to be behind bars."

"Well, it wasn't totally unprovoked, was it? Although, I think Colton went too far, he was protecting my honor."

"What are you talking about?"

"You sleeping around, and playing me for a fool that's what."

"Other women? I have not seen other women, only you. I thought we liked each other."

"Sure, dig yourself in deeper. I have proof you are cheating."

"I swear on my Mamma's life, Madison, I have not been with another woman since meeting you. What do you mean proof?"

She looked deep into his eyes searching them, a frown creasing her brow.

Lucio struggled to get up and sat on the veranda swing touching the bruised and broken skin on his face and chest as he watched Madison go back into the house. He spat out blood and touched his nose and winced.

"Don't go anywhere. I'll be right back." She returned with the battered camera.

"What is this?"

"The remains of a camera I threw across the lawn. I hope it will work so I can see your reaction."

She flicked the button, and the camera shuddered to life. The display screen was divided by a long crack, but it didn't obscure the images it contained. She handed it to Lucio and then watched for his response.

"So now tell me you are not guilty."

He looked at the hazy images of his motel room. "This is... not what it looks like, *bella*. I swear. Can I explain?"

The sarcasm in her voice pierced his heart. "Oh, please do, I'm a sucker for a good story."

"This girl, Ginny, came to my motel scared and frightened. She told me she'd been attacked. I could not leave her outside in that state. I admit I comforted her but only that, I swear it. When I tried to persuade her to go to the police station, she said her brother would pick her up. She did not stay long."

"Wait a minute, Ginny? As in the woman from the coffee shop?"

"Yes, the same girl who served me."

"Now come on, she's a right pretty girl and she sure isn't shy. You could have invited her."

"I did not invite her, Maddy, she bumped into me earlier outside the motel while I was unpacking but I did not invite her into my room. Although, she was quite insistent in wanting to come in. She flirted a lot, was very suggestive. It was over an hour before she pounded on my door again, I'd just got out of the shower. She was dirty and had scratches and welts all over her. You can see them here - look."

Lucio held the camera toward Madison urging her to see the image. She was watching his face for any telltale sign he was lying.

"So, you are telling me Ginny just happened to knock on your door rather than anyone else's? I know she was flirting with you at the café but why would she pretend to be attacked just to get into his bed?"

"She knew which room I was in, as the door was open when I unloaded my suitcase to let in some fresh air. She stood at the door suggesting a good time, but that does not mean I slept with her or invited her in for anything but real concern at her distress. Please believe me."

His heart sunk at her next words.

"I don't know what to think Lucio. I've had my heart broken before because I was too trusting. I need to think about this. Let me get some water and gauze, I can clean those wounds."

"There is no need for you to think, Madison. It is obvious you do not trust me. Stay with your dirty cowboy."

He stood up and pushed past her. Her attempts to persuade him to stay fell on deaf ears, he stormed off to his car, and immediately the tires were spitting gravel as the car raced down the drive.

Madison sat on the swing seat, her mind whirling with opposing thoughts. *Was Colton right about Lucio? Was he a Romeo taking advantage of any woman he could charm? Lucio had looked her straight in the eye when he professed his innocence. Could someone who was lying do that?*

The plume of dust from Lucio's tires had settled by the time Madison moved from the veranda. I've lost him. Damn, Colton! I know he was trying to protect me but his actions were more than a little overboard. It's been a long time since I've seen Colton violent. Beating up bullies at school is one thing but this, this is not right.

Later, she sat pushing her food around her plate at supper, deep in thought. *Am I so charmed by Lucio, I believe him no matter what, or is he innocent? Colton has shown me the depth of his feelings, but his vicious attack was frightening. Yes, he had been wild in high school, but he's calmed down a lot since then, or has he? Is he hiding a violent streak?*

"You can over think things, you know, Maddy? Why not sleep on it?"

Her father's words penetrated her confused mind.

"Sorry, Pops, maybe you are right. I can't seem to pinpoint something important. I just go round and round in circles. Is Lucio a player? Is Colton safe to be around? Which one truly loves me? Which one can I trust?"

"You will only make yourself crazy. Go and rest. Things will be clearer in the morning."

"You're quite right, Pops. Good night. See you in the morning."

Madison tossed and turned all night. Something didn't ring true about the events of the day. *What was it?* No matter how many times she went over each conversation and accusation, she could not pinpoint the reason for her uneasiness. The glimmer of truth was just beyond her thoughts. A while later, mentally exhausted she fell into a fitful sleep.

Chapter Twenty-Five

L ucio returned to the motel, anger fueling his thoughts and actions. Inspecting his battered face in the bathroom mirror, he saw the deep split in his lip. His skin already showed signs of discoloration as bruises emerged. He ripped off his tattered and bloody shirt and threw it into the trash. A thin film of congealed blood covered his face and neck, carefully avoiding his lip he washed off the blood. *That man is a danger, a maniac - how can Madison not see that?* As he moved his mouth, the split in his lip began to bleed again. *I do need stitches.* Lucio picked up the phone on the bedside table and called the reception.

"Hello, Sir, how may I help?"

"I need medical assistance, is there a doctor's practice nearby or a hospital?"

"Do you need an ambulance? I can call right now."

"No, no it's not that serious but thank you. I will come by and pick up directions in a moment."

The young receptionist looked shocked as Lucio approached the front desk. "Oh, my goodness, what happened to you? Are you sure you don't need an ambulance?"

"I'm sure that is not necessary, do you have directions to a doctor's office? I will go now before it gets too late. I think my lip will require stitches."

"Here I've written them down and I called to say one of our guests would be arriving. If you need anything, please let me know."

Anger seething in his chest, Lucio swung the car onto the road and turn the wrong way. He realized his error in direction when he passed the town limit sign. Finding a gravel track some way further on he made a U-turn and sped back the way he'd come. His lip throbbed painfully, and stiffness was settling into his back. In his rush, he almost missed the turn and swung the car in a wide arc only just missing a mini van on the other side of the road.

The driver's eyes grew wide, and Lucio understood the expletive she used. He raised his hand in apology and drove into the doctor's practice parking stall relieved to see the 'Open' sign displayed. He swung the door open crashing it against the wall. A nurse in a pink uniform clasped her clipboard and shrieked.

"Is the doctor still here? Have I missed him?"

The nurse looked at his battered face, picked up her clipboard and calmly spoke in a professional tone. "No, he's still here. Please come and sit that lip looks sore. Let's get some details and I will notify Dr. Cummings you are here."

After stating his name and that he was a guest at the motel, the nurse led him into the doctor's office. A middle-aged man with a shiny dome of a baldhead greeted Lucio.

"Well, you have been in the wars. Let's take a look at that lip first then we can see about any other injuries."

Once the doctor examined him, he administered a local anesthetic and put three stitches into Lucio's lip. As the doctor treated him, Lucio remained silent. When the doctor tied the last stitch, he asked Lucio to remove his shirt and manipulated his shoulders and neck.

"Well, you will certainly be sore and stiff by this evening. I will give you some muscle relaxants and pain medication. Do you want to explain what happened?"

"A complete maniac attacked me, an unprovoked attack I might add. I will see him charged for this."

"Is this a local man you are talking about? I know them all one way or another."

"His name is Colton, and he works at Willow Sway Ranch."

"Colt did this to you! He's always had a temper that I cannot deny and over the years I've treated several boys he got into scuffles with, but that was in school and certainly not recent. This is extreme. What were you fighting about, if I may be so bold?"

"I was not fighting. In fact, he charged at me along the veranda like an animal, grappled me to the floor, and then proceeded to punch me before I realized what was happening. Even when Madison screamed at him, he kept punching as he held me down. He is unstable. He should be locked up."

Doc Cummings looked at the stranger's injuries. "Colton had made a mess of other men's faces in his time as a wild child in his youth, but I thought he'd tamed down, but this is by far the worst. Take two of these now and before you go to sleep, they will ease the pain and swelling. Come back in the morning so I can check on those stitches, I don't think you will have much of a scar, not like the one on your side anyway."

"Thank you, Doctor. I will see you in the morning."

His lip throbbed as Lucio drove back to the motel. Once in his room, Lucio showered taking care not to rub too hard on his injured skin. He saw bruising up his back and across his shoulders in the bathroom mirror before it steamed up. No matter what Madison said, Colton was dangerous - old friend or not.

Chapter Twenty-Six

With the faint light of dawn piercing through the curtains, Madison sat bolt upright in her bed. *How did Colton know Ginny and Lucio were naked or almost anyway? I didn't think he'd seen the photographs on the camera.* There was something going on with Colton and she was determined to find out what. She managed to snooze until she heard her father downstairs.

As Madison entered the kitchen, the coffee aroma filled the room. Fat spat out of the frying pan as her father cracked eggs into it. Madison poured a mug of coffee and sipped.

"Did you manage to get any sleep, Maddy?"

"Not a brilliant night's sleep but I did manage to get a little shuteye, thanks Pops. I think a cup of this coffee will keep me awake. I sure need something. How many scoops did you put in?"

"It's only a couple, heaped. You know I like it strong."

She remembered the chat with Doc a couple of days earlier, which had settled her worries. He'd reassured her, her father was in good health, but his diet required some adjusting. "Now, Pops, you know the doc said you're supposed to cut down on the fat, salt, and caffeine."

"At my age there has to be some enjoyment in my day. Now, stop your fussing, one egg or two for you?"

"That's another thing. You need to poach those eggs instead of frying them. I'll have two please."

Madison gave her father a lighthearted nudge as she gathered the cutlery, place mats, and ketchup. She left the salt on the shelf on purpose. With the table set, she sat down and pondered whether she needed to mention her suspicions about Colton.

"There you are, Maddy, best meal of the day."

She stabbed her yolks to let the yellow liquid run over the buttery toast. She looked up at her father. *I'll have to substitute butter for olive oil spread too. That'll go down like a lead balloon.*

"Thanks, Pops, it looks delicious but I'm afraid it's just a heart attack on a plate. We both need to eat healthier, you know?"

"Stop worrying, Maddy. Just enjoy it, I will."

Afterwards with her hands deep in the soapy dishwashing water Madison thanked her father for making it. Wynne went upstairs to dress. He was shuffling one foot as he left the kitchen. *He's getting older. You need to start paying more attention.* Once the dishes were dried and put away, she went up to her bedroom. Her father's door was slightly ajar. As she walked past, she stopped in her tracks. He was sitting on the edge of his bed holding his chest. *Oh, no!*

Without the mandatory knock on his door, Madison rushed in. "Pops, are you all right? Shall I call an ambulance?"

"What? Good gracious, girl, you scared me half to death. What are you talking about, an ambulance?"

"You are holding your chest, I thought...oh, Pops, you frightened me."

"Now come here and sit down. I was talking to your Ma. I do it every morning. I hold my heart 'cause that's where she is, in my mind anyway. I'm fine, quit you're worrying."

Madison's tears fell from her chin onto his dressing gown sleeve. "I don't know what I'd do without you, Pops, really I don't."

"Well, I intend to stay around for quite a while yet, so stop your fretting. Come on, buck up we have two clients coming with mares in an hour."

With a loud sniff, she brushed a couple of tears from her cheeks.

"All right, panic over. I'll meet you in the breeding shed later. Don't worry yourself about me, girl."

His stubble brushed against her cheek as he gave her a quick kiss before releasing her from his embrace. She smiled and walked to her room. Showered and dressed, she made her way to the stallions stable. She pushed her earlier suspicions of Colton to the back of her mind. Loud snorts welcomed her. Titan certainly lived up to his name. He was a magnificent animal - all seventeen hands of him. Jet-black, apart from a white blaze the length of his nose, Titan was the first choice for many clients.

"Hello, my beautiful boy. You know what today is, don't you? Girlfriend visiting day, you lucky boy. Let's get you brushed and looking even more splendid."

Madison worked hard to make Titan's coat shine and braided his mane and tail. By the time she heard the horse trailer's coming up the drive, Titan looked spectacular.

"There, no mare will be able to resist you now, Titan."

She led him into the breeding shed, a tight grip on his lead rope as the stallion threw his head in excitement. "Steady, boy."

"Here, Ted and I will take him, Maddy he'll be dragging you around in no time. Once he smells those mares, he'll be too much of a handful for just you."

Relieved, Madison gave the lead rope to Colton. Titan knew what the shed was for, without a doubt. She walked towards the horse trailers and saw her father talking to two men wearing Stetsons.

"Here's my daughter, Madison, she just won the barrel racing championship on a mare sired by Titan."

"Pleased to meet you, darling. My name is Aubrey Stokes, and this is my good friend, Alan Chambers. We've seen you in the arena and you're sure one fine rider. You look real good mounted."

Madison took an immediate dislike to Aubrey Stokes. His sly innuendo and the dried saliva at the corners of his lips made her shiver. She nodded a greeting and looked toward her father for direction. He spoke directly to Alan and Aubrey.

"Are we ready to present the mares?"

"Alan, you take your mare in first. I'll stay a while with this delightful young woman."

Madison averted such a situation by turning to the other rancher. "I'll escort you Mr. Chambers. My foreman has the stallion in the breeding shed already. I'm sure this won't take long. Titan performs well." Before Aubrey could sneak in another innuendo, Madison walked Alan to the rear of the horse trailer.

"It is best to lead your mare straight to the breeding shed, Alan. She will get nervous if we hesitate."

"Thank you for your advice, Madison, but I can assure you this isn't my first time. I'll share a trick with you. Make up a mixture of olive oil and essence of lavender and smear it on his nose. It keeps him calm, and he doesn't smell the mare until the last minute."

"I've never heard of that. Where did you pick that one up?"

"Unfortunately, I have to credit Aubrey. The old letch."

"He has other talents other than making women feel uncomfortable then?"

They laughed in unison as Alan led his mare out of the horse-box but stifling their giggles as they passed Aubrey and Pops chatting together. With a determined stride toward the shed, Madison opened one huge door while Alan pulled at the mare's lead rope. They could hear Titan snorting. The mare neighed loudly - a good sign. Titan answered with a deep whinny in anticipation. Colton and Ted struggled to hold Titan as the mare trotted up to him.

Alan commented, "I don't think we'll have any trouble with this siring."

The horses performed while the humans observed. Colton stood to one side while Madison stood between the two men and chatted.

"He is magnificent, Madison. Your father has some good stock here."

"Thanks, Alan. The family has worked hard to breed strong healthy livestock without any rogues for a couple generations. My grandfather brought a couple of horses from a Spanish breeder to add to our breeding line."

"We will continue to have the very best horses at Willow Sway Ranch for a long time yet. Won't we, Maddy?"

Colton's arm rested on Madison's shoulder. She wanted to brush him off but thought best not to in front of a client, but his insinuation riled her. *How dare he imply he and I are a couple? I'll play nice for now.* When she answered she emphasized the 'I' in her sentence.

"Yes, I will run the ranch in line with all the knowledge my father has taught me, Alan. I intend to have a great breeding stock for many years to come."

Alan's puzzlement at her statement showed in his face, but Ted's shouting for Colton to help him, interrupted further discussions. Titan stamped his hooves and tried to mount the mare again. Dust billowed into the air around the stallion's hooves.

Alan and Madison pulled the mare away while Colton and Ted held the stallion.

"Serves us right for chit chatting, I suppose. I'll get this girl back to her trailer."

"I will follow you out, Alan. I have to bring Aubrey's mare over next."

As they exited the breeding shed, Aubrey and Pops met them, their shoulders peppered with raindrops.

"What's all the excitement?"

"Titan's proving to be an over eager participant, Pops."

"Best we get this mare in there then."

The soft summer rain damped the atmosphere as Aubrey led the dappled grey mare into the shed. Titan's snorting echoed around the walls as he saw the next mare.

Relieved at not having to suffer Aubrey's letch full old eyes, Madison walked back to Alan's trailer with him, hunching her shoulders as the raindrops fell.

"I hope you don't mind me saying, Madison, but you have a fine man there in Colton. He is an excellent employee."

"Really, do you know him?"

"Yes, he worked for me for a couple of summers quite a while back now. He was young but willing to learn the ropes and worked damn hard. He was on a work program."

"I've known Colton since high school I don't think he ever mentioned working at another ranch, or stables. What program?"

"Damn, maybe I shouldn't have said anything. Believe me he is a great worker."

"It's all right, Alan, Colton is almost family, and we've known him a long time."

"He was placed at my stables for a teen rehabilitation program. He worked well and showed me he had turned his life around in just a few months. He had a way with the horses even then calmed them down when no one else could. It's rare to find someone like him, ready to work and a passion for the ranching life as well as empathy with horses all rolled into one. It will be good for your ranch to keep hold of him."

"Yes, Colt sure is a rancher through and through and there is no doubt about his abilities with the horses. I wonder why he never told me about the program."

"I expect he was ashamed. We all make stupid mistakes when we are young. I can assure you when he left my place, he was a responsible, hardworking man. I even asked him to stay on permanently, but he told me he had a girl and a home to go to. Now I see why he wanted to be here, you're a fine pretty girl."

"Thanks, Alan."

"Well, I hope I didn't speak out of turn."

"No, that's okay."

Worried thoughts rolled over in her mind. *How many more secrets have you got Colton? You loved me even then? It must be torture seeing me every day and knowing I'm not interested. Oh, Colton. Have I misjudged you? It was obvious Alan couldn't praise you enough.*

Pops and Aubrey joined her and Alan a short time later in front of the office. Money for stud fees was exchanged and the two cowboys drove their horseboxes away. The rain was steady, and rivulets were forming in the trailer tracks.

"That was a good morning's work, Maddy. Let's have a beer to celebrate."

"It's just past noon, Pops."

"You only live once. Come on, placate your father."

Father and daughter strode over to the green roofed ranch house, which was nestled between two tall pines, trying to dodge the rain as they went.

Madison's mind was full of conflicting thoughts. *I've lived here all my life, and I still love it. Would Lucio expect to take me away to Italy? I don't think I could bear being away from Pops for long periods of time. What if Lucio never comes back? Ought I to hang my heart on a handsome face? Would Colt's behavior be enough to scare him away? Does Lucio think so little of me? Could our relationship work or am I deluding myself? Colton knows me so well and can handle any situation that comes along on the ranch. Colt has shown me how much he cares for me. I would always be safe with him. He's always protected me. I need to stop dreaming and face practicalities. His reaction to Lucio was extreme but doesn't that just show the depth of his feelings for me - he was protecting me from harm - again.*

With beer bottles in hand, father and daughter sat on the veranda overlooking the driveway, lawn, and paddocks. Dark grey clouds in the sky released their raindrops cooling down the earlier heat of the day and dampening the parched earth.

"Nice and cool, just the way I like them. There's nothing like a swig of beer to commemorate a good day's work."

As they sat on the veranda, they watched Colton and Ted lead Titan to the paddock. Colton was stroking the stallion's neck and talking to him in a soft calm voice. The horse kept swinging his head toward Colton in response.

"Colt really has a way with the horses, doesn't he, Pops?"

"For sure, never seen anyone calm a stallion down like that after breeding. One of the reasons I thought he would make a good ranch manager."

She let out a sigh. "You're right, Pops. He is the right choice." *I know you will be happier knowing I married a rancher and someone you're familiar with. His lost of control, that angry exchange I'm sure was only fueled by whiskey and jealousy, a one-time thing.*

"What made you change your mind?"

"I've had time to think, that's all. Why not ask him to come for supper like you suggested and you can tell him then?"

Madison sipped her beer, her exterior calm but her mind plagued with troubling thoughts. *I'm deluding myself that a man like Lucio would want a girl like me. I've made bad decisions before and paid the price with heartbreak. For all I know Lucio might have a girl in every rodeo town and use that smooth accent to charm their pants off. Well, he didn't fool this one. Why did I not listen to Colton and Pops sooner? They have better instincts than me. It's obvious they both love me.*

Chapter Twenty-Seven

The bubbling pans of water filled the kitchen with steam. Madison dropped three sizable lobsters into the largest pot and secured the top. She stirred up butter cubes until they melted and then poured the clear liquid over lemon zest. A large mixed salad chilled in the fridge and the seldom used dining table was set with a fresh linen tablecloth.

Satisfied everything was under control, Madison ran upstairs to have a quick shower. Once dressed, she picked up her mother's photograph. *You and Pops married young, and you were both so happy together. I'll make Colton and me work for your sake Ma, and for Pops. He only wants the best for me I know that.* Lucio's handsome face popped into her mind. *A pretty face will fade but a loyal, loving, and hardworking man will stand the test of time.*

A firm knocking on the front door brought Madison out of her musings. *That must be Colton. He's early.* She approached the door puzzling at the blurred shape on the other side through the frosted glass panel. She opened it to find Lucio holding a large bouquet of flowers.

"Maddy, my *bella*, I come to apologize. I was angry but it was no excuse for treating you in such a way."

"Lucio? What are you doing here?"

He looked surprise by her question. "To apologize to you, I lost my temper with you. His actions made me lose myself in anger. I am asking for your forgiveness."

Her head jerked backwards, and then shook side to side. "Come in. Oh, wait, maybe not. Let's go to the stable."

"Go to the stable, but why?"

Madison's mind was exploding with conflicting thoughts. *Had she misinterpreted Lucio? Was he as genuine as he seemed?*

"Please just follow me, quickly."

Her mind spun. I need to sort out my feelings. *Who do I love? Love? I don't really know Lucio. Colton has always been there for me and it is obvious he loves me a great deal. Do I risk him leaving because of an infatuation with a smooth talking, handsome, sexy Italian?*

Madison pulled Lucio into the nearest stable and closed the door. She flicked the light switch making the mares pop their heads up. The air filled with the scent of horse, hay, and pellet feed.

"Madison, please tell me what is going on. Why are we hiding in here?"

"I don't know where to start, Lucio. When you left, I thought you had gone for good. I didn't blame you. Ranch life is rough. I'm rough, just look at me. I'm not a sophisticated woman dressed in designer clothes."

"Wait, wait, what are you saying? When did I ever say I wanted such a woman? Beautiful women, all cold and distant in their allure, have surrounded me my whole life. They are as false as their makeup. I do not want that kind of woman. I want you with your vitality, humor, and natural beauty."

"Are you sure? I'm dirty more often than not and smell of manure, sweat and hay. The city life isn't for me. I find it hard spending an evening there let alone living in one. I couldn't jet set around and leave Pops, he needs me. We are so different, Lucio, it wouldn't work."

The bouquet slipped from Lucio's hand. He gazed into Madison's eyes and sighed.

"You want me to go? I will leave if that is what you want."

"Yes, get your foreign stink out of here before I give you another beating." Colton's voice was thick with threat. Madison and Lucio swung around to face him, standing at the entrance to the stable with a mare in tow.

"Don't say a word, Maddy. Not one word. You get out now. She has had enough of your sort. Treating her like dirt. How many others have you cheated on? She deserves a real man, one who loves her without secrets, not a traveling Romeo."

Madison's mind swirled with images of Colton and Lucio on the veranda, fists flying. The hours Colton sat with her as she cried over Daniel. Lucio's hand slipping into hers, pulsing with electricity. Colton telling her jokes and visiting old haunts to cheer her up. Lucio's kisses so tender and sweet but Lucio taking her away from the ranch, Pops, and everything she knew and loved. Her heart ached at the thought of leaving the only home she had ever known. Colton had shown her the depth of his love. *I can't make another mistake.*

Lucio looked at Madison. Her head moved side to side ever so slightly before she ran out of the side door towards the house.

Lucio saw Colton's face brake into a satisfied smile as he tied the lead rope to a hook.

"The best man won the girl and the ranch. Now get out of my sight and don't come back else I'll put you in a six foot hole and fill it with horse shit."

Lucio stood up straight and walked past Colton with clenched fists. "You might fool Madison, but you don't fool me. It's the ranch you want not her."

"It's a means to an end and some pasta twister's not going to spoil years of hard work and planning. I deserve this place after all the hours I put in. And anyway, Maddy knows me a darn sight better than you. She'll calm down once I get her pregnant."

Lucio swung for Colton, but the rancher managed to duck and swing to his right. The crack of a whip echoed in the stable. The arm of Lucio's shirt sliced in two. Blood beaded from the wound. Lucio let out a cry of pain. Colton raised the whip again, but Lucio managed to avoid it. He grabbed a pitchfork and pointed it at Colton.

"You are a mad, dangerous man. I will protect Maddy from you."

"I'm the one who's going to protect her from a low life Romeo. She's mine and so is this ranch."

The whip cracked above Lucio's head. He threw the pitchfork towards Colton and ran out of the side door and towards his convertible.

Chapter Twenty-Eight

M adison stood on the dark veranda as Lucio sped away. Her heart ached and tears welled. *He can't think that much of me if he won't even try to persuade me he loves me. He can't love me. Pops is right - Colton is the one I ought to be with. At least our worlds are the same. I was dazzled by his uniqueness, his newness – what was I thinking?*

Shaking her body and head to rid herself of the thoughts and pain, she entered the steam filled kitchen and placed the lobsters in the buffet server. Pops and Colton walked in together, their talk relaxed and amiable. She tried to clear her confused mind and gave them both an uneasy smile.

"Something smells wonderful. We're living it up in the dining room I see. Come on, Colt. Let's carry the plates in for Maddy."

Pops collected the plates and the butter dip and followed Colton, pushing the buffet server table. Madison followed behind with the salad bowl thinking, *we haven't used that server since Ma died. This house needs a family in it again, not two lonely people clinging to the past.*

Chins and fingers sticky with butter, and several bottles of beers later, the trio relaxed and regaled each other with jokes, before Wynne said, "Well, Colt, I suppose I need to tell you the reason we invited you over tonight."

"It wasn't just for this fantastic supper? This was excellent, Maddy, best lobster I ever had."

"Thank you, Colton. I thought I'd spoilt it."

Wynne smiled. "No, there's a reason we asked you here tonight, Colt. We want you to be the ranch manager. Well, actually to try out the position for three months. See how you like it and how it suits us. What do you say?"

Colton clinched his hands together under the table, inhaled and put a smile on his face as he said, "Are you serious? It would be an honor. You know I love this place. It's more like home to me."

"Maddy and I feel you have the talent and an obvious a strong work ethic to make this place even more successful. Congratulations."

Beer bottles clinked together in a toast. Colton smiled at Maddy. She smiled back but it did not reach her eyes. She stood up. "Wait until you see what I made for dessert."

Madison strode into the kitchen, gasping for breath. *Is this right? Have I made the right decision? Lucio was so sincere. He looked me right in the eye. That bouquet must have cost a fortune but it's not all about flashy cars and bouquets of flowers, is it? Who will run the ranch once Pops isn't here? What if Lucio wants me to live in Italy? I couldn't give up the ranch. Who has shown me they will protect and love me better than Colt? Get a hold of yourself. Going over it time and again isn't helping.*

Madison slid the huge apple pie out of the warming oven and carried it into the dining room. Once she placed it in the center of the table, she returned to the kitchen to collect the cream.

Back at the table, she sliced the pie into generous helpings and passed them around.

"I won't be able to move for a month with all this food. You don't want a fat husband. Do you Maddy?"

Her father's head swung upwards. "What's this? Are you keeping secrets from me, Maddy?"

"No, Pops. I think Colton forgot himself is all."

Her father looked at Colton, who was gazing at Maddy with a loving look. "Well, if you two young ones will excuse me, I need to sit in my armchair and have a snooze."

"I could join you, Wynne but maybe I will help Maddy instead. Shall I?"

"Thanks, Colt. That would be great. I'm not the best cook in the world but I can sure use a lot of pans doing it."

Colton carried the plates and empty beer bottles into the kitchen, a confident grin creasing his features. Without waiting for Madison, he ran the hot water tap and submerged the plates into the sink. Suds spilled over the counter as he washed each plate. She stood beside him drying the plates as he passed them to her.

He placed a finger on Madison's nose covering it in suds. She retaliated by scooping up a handful and spreading them over his back. Soon their bodies were covered in suds and damp patches, their laughter uncontrollable. Colton took Madison's face in his hands and kissed her lightly on her lips. Then stood still. She looked deep into his eyes then returned the kiss. Their kisses grew more passionate.

Madison pushed images of Lucio from her mind, although the urgency, the electricity of touch wasn't there. *I can learn to love Colt for Pop's sake, can't I?* She could feel Colton's excitement, his breath heavy on her face. He pulled her shirt out of her jeans and cupped one breast.

"Colton, stop, please stop, I can't do this now. Please."

Colton shuddered. "You're right, Maddy, I'm moving too fast. Sorry. I'll say goodnight." He placed a light kiss on her forehead and walked out in the cool evening air. Madison watched him leave giving a smirk as he adjusted his jeans, and then climbed up the stairs with slow steps, deep in thought. *Again, he surprised me. Maybe Pops' intuition is better than mine. Most men wouldn't have stopped but I still imagine Lucio. Surely, that's wrong if Colton is the one.*

Chapter Twenty-Nine

A night of conflicting emotions exhausted Madison. She questioned herself over and over. Questions were easy, answers were not. *A foreigner in a foreign land, or a good friend who knows ranch life and her past?*

In the morning, she yawned as she entered the kitchen.

"That's not my usual bright eyed, bushy tailed girl. Didn't you sleep?"

"Not a lot, Pops. How about some of that treacle you call coffee?"

As her father poured her a mug, Madison's cell phone rang. It was Lucio. "Thanks, Pops. I'll take this outside." Once she was on the back porch, Madison answered the call. "Hello, Lucio? I didn't expect to hear from you again."

"Maddy, there was a good reason for me leaving the way I did. Will you meet me tonight? I have something important to tell you."

"Why all the mystery, can't you tell me now?"

"It would be best told face to face. Please, *bella*, it is vital I talk to you."

"Well, all right. Where, and at what time?"

"Meet me at the Cartridge restaurant in town at eight?"

"Okay, I'll be there."

"I can get the taxi to swing by and pick you up, Maddy."

"No, that's all right, I'll meet you there."

Madison couldn't help smiling as her heart missed a beat. *Colton never makes me this foolish.* She walked back into the kitchen, where her father was sitting down to a plate of bacon and eggs.

"Yours is under the broiler, girl, keeping warm."

Although she had no appetite she took the oven mitt, retrieved the plate from under the broiler and placed it on the table. Sitting opposite her father, she played with her food for a while, pushing around the plate.

"No need to fool me. If you ain't hungry, don't bother. Bandit will appreciate it."

"Sorry, Pops. I think I'm much too tired. Think I'll get a couple more hours. See if I feel better after."

"You ailing or something. Have you got a temperature?"

"No, Pops, just plain old tired out. See you later."

She kissed her father on the top of his head and ruffled Bandits ears before laying her plate on the floor for the dog to consume the breakfast. Once upstairs in her bedroom, she pulled the covers up to her chin and closed her eyes. Lucio's smiling face flickered behind her eyelids then merged into Colton's laughing face. *What could be so important? Was Lucio going to give her good news or bad?* She fell asleep, too exhausted to wonder about what Lucio would say.

Chapter Thirty

Madison dreamed of Lucio riding Titan while she rode beside him on Amber Fire. Lucio dressed in jeans and a plaid shirt and a white Stetson. His dark hair curled at the nape of his neck. They tied the horses up and made love in long meadow grass. As she rolled over, Colton kissed her cheek, and they stood on the front porch holding hands. His rough hands clasped hers, and his scent was familiar and comfortable. She woke up refreshed but puzzled. *Which one is the one?*

Getting out of bed, she enjoyed a brisk shower to soothe her body and mind. Once dressed, she made her way to the tack room. Her father was busy rubbing leather oil into a saddle. Its aroma was familiar and made her feel at home. Saddles hung on custom supports along one wall and halters with bits along another. With the store cupboards' doors open she could see the many folded cloths and containers lined up above labels Colton had made when he organized it.

"Well, look who's up. Feeling better now, my girl?"

"Much better, thanks, Pops."

"That's good to hear. Take a cloth and begin on that saddle."

They worked together, rubbing oil into the leather for an hour or so. Darcy came in and asked for her father's help.

"I'm fine, Pops. You go. I can finish the rest of the tack."

Madison kept herself busy, but the hours dragged on throughout the day. She had to think of an excuse to leave in the evening. Several ideas came and went. At five o'clock, she saw her father walk to the house as she led a mare into the stable. *Well, now or never.* Walking to the house, she heard voices.

"Heh, Madison, Doc came over for a visit. You didn't put him up to it did you?"

"I certainly did not. Hi, Doc."

"Hello, Madison. I was over at Frank's and thought I could pop in. Your father is a suspicious old goat."

"Well, have a good visit. I'm going out so Pops will enjoy the company."

She noticed her father's puzzled look, but headed up the stairs before he could question her. She relished the creamy lather of a new fragrant shower gel, and let the water run down her body as she pulled her fingers through her hair. Out of the shower, she rubbed at the mirror to see her reflection. Wrapped in a towel sitting on the floor she blew the hairdryer at her hair as she shook her head. When her hair was dry, she made a parting to one side and fixed a hair slide to make a sweep. Looking through her wardrobe, she chose black jeans and a crisp white shirt with tiny pearl earrings. As she descended the stairs, Doc and her father were talking in the living room. Tiptoeing across the hallway, she called out her goodbye from the front door.

Her heart beat faster the closer she got to the restaurant. The restaurant's name was lit with blue and gold light the reflections glittering on puddles from the earlier downpour. She parked the truck and looked around the parking lot. Lucio got out of a taxicab as she cut the engine. He walked up to her and clasped her hand in his.

"Thank you for agreeing to come, Maddy."

"You sounded so concerned. I thought it best."

"Shall we go in?"

"Yes, of course. Where's your rental car?"

"It's being repaired. All four tires were slashed and the paint-work gouged."

"Oh no, how dreadful. When did that happen?"

"Last night at the motel."

"What the heck? Do they have security cameras? Maybe they can find out who did it."

"I think I know who the culprit is, but enough of that for now."

Lucio held out his arm and Madison curled her own arm around it. The tingling sensation thrilled her as their hands touched. *We fit together just like two jigsaw pieces. We are different shapes but make a new form when linked.* She smiled inwardly at her fanciful thoughts.

Lucio dropped his arm to allow Madison to enter the restaurant but put his hand on the small of her back. *Another electric moment – just his touch has me excited.*

A server welcomed them and escorted them to a booth at the back of the dining room. The interior was painted in darker colours, with small wall scones holding mock flickering flames, and the linen was navy blue. Maddy identified the mingling aromas of steaks cooking, fries, and chocolate.

The server lit a candle in the center of their table and asked for their drink order. Once she left, Lucio reached over the table and held Madison's hand, his face full of concern.

"You must leave the ranch, Maddy, you and your father, as soon as you can."

"What are you talking about? It's our home. We would never leave."

"I feel sure Colton means to harm your father and coerce you into marrying him so he can own the ranch. I fear once he has it you will be in danger, too."

"Now, come on, Lucio. I know Colton has been rather less than welcoming to you to say the least, and I can only apologize again for his violent attack, it was a onetime thing. I'm sure he would never harm Pops, or me. I've known him since we were in high school together. Colton saved me from bullies, he wasn't one of them! He's almost family to me and Pops. You are overreacting."

"Maddy, he whipped me. He is dangerous and I am certain he will not stop until the ranch is his. Please leave."

"Wait, what? He whipped you? When?"

"In the barn after you left the other night. I left as soon as I could. Look."

He unbuttoned his shirt cuff and rolled back the sleeve. There was a large welt on his forearm.

"Lucio, I don't think Colton is capable of that. He has been a good friend and protected me when I was most vulnerable. I can't believe he would do such a thing."

"He is capable of more than this, I am sure. You did not see the hatred in his eyes, Maddy. He was possessed, mad. I am certain he would stop at nothing to get what he wants. It took me a while to figure it out, but I think he staged Ginny visiting me in the motel. It was Colton, who took the photographs and then made sure you found the camera. Why else would it be there?"

She felt torn between feelings of loyalty and love. She could not believe Colton would do such things. She had worked beside him for years and been friends for longer than that. The Colton Lucio was describing was not the man she knew.

"This is not real. You're wrong. I'll confront Colton. There has to be an explanation. Why would he have taken such photos?"

Madison looked up at Lucio, realization crossing her face. *Would he go to such lengths to get rid of Lucio? No, not Colton, he wouldn't.*

"Madison, do not go near that mad man. He will stop at nothing to get what he wants, and that thing is your ranch."

"No, I can't believe this. You must be making this into something it isn't. I know Colton. He protected me in high school. I don't believe he would do anything to hurt my father or me. You are wrong. I'm going to talk to him, right now. I'll get to the bottom of this. It's just plain jealousy on both your parts and I'm the prize. Don't I have a say in who I want to love? I'm not a toy to be fought over - pulled back and forth."

She didn't wait for Lucio's answer but ran out of the restaurant and to her truck without a backward glance. Gravel spitting out from her back tires, Madison raced out of the parking lot and toward the ranch. Unaware of Lucio's frantic waving in a bid to stop her, anger raged through her body.

With no moon, Madison could only see what her headlights illuminated. All of a sudden, a large object appeared on the road in front of her. A deer stood frozen in the blazing lights. She swerved to miss the animal. The truck jolted onto two wheels, down into a ditch and then rolled. She screamed as the truck pitched over and her head struck the side window. Blackness enveloped her.

She woke to stabbing pain through her legs as she regained consciousness. The aroma of gas stung her nose. She tried to move, but the steering wheel held her down fast. The view through the windshield disorientated her. In the pale moon light, she saw the trunk of a tree, lying in a diagonal across from the windshield. She cried for help. *Lucio would come. He would be there for her even though she had sped off after their disagreement at the restaurant.*

Taking a deep breath, she pushed her body upwards. She was stuck tight and no room to move either way. She pushed at the door, but it was stuck fast. *Where was Lucio? He would have followed me, wouldn't he? Well, maybe not immediately. You met him at the restaurant, but he would have called another cab and given chased me, right?*

She looked around for her purse but could not see it in the dark. If only she could reach her cell phone. An owl hooted somewhere above her. She strained to hear any engine noises but heard no vehicle sounds at all. Fear gripped her. *Someone will drive by and see me. They will.* Trying to pull herself free again, she realized she no longer had sensation in her legs. They were numb, just a dull ache in her lower back. *That's not good, is it? Oh, God what if I've made an injury worse by struggling?* Her screams burst into the night air again and again until her throat became raw. *Please help me, someone. Please.*

Bright lights washed across the interior of the car. Madison yelled out, hoping the driver would either hear her or see her vehicle. In anticipation, she listened to the engine noise getting louder and louder in-between screaming as loudly as she could. *It's not slowing down. No, don't drive past. See me. Please see me.* The car's engine noise began to fade as it passed by. The aroma of gasoline became stronger. *What if the truck explodes and I burn to death? Oh, please, don't let me burn. Think, Madison. What can you do apart from screaming?* Her red jacket lay just in reach hooked on the side of the passenger seat. Using her fingertips, she edged it toward her until she could get a good grip on it. Orientating herself as best she could, she pushed the jacket through the broken side window and flung it upward, so it lay on the truck's roof. A glimmer of hope shone. Maybe the bright color will show up in someone's high beam.

The owl hooted again, and Madison heard an answering call. A blast of wind rushed through the broken window. She shivered. She was so cold and sleepy. *Don't sleep. Stay awake. What if I never wake up?* Madison forced her eyes open and took deep breaths even though the cold hurt her lungs. A distant hum grew louder. Light spread across the car's interior again. Madison shouted out as loud as possible. Tires crunched on gravel. *Yes. They've stopped. I'm safe.* The beam of a flashlight washed over the truck and settled on her door.

"Is anyone in there? Hello?"

"Yes, here. I'm here. I can't move my legs and the steering wheel has me pinned in. Please help me."

A light flashed in her face before a large hand entered the side window. Grateful, Madison gripped it.

"Thank you for stopping. Can you get me out? There's gasoline leaking somewhere."

"All right, Miss, stay calm. My name is Carson. What's yours?"

"Madison. You can get me out, can't you?"

Carson tugged at the driver's door. It did not move. He tried kicking the handle, but the door resisted his attempts. "I'm going to the other side to see if the other door opens. Maybe I can get you out that way. Your truck is on its side but let's hope the passenger door is not wedged against the bank."

"Please be careful. I can smell gas."

"I sure will, Madison, just sit tight."

Carson shouted, "Call 911, Ricky, and then come on down here. There's a girl stuck in here."

A younger voice answered, "Be right there, Carson."

Another beam of light entered the truck's interior and a younger man's face appeared at her side window.

"Heh, I'm Ricky. We'll have you out of there, don't you worry. The rescue trucks are on their way. Okay?"

"Yes, thank you. I'm Madison. I feel better knowing someone is here with me."

"Where did Carson go?"

"He's gone to the other side to see if the passenger door will open. Can you hear us, Carson?"

"Yep, I'm here, I just needed to make my way around without plunging into the mud and getting myself stuck. Ricky, come on round the front."

"Okay, be right there. Hang tight, Madison."

She heard the two men discussing how to open the passenger side door. The groan and creak of metal sounded soon after as they pulled at the twisted door. She could hear them grunting with effort and the sound of frustrated kicking echoed through the truck's cab. After a while, silence fell on the scene.

"It won't budge, Madison. If only I had driven my truck tonight, Ricky. There's a crowbar in it, which would have made short work of this door."

"Are you sure you can't open it? What if the gasoline alights? I don't want to burn alive. Please try again."

The two men must have recognized the despair in Madison's voice. Carson's deep voice rumbled. "Don't worry, we'll stay with you. The fire and rescue truck will be here soon."

"Let's check out where that gasoline is coming from. We might be able to stop its flow."

"Good idea, Ricky."

"Thank you so much. I hope the rescue crew hurry up, I can't feel my legs."

The men moved around the truck, talking quietly. She couldn't quite make out their words.

Carson called out, "I've put the gas cap back in place. That will stop any more gas pouring out, anyway."

"Yes, best we let the crew know it flowed out though, Carson, just in case the thing goes up."

Carson made his way back to Madison's door, just as sirens broke through the night. "Here they come. You'll be out in no time."

Madison held his hand tight, tears flowing in relief. "I want to be out of here. Thank you for stopping and helping."

"No problem at all. You'll be good as new in no time."

Carson leaned on the truck door, holding Madison's hand while Ricky scrambled back up the ditch to stand at the roadside and direct the fire truck. The sirens and flashing lights filled the air with sound and an alternating red and blue glow. Ricky shouted as he led a couple of firemen down to the truck. "Here! It's down here."

"Thank you, sir. We will take over now."

Carson leaned in as far as he could and told Madison everything would be all right before he slipped his hand from hers and disappeared. A uniformed man appeared at the truck window.

"Hello, Madison, isn't it? Ricky told me you are the only passenger. Is that right?"

"Yes, yes, it is. You can get me out now, can't you?"

"We will get you out but first I need to find out if you have any injuries and if you have an idea what is stopping you from moving."

Madison explained the numbness in her legs, and how the steering wheel pinned her into the driver's seat.

"Right, we will need to use some cutting tools to remove this door. It will be noisy but don't worry."

"As long as you can free me, I will be happy. Did Carson or Ricky tell you about the gasoline?"

"Yes, they did, one of my colleagues is inspecting the rear of the truck to evaluate if there is any risk. You have nothing to fear. We have the situation under control."

Madison was relieved knowing that soon they would have her cut free. Within minutes, there were several firefighters at the side of the truck. She felt calmer with them there. They inspected and discussed the position of the vehicle and her proximity to the door, all the while ensuring she understood what was happening. *Just hurry up and get me out of here.* An ambulance arrived just before the fire crew began cutting. A medic assessed Madison's position and injuries. She told him her legs were numb. He nodded, told her everything would be all right, then turned to the fire crew advising them that once he placed a cervical collar on her neck they could begin cutting. *A collar? Does he think my back is broken? I could feel my legs earlier.*

"Please tell me I won't be paralyzed," she begged.

"Now, don't worry yourself, we always put a collar on vehicle accident victims as a matter of course. There could be many reasons your legs are numb. Don't worry about it. We can get you checked out at the hospital."

Madison's fears eased at the medic's words. It took another forty minutes of preparation, wrenching and cutting before Madison was finally free from her temporary prison. Two medic's placed Madison on a body board and strapped her in even though Madison assured them she could move her upper body.

"Procedure, Miss. Please lie still and we will have you in the hospital in no time."

As the medics lifted her into the ambulance, Madison saw Carson standing to one side of the rear of the ambulance.

"Can you find my cell phone? I need to call my father."

"I'll take a look for you."

"Thanks, Carson. It's in my purse, somewhere down there."

Madison motioned with her head and the medic was immediate in his admonishing of her action. The two medics pushed the stretcher into the back of the ambulance and began shutting the doors. "No, please wait. I need my cell and purse."

Carson appeared at the open door, gasping for breath. "Found it. Here you go. Good luck to you."

"Thank you for everything and tell Ricky thanks as well."

"I sure will. You'll be just fine, just wait and see."

The door closed as the medic jumped in the back to sit with her. The ambulance siren wailed, and the vehicle moved away from the crash site.

"Let's take a proper look at you, shall we?"

Madison watched the medic take her blood pressure and pulse, then asked her to move her toes. She wiggled them. His smile creased his lips but did not reach his eyes. Then he asked her to gauge her level of pain from one to ten.

"I feel sore but not much pain, maybe a three."

"That's good. We will be at the hospital shortly. Try to relax."

"Can I phone my father?"

"Sure, just be quick, okay?"

He rummaged in her purse and found her cell and then pressed the keys of the number she gave him, and then held the device to her ear. *How would she phrase where she was without causing too much worry for Pops?* The phone was picked up at the other end.

"Hi, Pops. Now please don't worry. I had an accident but I'm in safe hands in the ambulance. We're going to Thorns General. Can you come?"

"Good God, Maddy! Of course, I'll be right there. Are you sure you are all right?"

"Feel like I got thrown but I'm used to that. Please drive safely."

"I will, see you in a while."

Madison glanced at the medic who hung up the call. She felt lightheaded suddenly. "I'm not feeling too good. I'm all fuzzy in my head. Will I be okay?"

"It happens quite often once the adrenaline wears off. Just relax and let everyone do their job."

A while later, the sirens wailing ceased and Madison realized the ambulance had stopped. The doors opened and bright lights overhead blinded her. The medics took the stretcher out of the ambulance and rolled it through the hospital emergency doors. She closed her eyes. *I'm so sleepy.* Before she lost consciousness, she felt herself lifted and placed down again.

Chapter Thirty-One

When Madison sped out of the parking lot, Lucio frantically ran back into the restaurant to grab his cell phone. With no vehicle to chase after her, he needed to phone a taxi right that minute. Fear filled his mind. *What would Colton do when she confronted him.* His jaw tight, he jabbed at the device several times trying to remember the taxi company's number. He would never forgive himself if anything happened to Madison. He had to get to the ranch as fast as possible.

The taxi arrived at the restaurant nearly fifty minutes later, Lucio jumped in furious it had taken so long. Without waiting on an explanation, he instructed the driver to head toward the ranch. The driver opened his mouth to tell his fare he'd been stopped on that same road due to an accident, but the man just said, "I don't want to hear it just hurry."

By the time, the taxi driver reached the scene of the accident the emergency crews had left, and a tow truck's flashing yellow lights marked the spot as the recovery vehicle personnel worked on pulling the truck out of the ditch. Due to his distraction and anxiousness, Lucio did not pay any attention to the vehicle.

When they arrived at the ranch, they nearly collided with Colton's truck as he raced out of the ranch. Both vehicles braked hard to avoid a collision.

When Colton saw the taxi's passenger, he rolled down his window and shouted, "You've done enough damage, get out of here. If she lives, I'm the one she will marry not some Italian Romeo cruising around breaking girl's hearts. If I see you again, I'll shoot you make no mistake."

In a cloud of dirt and gravel, the truck sped away, leaving Lucio and the taxi driver coughing up dust. *What did he mean if she lives, what happened, where is she?* The taxi driver turned to him.

"Are we staying or going?"

"We need to go but I don't know where to. I need to think."

"Well, while you're thinking, I'm taking us back to town. I wouldn't be surprised to see that jerk in a ditch as well."

"In a ditch, you saw someone in the ditch?"

"I tried to tell you when I picked you up, that was the reason I was late, a truck rolled over into the ditch and I had to wait for the fire crew and ambulance to clear a way through."

Lucio's heart sank. *Oh no, Maddy was it you? No wonder Colton is mad.*

"I need to go to the hospital now."

The driver made a U-turn in the drive tearing up some of the lawn as he did so, as if the sooner he got this fare out of his taxi, the better.

The silent drive to the hospital increased Lucio's anxiety, so when the vehicle came to a stop at the entrance doors, he leapt out after tipping the driver generously. He strode purposely into the hospital reception and asked where he could go to find Madison Beauchamp.

"I cannot release patient details, sir, unless you are family. Are you family?"

"No, but I'm a close friend."

"Sorry, Sir, unless the patient or family gives us permission, we are unable to give out details. I can send a message if you like?"

He barely controlled the anger seething within him. "Yes, please I will wait here."

Frustrated and worry mounting, Lucio paced the waiting room. With every phone call the nurse took he hoped it would be the one allowing him to see Madison. An hour later, the nurse called him over.

"Hi, look I'm sorry but the family have said no visitors at this time. Maybe come back in a day or two."

"Can I get a message to her? Can you tell me how she is? Anything?"

"Well, I already sent a message up, sir, and you got their answer. The patient's condition is confidential, so best to wait and come back another day. Okay?"

Disheartened Lucio looked around him at the waiting patients and the nurse's efficiently guiding them one by one into curtained cubicles. He had no option but to return to the motel and wait.

Chapter Thirty-Two

"Madison, can you hear me? My name is Doctor Hanson. Can you open your eyes for me?"

It was a struggle, but she managed to open her eyes to see a female doctor and several nurses around her.

"Is Pops here yet? Where's Pops?"

"Who is Pops, Madison?"

"My father."

"Yes, he is here waiting in the other room. Once we have you stabilized, he can come and see you. Now can you wiggle your toes for me?"

She nurses removed her clothes, took her pulse, and inserted needles before blackness encompassed her. A warm hand was holding hers when she regained consciousness.

"Pops, is that you?"

"It's Colt, Maddy, he's just talking to the doctor. I'll get him, all right?"

She murmured back unable to speak or move. Sleep returned. A cooler hand was holding her other hand when she woke up again.

"Pops, are you there?" She couldn't seem to focus her eyes.

"Yes, Maddy, I'm here and so is Colton. We've stayed with you the whole time. How do you feel?"

"Rather lightheaded and sore. Colt is still here?"

"We've taken turns sleeping here with you and keeping the ranch going."

"Turns? What are you talking about? I've only been here over night."

"Actually, Maddy, it's been six nights. The doctor needed you to lie still so she kept you asleep."

Madison couldn't quite process his words. "Six nights, I've been here. What are you saying? Are you serious?"

"Yes, it was to help your back."

Pops shushed Colt's comment.

"What's wrong with me, Pops?"

"Maybe we can talk about it when you're feeling a bit better. Just rest now."

Fear bloomed in her chest. "Pops, what's wrong? Tell me please."

Madison saw her father look at Colton and then rub his own face as his brow creased. *This isn't good. What if I'm paralyzed?* Madison felt cold dread rise in her chest her heart rate increased. She wanted to scream.

"Doc Hanson said we should wait until you were stronger, Maddy. Look, I'll go and find her."

"How bad is it, Pops?" Madison squeezed her father's hand. Her eyes pleaded with him as tears trickled onto her cheeks.

At that moment, the hospital room door swung open, and the white coated figure of Doctor Hanson walked in with a smile on her face. It dropped when she saw Madison, Pops, and Colton's expressions.

"Mr. Beauchamp, what is going on?"

"Madison wants to know, doc. I was about to come and find you."

"I see. Well, let me take a look at you, Madison, then we can talk."

"Tell me. I have to know. What are you keeping from me? I'm paralyzed, aren't I? Tell me."

Madison's outburst made her father grip her hand even tighter. Colton looked down at the floor and the doctor moved to her bedside in a couple of quick strides.

"Madison, please stay calm and still. Your imagination is without doubt conjuring up worse scenarios than the actuality. Please let me assess you and I promise we will then talk."

Pops nodded at Madison, and she sniffed back more tears. He released her hand and walked out of the room with Colton. She tried to return Colton's smile. The doctor read through Madison's chart, took her pulse and pushed her feet. *I didn't feel that! Oh, my God, I am paralyzed.*

"Madison, it's not good but it's not as bad as you imagine. Where you were pinned into your seat by the steering wheel, the pressure, and I suspect your struggling to some extent caused a reaction of the tissues compressing your vertebrae. In essence, they clamped down and became rigid. In order for your body to heal itself, we required you to be as still as possible. The paralysis will not be permanent."

Madison burst into tears. She touched the doctor's hand and squeezed tight showing her gratitude. Between sobs, she thanked her again and again.

"Madison, you need to calm down and relax. The more relaxed your muscles are, the quicker they will return to normal function. We will start physiotherapy tomorrow."

"How long before I'm walking and riding again?"

"Riding?"

"Yes, I'm a barrel racer. I will be able to ride again, won't I?"

"Let's get you walking again and strong and healthy. I will review you in a month, but in the meantime, it would be best if you utilized a wheelchair."

"A wheelchair? But I will be able to walk again, promise?"

"Yes, Madison, you will but you must follow instructions and be diligent with your physiotherapy. Now, let's get your father back in here, shall we?"

Madison thanked the doctor, who opened the door to let her father and Colton back into the room.

"Mr. Beauchamp, Madison is aware of her condition and I'm sure, with proper care, she will be walking in no time."

"Thanks, Doc."

Madison smiled at her father as he sat next to her bed and grasped her hand. Colton stood at the other side of the bed, twiddling with his truck keys.

"Now, that will get on my nerves. Sit down, Colt. Thank you both for being here. Now I know this isn't permanent, I feel much better."

As they chatted, telling Madison of the goings on at the ranch, she could not help but wonder where Lucio was. *Did he visit me? Did Colton scare him off? I can't ask either of them.* After an hour, a nurse appeared and recorded Madison's pulse, blood pressure, and took out her intravenous drip.

"If you don't mind, gentlemen, I think it's about time my patient had some peace and quiet."

The nurse smiled kindly at Pops and Madison could see a definite twinkle in her eye when she looked at Colton. *Maybe I can cultivate a relationship between those two. If Colton has a girl, he won't need to fixate on me. That's if Lucio wants me anymore, wheelchair and all. Would I fit into his jet set lifestyle in a wheelchair? Who am I fooling of course not but I'm no good on the ranch either. I'm useless to everyone now, even Pop's.*

With goodbyes said, her father and Colton left for the evening. The nurse told her supper would be served in thirty minutes, and walked toward the door. Madison was desperate to see her cell phone so asked if the nurse could retrieve it.

"Not supposed to use them in here. The ICU has too many monitors to allow cellular connectivity, but if you are quick, okay?"

"I promise. I need to see if my boyfriend has texted me."

The nurse opened Madison's side cupboard, and handed over her purse. Delving into the pockets one by one, Madison became anxious. *Where was it? She had used it to call Pops from the ambulance.*

"I can't find it. Is it in the cupboard?"

The nurse searched through the small bedside cupboard. "No, not in here. Shall I look through your clothes?"

"Yes, please. Thank you. Sorry to be a pain."

"No problem."

Madison watched as the nurse went through the pockets of her jeans and jacket. She did not find the cell phone.

"I'm sure it will turn up. Maybe your father took it to charge it up?"

"Doubtful. He's not into technology."

"Well, don't worry about it. I'm sure it will turn up. Now, do you feel like eating something? We've taken out the drip so you can eat."

Madison tried to focus, though her brain was still fuzzy. Did she feel hungry? Somewhere deep inside she found the answer. Yes. Extremely hungry!

"I would love something to eat. Thanks."

The nurse pushed a button and raised the top half of her body up a couple of notches. "Sorry, I can't go up higher, doctor's orders. At least it isn't soup." The nurse gave a short laugh.

Madison smiled back at the joke. "I think I'll be able to manage it, somehow."

"Good. I'll be back in a few."

The nurse returned with a wheeled trolley and a covered tray upon it. She maneuvered the hospital tray table until it was close to Madison's chest, and then uncovered a plate of beige blobs and a small cup of jello. She laughed at the expression on Madison's face.

"It's not brilliant but it fills a hole. Try to eat some. I'll be back in a while. Press the button if you get into difficulties."

Madison picked up a fork and poked at the blobs trying to determine what the food could be. She put a small amount on her tongue. The consistency was soft mash, and it had a feint taste of potato. *I can't eat this. Maybe Pops can bring in some proper food.* She pressed the button and another nurse came in.

"Hi, is it possible to make a phone call?"

"Of course, I'll bring it in."

The nurse maneuvered an old trolley into her room. "It's quite ancient but it works. Not every patient has a cell phone. Hard to believe, I know."

Once the nurse had left, Madison dialed the house number.

"Hello?"

"Hi, Pops, it's me…"

"Is everything all right, I can be there in forty minutes."

"Calm down, Pops. Yes, I'm fine apart from the food being disgusting. Could you bring me something?"

"Leave it to me. I'll get something good and tasty."

Relieved, Madison hung up and pushed the small table away. *If Lucio thought anything of me, he would have been here. Did I misjudge him? Was Colton right all along?*

Madison dozed until the door opened and Colton walked in carrying a large carrier bag. Madison hid her surprise. The aroma of fresh pizza filled the room.

"I brought your favorite. Shall I put it on here?" He motioned to the table. Madison nodded.

"Thanks, Colton. Where's Pops?"

"He asked me to come over with the pizza. He apologized and said he will be over in the morning."

"Really? I thought he would come."

"Sienna went into labor, and he wanted to stay with her. Cody was on his way when I left."

"Oh, that explains it. Sienna is a favorite of his, and she did have trouble with her last foal. Well, thanks for this, its way better than the slop on that plate. Colton picked up the plate cover and screwed up his nose at the blob underneath.

"That just looks nasty. What is it?"

"To be honest I'm not sure. I tried some and it sort of tasted like potato."

"You could have fooled me. Let's enjoy the pizza while it's good and hot."

Her room filled with the aroma of spicy pepperoni and melted cheese. Her stomach grumbled. She watched him devour slices of the pizza, licking his lips and smiling. He talked about her father rushing to Sienna's side and shouting orders as he did. The atmosphere was comfortable and friendly. Madison relaxed and enjoyed the spicy pizza and his company.

He is a good friend. It's pleasant between us but is that enough? I don't feel that excitement for him like I do for Lucio. When Lucio touches me its literally electric.

A nurse popped her head around the door and asked if Madison had finished with her supper. When she saw Colton, she came into the room and began straightening the bedclothes, checking on Madison, but all the while making idle chitchat and glancing at Colton. Madison could see he was enjoying the attention so lay still, observing the exchange.

Wow, another nurse making eyes at him. Why am I seeing Colt in such a different light? All these girls seem to be drawn to him. Are we too familiar that I don't see him?

"We won't get into trouble having pizza in here, will we?"

The nurse's eyes twinkled at Colton as she answered, giggling. "No, it happens a lot. Not surprising with the stuff that comes out of the kitchen."

"I looked at Maddy's plate. It looks disgusting. What is it supposed to be anyway?"

"Believe it or not, beef stew and mashed potato."

"Beef isn't beige…!"

"Yep, I know. I'll take it away. You have another ten minutes, and then you need to go."

"Not a problem, thanks, nurse?"

"Oh, call me, Rachel. Use the buzzer if you need anything."

Rachel was looking straight at Colton when she spoke. When she left the room, she couldn't help but tease him.

"You have another admirer by the looks of it. The other nurse was making eyes at you, too. Way to go cowboy."

"It's just innocent flirting, Maddy. You know I only have feelings for you. Once you are home, I can take proper care of you."

Madison smiled unsure, how to respond. She knew Pops would look after her of course but Colton's remark had an underlining forcefulness to it. *Is he really looking out for me or only what a relationship with me, could give him? Could Lucio be right?*

Colton stood and kissed her on her forehead. "You sleep well now, you hear? Pops and I will be back tomorrow."

"I'll try to sleep. Thanks for the pizza, Colt, it hit the spot."

As she fell asleep, Lucio's face appeared, smiling and gorgeous as ever. His arms were stretched out before him reaching for her. She so wanted to run into them and feel his warm embrace. She felt at home in his arms.

Chapter
Thirty-Three

Ten days later, after promising Doctor Hanson she would not walk for another week without help, Madison was discharged. She'd made good progress with the physiotherapy, but still required pain medication. Colt and her father made up a bed in the living room, so she didn't have to struggle up the stairs. She felt helpless and a burden to them both.

"There, you have everything you need within reach, I think. TV, radio, magazines, books, and I even found the little bell your Ma used."

"Don't you think this is a bit over the top, Pops? I can wheel myself around in the wheelchair, you know."

"The more you rest the better your recovery. That's what Doc said."

"All right, I'll do my best, Pops."

"I even bought you a new cell phone."

"You didn't have to do that, Pops."

"Well, your other one didn't turn up, did it?"

"No, even after the hospital administrator investigated all the staff. I felt bad about that."

"Well, someone must have taken it, Maddy. If you were asleep, it would have been easy to slip into your room, but why didn't they take the cash and your credit cards?"

"I know it was odd. Well, thanks. Did I get my old number or a new one?"

"It's a new one, I believe. Don't ask me how to work the thing. I got the guy in the store to enable it, wherever that means. He wrote down your new number on the box, see on the side there. Now, how about a nice cup of coffee?"

"Thanks, Pops. That would be great but maybe not too strong, don't think I'm up to that just yet."

"I'll be right back with a weak coffee. It might take me a few tries mind you."

Madison opened the cell phone box and read the instructions, then began pressing buttons and entering the few numbers, she knew off by heart. *I can't remember Lucio's number, but then I don't need it, do I? He never called or visited me.*

She felt a pain in her heart as she realized what his absence meant. It was obvious he wasn't interested enough to bother coming when she was in the hospital. *Did he know where I was? He would have called the house if nothing else but Pops, never mentioned a call from Lucio. In fact, he hasn't mentioned him at all.* Her father returned with two mugs of coffee and a plate full of pastries on a tray. *Should I ask?*

"There, we can enjoy a mid-morning snack before I go back out, if that's all right with you?"

"Of course, Pops. You can't stop running the ranch. Did you hear from Alan or Aubrey?"

"Yes, I did. Both mares are in foal. Titan will be a father again."

Madison sipped her coffee relishing the taste. It was not as strong as her father usually made it but still a lot stronger than the hospital supplied. She picked at an apple pastry but did not have much of an appetite.

"If you have everything you need, I'll see you later, duty calls as always. Just remember to call the office number if you need anything, although Colt said he will drop by from time to time to check on you."

"I'll be fine, Pops, honest. Everything is close to hand, and I can wheel about too." *Pops would have mentioned Lucio, I'm sure of it. He couldn't have come around after all.*

She watched her father walk past the window on the veranda and disappear from view. For the next couple hours, she flicked through TV channels and tried reading a couple magazines. Nothing kept her interest. She longed to be outside. Bandit lay beside her relishing her company, but fear invaded her thoughts. *What will happen if I don't fully recover from this injury? Could I live without being free to go outside, to walk and ride again? I couldn't cope confined to this contraption forever. I will get better I just need to believe that. The physiotherapy sure is hard, though.*

Rolling her wheelchair past the living room furniture, she managed to reach the front door with some effort. With a bit of maneuvering, she opened the door, and pushed the screen door open with one footrest. The fresh air felt so good. Across the driveway, the willow trees gently swayed. She remembered her father telling her, as a child, how her mother came to love Willow Sway Ranch after watching those same trees blow in the breeze. *Could I manage to wheel myself all the way down there? I have to get out being cooped up inside is driving me mad.*

Determined to try, Madison wheeled down the ramp her father had made especially for her return home. The gravel driveway jarred her back and she stopped several times to wait for the pain to subside. She reached the lawn and pushed hard on the wheels. *I ought to have taken an extra pain med - well too late now.*

"It's not a good idea to strain yourself. Isn't that what the doctor told you?"

Madison turned to the young ranch hand. A bead of sweat ran down her cheek. "Oh, Garner, I can't bear to be cooped up inside any longer. Can you push me down to the steam, please?"

"Well, as long as I don't get into trouble."

She thanked the young man and gritted her teeth as he pushed her over the lawn to the overhanging willows. The uneven ground jerked her up and down, sending pain through her back, but it was worth it to be outside. Once her wheelchair was positioned under a willow, Madison gripped his hand.

"Thanks, Garner. I'll shout when I want to go back."

"All right, but I could stay with you, just in case, you know?"

"Really, I'm fine. Thanks again."

The feel of air brushing against her face was wonderful. *I could never spend my time working in an office or inside all the time. I need to be outside. What if I can never ride again? Life confined to this wheelchair is not worth living. I'm not sure I could bear that. Oh, Lucio wasn't your love for me strong enough? Was I a passing fancy like Pops and Colton say?*

Madison didn't stop the tears flowing down her cheeks and onto her useless legs.

Chapter Thirty-Four

"Where's Madison? Garner, have you seen her?"

"I pushed her down to the stream, Boss, said she wanted some quiet time."

"She's not alone, is she?"

"Ummm...well yes, Boss, I didn't think."

"No, you didn't think Garner, damn fool. With her state of mind, she could very well be floating face down by now. Hurry, we need to get over there."

"Boss, she seemed fine to me."

"I know my own daughter, damn it. Best we ride there. It'll be quicker."

Colton overheard Wynne and Garner. *This is my chance to make her mine.* Roping the nearest mare, he jumped up and rode bareback towards the stream moments before Wynne and Garner appeared at the stable entrance. He was half way to Madison when the other two men emerged from the stable. His call startled Madison out of her reverie.

"Madison! Madison, are you all right? What are you doing down here."

"Of course, I'm okay. What's the matter?"

"Garner told your father you were down here alone. Scared him, you being all depressed and all."

Colton looked behind him. He had a couple minutes at most. Sliding down from the mare's back, he approached and then knelt beside Madison's wheelchair, and looked up at her. *Perfect, Wynne will think it's a proposal and will, with any luck back off for a few moments.*

"Madison, I know we've had some upsets lately, but I want you to know, you mean the world to me. Whatever I need to do to make you happy, I will do it."

From the corner of his eye, he saw Wynne hold out his arm to Garner, and they slowed their horses to a stop. With her back to the other two men, Madison was oblivious to his conniving.

"Colt, you are a good friend and I'm guilty of not always treating you fairly. After Daniel and now the Lucio fiasco, I need to count myself lucky you are still around picking up the pieces."

"Madison, you don't need to answer me now, but will you be my wife?"

"Oh, Maddy, Colt is a good man, he would look after you and the ranch so well."

Colt saw how her father's voice shocked her further than his statement. They both turned to face Wynne and saw a broad smile on his face. Her shoulders sagged.

"Colt, can you give me a few days to think about it? Apart from everything else these pain meds have my head all over the place."

"Well, of course. Now I think it's time you were back in the house, rains coming."

Colton passed his mare's lead rope to Garner and took hold of the wheelchair handles. *Keep it light. The ranch is within your reach now.* As he pushed Madison back towards the house, he tried not to look smug. Wynne and Garner rode beside them for a while and then headed off towards the stable. Once he had Madison back on the veranda, he turned her around and said,

"Well now, what can I get for my girl? Coffee, or can you have a beer?"

"I'd love a beer, but doctor's orders and the medications don't allow it. Coffee it will have to be. Thanks, Colt. I'll take one of those tablets now that ride over the lawn has my back complaining."

Colton was busy making the coffee, when a cell phone vibrated in his pocket - Madison's cell phone. The battery was almost dead, he wouldn't recharge it again. He scrolled over the text messages. There were twenty-seven from Lucio and another fourteen voice messages from him. Colton clicked a button and then put it back in his pocket. He heard another faint beep. *Another message she will never get.*

He looked around the kitchen and then walked into the living room. *Needs a lot of upgrading but I'll be happy as a gopher in soft dirt here. Once Madison's pregnant, she'll be bound to the kid, and this place, as well as me. No way, she'll divorce me and split the old homestead.*

Once the coffee had brewed, he filled two mugs and took them out to the veranda. Madison had fallen asleep. *Damn strong drugs those. I have to get me some of them. They might come in handy sometime.* Careful not to wake her, Colton placed the mugs down on the table and descended the steps, an idea formulating. In the office he made a call.

Pleased with himself, he arrived at the main house at suppertime carrying lots of containers of Chinese take away.

"I wasn't sure what your favorites were so brought one of everything. I hope that's all right, Wynne."

"Sounds great to me, Colt, saves me trying not to burn something. I can do a fair breakfast but that's about it. I think even I would get tired of bacon and eggs every day, twice a day."

With Wynne's help, Colton arranged the containers on the dining table and placed plates and forks for them all. The smell of caramelized sugars, simmering broths, fragrant spices, garlic, and soy filled the dining room from the opened containers.

Madison came to the table, and they all dug into the boxes sampling each one and deciding on favorites. There was so much left, Wynne called down to the bunkhouse for the ranch hands to come up to the house and grab some. The four men arrived soon after, filling their plates with wide smiles and thanks before departing. Colton offered to wash up and told Madison and Wynne to go watch television.

"I can help you, Colt."

"No, Maddy, go and sit with your father. This won't take me long. It's only a few plates and all the rest can go in the garbage."

When Madison wheeled into the living room, he listened at the doorway, hearing her father say, "Have you made a decision on Colt's proposal?"

"Pops, really give me some time. He only asked me this afternoon."

"When it's right, it's right. Your Ma said yes right there and then."

"That was different, Pops, you fell in love. I've known Colt solely as a friend and it'll take some adjustment to think of him in any other way. Let's just enjoy the evening, shall we?"

Colton tiptoed back to the kitchen sink and felt his cell phone vibrate in the opposite pocket of his jeans. Drying off his hands, he read the text message on the display.

Honey, I need your sweet loving. Baby wants it so bad. Give it to her.

He groaned. Damn Ginny, she'll ruin everything. If Madison, or worse the old man, find out about my many night visits, my plan may be ruined. Ginny was insatiable though and he sure enjoyed her adventurous nature. Once he was married to Madison, he could indulge Ginny once in a while.

Give me two hours. I'll be over to your place at ten.

Colton tugged at his belt and went into the living room.

Wynne put one finger up to his lips and whispered, "She's fallen asleep. Those drugs are mighty strong. Can you lift her into bed?"

"Sure, I can, Pops."

Colton saw the pleased look on Wynne's face when Colton used Pops instead of Wynne, or Sir. *Yes, I have him on my side. It's just a matter of time before Maddy agrees.* With care, Colton lifted Madison out of the wheelchair and laid her down gently, pulling a blanket over her.

"Thanks, Colton, and thanks for a mighty supper as well."

"It's my pleasure, sir."

"None of that, Pops it is from now on. Night, son."

Colton sang along to the radio all the way to Ginny's place. He was more than happy. The ranch was within grasp, and he was going to get laid. The evening couldn't get any better.

Chapter Thirty-Five

L ucio typed another text message and willed it to find Madison. After so many days and no word at the hospital desk as to her condition, he was frantic to see her, to explain his absence. *She will think I have abandoned her - if only I could see her just for five minutes.* He stared at his cell phone display hoping a message would pop up. Five minutes later with no answer, he put the phone in his pocket and walked to the boarding gate. He'd delayed going home long enough and now he needed to return to the factory. His business required his attention. As the plane rose above the clouds, he gazed down at the flat plain below, buildings dotted across the land and dusty tracks connecting them. *I will return Maddy, I promise.*

On his return to his Italian home, Lucio immersed himself into the new product line and investigated a new site for a second factory. With no word from Madison for weeks, his hopes died piece by piece. He second-guessed, her feelings, his feelings - *was their attraction solely based on the cultural differences, the unusual, the suddenness of the attraction?*

As the weeks passed and his plans for expansion demanded his attention, he thought less and less about Madison but only during the day. At night, his dreams were filled with her beautiful eyes, her silky auburn hair and the softness of her skin. They rode across lush Italian pastures, drank bold red wines, ate fresh pasta and made love in a multitude of places. He showed her the places of his childhood, walked along the lakeshore where they dipped their toes into the waves and kissed until their lips were sore. In the mornings, he felt his heart ache at the realization it was just another dream that his love was only in his imagination.

One brilliant sunny morning, he arrived at the factory to see a new batch of tanned leather arriving and walked to the inspection office. With a nod of greeting, he questioned the quality manager.

"Is this the newest batch from Senor Bachini?"

"It is but part of the batch is quite unusual, I think he may have delivered part of someone else's order. Did we want a pale green? I cannot see it on the order form. The rest of the order is correct just this small quantity."

"Let me take a look, Palo, it is certainly not a colour I would have ordered but seeing it, I do have a use for it. Check with the supplier to see if it is a mistake, but if we can buy it let me know."

Palo nodded his agreement and went to make the call. Lucio ran his hand over the pale green leather. The smoothness rippled under his touch. If he'd wanted a sign, this was it. Instead of going to his office, he detoured to the design room and discussed what he required with the two graphic designers. He felt happier than he had in weeks, with a plan in mind his hope rose again. He would know once and for all if his gift was returned.

Chapter Thirty-Six

A sharp rapping on the front door alerted Madison to a visitor. As she wheeled up to the door, the rapping sounded again.

"All right, rein it in will you."

An admonished looking delivery driver apologized when he saw her wheelchair. "I'm so sorry. I didn't know. I have a parcel for a Miss Beauchamp."

"That would be me."

"Can you sign here please?"

With the electronic device signed, the delivery driver handed Madison a large box and descended the veranda steps back to his truck.

Who's sending me stuff? She ripped at the paper to reveal a large rectangular box. As she lifted the lid, her heart did a flip over. Inside was the most beautiful pair of boots she had ever seen in a soft green and tan coloured leather with willow tree details.

"Lucio," she whispered, awestruck.

Only Lucio could have sent them. No one else knew her dream of having customized boots. *When did he send these? It couldn't have been before her accident, before that dreadful night.* She looked through the box for a card or a letter. There was

"

nothing. *I can't even call him I don't have his number. Think girl, how can you contact him?* She smacked her palm to her forehead. He would have a website, maybe she could message through that but her laptop was upstairs. *I have to get it. I have to contact him.*

Madison wheeled herself to the bottom of the stairs and eased herself out of the wheelchair. Sitting on her bottom, she got up the stairs one by one. Sweat beading on her brow and upper lip as she hauled her body upward. Using the banister at the top, she raised herself up wary of her weakness and shuffled to her bedroom by bracing herself against the wall and guiding her movements with a hand along it. By the time she got to her bed, she was exhausted and dizzy.

Taking a tablet from her pocket, she dry-swallowed it and lay on the bed waiting for it to take effect. Once the dizziness and dull ache eased, she rolled over and sat up anxious the spinning sensation did not return. Opening the lid of her laptop, she typed in her password and then opened the search engine. She typed in Calligaris Avvio Inc. and waited for the search to complete. A website popped up. Madison found the Contact Us page. There was no direct message option to Lucio, so she typed a message into the general mailbox. She pressed send. *Now all I can do is wait. I hope Lucio gets to see the message.*

She felt alive again knowing Lucio did remember her. The next few days were agony as she waited for a response. She checked her email dozens of times a day. Her happier outlook pleased her father. She knew by his querying looks and secret smiles, when he thought she wasn't looking, that he was thinking she was going to accept Colton's proposal.

Doctor Hanson visited two days later and was pleased with her progress. Madison was walking with a couple of canes for extended periods, thanks to a great physiotherapist and her renewed determination.

"Now, don't overexert yourself walking, Madison. It will come in time, but you are doing remarkably well, just be patient."

"When do you think I can ride again, doc?"

"I would prefer you didn't ride for at least another month and only when I have seen new X-rays."

"A month! Doc, I'm doing well. That's such a long time. I'm more at home in the saddle than walking."

"Madison, I understand you are chomping at the bit, literally in your case, but spinal injuries are a serious issue, and healing must be complete before any form of strenuous exercise is performed."

Madison nodded her agreement and smiled at the doctor's horse reference. Over the next few days, she concentrated on her exercises and walked as often as she could, first with both canes then just one. With each day's passing, she became more despondent. *Why hadn't she heard from Lucio? He must have received her message by now.*

A week later Madison's cell phone buzzed notifying her there was a text message. With a towel wrapped around her, she picked up her phone from the bedside table. *Who could be messaging me this early?*

Maddy, I got your message, but I can't come to the ranch.

We have things to say.

Meet me at nine o'clock today at the Faulkes Bridge.

L. XXX

Madison's heart beat faster. *He does love me, or at least cares enough not to give up. What is he going to tell me?* She pressed the keys confirming she would meet him. When she looked at the time, she realized she only had forty minutes to get dressed and make her way to the bridge. After a frantic search through several shirts, she was hot and bothered with excitement. She gave her hair a quick dry. *Calm down - breathe girl.*

Her father was at the bottom of the stairs looking through the mail when she eased down them as fast as she could with one cane.

"What's the rush, this early?"

"I forgot a hairdresser's appointment. See you later, Pops."

"Really, you didn't mention it. I could drive you."

"Don't fuss, Pops, I'm able to drive myself. See you later."

Her father shook his head in disbelief standing at the open front door, watching as she climbed carefully into the truck.

Anxious she would be late, and Lucio would leave, Madison drove faster than was probably safe on the back roads to the bridge. It would save her some time, as the main route would be filled with morning rush hour traffic. She breathed a sigh of relief when she saw the bridge in the distance. *He'll wait, he must.* A cherry red car sped past her in the other direction. She recognized its driver. Madison screamed as she slammed on the brakes making the truck fishtail to a halt in a plume of dust. Her back gave a painful twinge.

"No, Lucio, stop, I'm here."

The dust cloud behind her obscured her view. *Please be there when the dust settles, please.* She opened the car door and stepped out. A shape moved within the brown cloud. *Is it him? Please let it be Lucio.* The figure appeared waving his arms to dispel the dust and pat some off his shirt.

"Madison? I thought you were not coming."

"Wild horses would not have kept me from meeting you. You didn't leave me much time to get here that's all."

Filled with relief, Madison walked to Lucio leaning on her cane and then threw her arms around his neck. Savoring his cologne and firm, muscular body but also the nearness of him felt right.

"It is so good to hold you again, Maddy, and see you are wearing my gift. But why are you using a cane?"

"That night when I sped off from the restaurant, I crashed into a ditch. I was lucky someone stopped to help me. I hoped you were following me. Why didn't you?"

"I would have followed you if I'd had a car, but I could only wait on a taxi, which was delayed by what turned out to be your accident. When I tried to call your cell, there was no answer. I tried repeatedly. I swear to you, I text you and called most of the night and for days afterwards. I pleaded with the nurse at the hospital reception to get a message to you but there was no reply. When you didn't answer I thought we were *finito*. I waited as long as I could, I even delayed going home."

Madison looked up into Lucio's eyes. *There, that is it, true love. He did try to see me, why did I doubt him. Why didn't Pops or Colt tell me or let him come onto the ward? Surely, one of them got the messages.*

His brow creased. "What did you injure?"

"It was my back, compressed vertebrae. For a time, I was in a wheelchair."

"My darling, *bella*, I would have come to the ranch again but..."

"Again? What are you talking about?"

"I came to see you. Colton met me at the gate and told me you had gone away. I had no way of proving if it was the truth or not. I drove around to the other side of the paddocks and watched for a couple of days, but I never saw you. I then thought he might have told the truth."

"I was in the hospital for some time and then confined to a wheelchair in the house."

Madison leaned on her cane, a slight grimace on her face. He caught her elbow and said, "Maybe you need to sit. I want you to listen to what I have to say and once I am finished you can speak. I want you to know I am sincere in what I am about to say. It is for your protection."

"My protection, what is this?"

"No speaking, remember?"

Madison opened her mouth to ask another question but with a tender finger on her lips Lucio, silenced her. With an arm around her waist, Lucio escorted her to the car, opened the passenger door and let her sit. He walked to the other side and sat in the driver's seat, then turned towards Madison.

"You must listen to me. I believe Colton is using you as a means to own Willow Sway Ranch."

He held up a hand when Madison began to speak. "I know you dismissed what I said at the restaurant and if I had known what happened next, I would have stormed that hospital and run into every ward to find you. You have to believe what I am telling you is the truth. Colton admitted, to me the day you and I were in the stable and he interrupted us, that he is only interested in owning the ranch, anyway he can.

Madison shook her head but remained silent.

"That day you ran to the house if you remember, I saw his true nature. He threatened me again when I came to find you. When he told me you were away for an extended vacation, there was no way of knowing if it was the truth. He said that if I ever returned, he would kill me. I am convinced of this, Maddy, one hundred percent. His eyes bored into me with such hatred and menace that I knew I had to leave and leave fast. He is a dangerous man Maddy, and I believe you and your father are at risk from him. He will stop at nothing to own Willow Sway Ranch."

"Lucio, wait you are blowing all this out of proportion. I know Colton has a temper and he has feelings for me but in my heart, I only see him as a friend. Lucio, I've known him since high school, he would never hurt me, or Pops, I'm sure of it. When he attacked you, he was protecting me from someone he thought had betrayed me."

"Are you sure? The man who confronted me was obsessed and crazy. We both know he is violent. I do not doubt he could cross the line to get what he wants. You must use extreme caution around him. I could not bear to...see anything bad happen." There was hesitancy in his voice.

"I really don't know what to do now, Lucio. Ought I to confront Colton?"

"No, you must not. There is no way of knowing what extreme action he may take. I am convinced he is a dangerous man, Maddy. Maybe it would be best to advise your father."

"That will be a huge problem. Pops has just given Colton a three-month trial as ranch manager. He thinks highly of Colton. Then Colton..."

Madison looked down at her boots. The fancy boots Lucio had sent her.

"What did he do, Maddy?"

"Proved beyond doubt he cared about the ranch and me to my father. Oh, Lucio, if you had seen how happy my father looked when he thought...well, when he saw I might have a happy future on the ranch."

"Your father expects Colton to marry you and run the ranch, yes?"

She turned her head unable to look Lucio in the eye. She had let her father and Colton convince her she was wrong in wanting Lucio. They told her a foreigner, and a stranger at that, could never be the right one for her. Sitting beside him now, she was ashamed of listening to her head and not her heart. It beat for Lucio. Her body yearned for him like no other. His hand cradled her chin and raised her face to meet his.

"Madison, my sweet *bella*, I am not frivolous with my love. We have known each other a short time but deep inside I know we are meant to be together. Do you not share this feeling?"

"Yes, oh Lucio, yes, I do. It doesn't make sense, but it feels so right - deep down a real connection, like my soul has known you forever."

His lips brushed hers as his fingers caressed her neck and ran through her hair. Their bodies pressed together as the intensity of their kiss increased. Madison's body was on fire, tingling and shuddering. *I have never felt such passion. Is this what real love feels like?* Hands explored, lips tasted until their intimate world was disrupted by a car horn and a shout from the driver.

"Better get a room, you two."

Madison swung around and grimaced to see who was taunting them and her heart fell. *Not Ted of all the people. He's bound to tell Pops and Colton.* She held up her hand in an attempt to stop Ted from driving on, but he did not stop.

"There goes our element of surprise. Ted will tell the whole crew at the ranch including Colton and Pops. What do we do now, Lucio?"

"You have to advise your father first. Can you call him?"

"I'll try but if he's not in the house, I have no other means of contacting him. He refuses to buy a cell phone." Madison pressed the buttons with a stress-fueled urgency and prayed hard her father would pick up the phone. With no answer, she hung up the phone.

"I need to go home, Lucio. If I use the back road, I might be able to catch Ted before he speaks to anyone."

"It is urgent that you go, Maddy, but my heart, my arms want you so much it hurts."

His passionate kiss radiated heat on her lips before she pushed him away with reluctance in her heart.

"Meet me here at five o'clock, all right? If I had a choice I would stay forever."

Their hands loosened and slid through to the fingertips unwilling to break their touch. She opened the car door and pushed herself up with the cane then turned to walk away.

"Until later, my *amore*, my Maddy."

She smiled then got into her truck as quickly as she could and sped away. The track was deeply rutted but she did not slow down. Her body jostled up and down, and side-to-side as she drove nearer and nearer to the ranch, plumes of dust billowing behind the vehicle. She ignored the dull pain in her back. She could take pain medication later. To her right she saw another dust trail. Hoping it was Ted, she planned to cut him off at the rear barn.

With practiced ease, Madison ground the truck to a halt behind the old barn and eased herself out of her vehicle just as Ted's truck drove up to the bunkhouse. She raised a hand and called out to him. Bending over to ease the throbbing pain in her back, Madison felt relieved at the sight of the middle-aged, broad-shouldered rancher.

"Heh, Ted. Can you come over here for a minute?"

Ted smiled and walked toward her. "What are you driving, a time machine?"

"Ted, I need you to keep quiet about what you saw earlier. It is of vital importance to Pops and me. There is a lot at risk."

He put his hand on her shoulder concern clouding his features. "Hold on a minute, why all the melodrama? I've known you since you were a young kid and you've never been this serious about anything. What's going on?"

"Ted, I can't tell you all the details yet but please don't say anything about seeing me with Lucio. Please."

"All right, if it's that important to you, I'll keep my lips sealed. If you are in some trouble, you tell me though, girl. I might be getting on in years, but I've still got a pretty good punch."

"Thanks, Ted. I'm sure it won't come to that. Well, I hope not."

"Sounds more serious than you're letting on, Madison, are you sure I can't help?"

"If I think you can, I will let you know, Ted, I promise."

Ted gave Madison's shoulders a friendly hug before he walked over to the bunkhouse. A deep crease showed on his forehead as he thought of possible scenarios. Madison breathed a sigh of relief. *One hitch adverted, one more to go.*

She got back into her truck and drove at a more sedate speed to the ranch house. It was mid-morning, and she knew her father would be out on the ranch somewhere. She was anxious to find him. Lucio's words had made her nervous and afraid. If Colton were as desperate as Lucio thought to get ownership of the ranch, there was no knowing if he would be able to control his temper with his goal almost within his grasp. Her father was a strong man from years of hard physical work but certainly no match for Colton. He had always been big and muscular and ploughed through opponents at high school football matches with ease. When Madison befriended Colton, the bullying stopped. He became her protector, and she was deemed acceptable with her association, although Madison never involved herself with the cheerleader crowd. She was more comfortable in jeans and shirts rather than the pretty dresses and tons of makeup preferred by those girls. Madison knew they only tolerated her because of Colton, and she had been grateful for his friendship. *Where had it gone wrong? Why was he so obsessed with owning the ranch? She and Pops had treated him well, treating him like family. Would she be able to dissuade Colton in his fixation?*

Chapter
Thirty-Seven

With her truck parked in front of the house, Madison scanned the nearby paddocks and stables for any sign of her father. Just as she was about to turn towards the veranda, a familiar Stetson broached Titan's stable door and turned the corner of the building. Madison knew her father would not hear her if she called out so she hurried across the yard as best she could, leaning on the cane for support. Her back ached a great deal now, she would have to take some pain medication soon, but first she needed to talk to Pops. Clouds threw shadows across the paddocks, horses grazed, and all looked normal.

However, as she drew closer to the stable, she heard shouting. On entering the stable her father's raised voice startled her. She had not heard him shouting in a very long time.

"I've always treated you fairly and like family, Colt. What are you insinuating?"

"Old man, you need to let new blood revitalize this place…"

"Less of the old, Colton, I have many more years in me before I even consider passing this ranch over to Maddy."

Madison hobbled as fast as she could all the while waiting for a reply from Colton. None came but a dull thud. Panic rose in her chest.

"Pops? Are you all right? Pops, answer me."

As she rounded the corner to the far side of the stable, she saw Colton lying on the straw strewn ground. Puzzled but anxious she looked for her father. He stood with one arm on Lucio's shoulder. Pops was red in the face and his breathing came in gasps, but he didn't seem hurt.

"Pops, are you all right? What happened?"

"Damn, Colt, implying all sorts of ridiculous things. He got me so angry and then he swung at me. Without this chap, I would surely be on the ground instead of Colton. I have no idea where this guy came from, just glad he is here."

Madison ran as best she could and clasped her arms around both men. Her tears flowed in relief.

"Heh, girl, I'm okay. Settle yourself. Best we do something about Colton before he regains consciousness. I've never seen such focused anger."

Lucio put his hand behind Madison's head and gave her forehead a gentle kiss before turning to grab a rope. "I think it might be best to tie him up and call the police. I expect he will be more than a little angry when he wakes up. I was lucky catching him by surprise, Wynne."

"That was more than a surprise right hook, my man. Yes, tie him up. Maddy, call the police, I will be pressing charges. I've never seen Colton like that. He was raging."

Madison dialed the sheriff's number on her cell while she watched Lucio and her father tie Colton's hands behind his back. Colt groaned a couple of times before opening his eyes. When he saw all three of them standing over him his outburst became vicious.

"Stupid bitch, you're going to regret choosing that fake man. All flashy clothes, and not a day's hard work in his life. You'll come crawling back to me, just wait and see. But I'll make you pay. Old man, I'll see you turning in your grave when I'm running this place and making loads of money. As for you, bastard pasta eater, you watch your back because sooner or later I'll get you."

Madison looked at Colton as he spat his threats trying to recognize the man before her. This wasn't the Colt she knew. He'd twisted into a foul, angry fanatic. She turned away, hurt and shock crushing her heart.

"I have to leave, Pops, I'm disgusted."

"Sure, go out to the drive. Direct the police when they get here."

"That will not be long now, I can hear sirens."

Colton struggled to get free at Lucio's words, but he was tied tight. "I'll tell them it was three against one. Wait and see. I'll get off and be back in no time."

A siren silenced him. They heard Madison shouting and then two police officers ran up to Wynne and looked down at Colton.

"Is this the man, sir?"

"Yes, officer, he attacked me and if it weren't for this fine young man I don't think I'd be standing, let alone breathing."

"We'll take him to the station, but if you can come down at your earliest convenience to make a statement."

The officers pulled Colton to his feet and escorted him to their cruiser. He remained silent but glared at the two men standing at the stable entrance. Once the cruiser drove away, Wynne turned to Lucio. "Thank you for your help, Lucio. Not sure I would have been able to defend myself against Colt's madness."

"My honor to assist you, Mr. Beauchamp, I am sorry our second meeting was under such circumstances."

Wynne took one of Lucio's hands with a firm grip in both of his. "Well, I'm not. Without your help, I'd be in poor shape and that's for sure. Under the circumstances, you need to be calling me Wynne. Now let's go up to the house. I need to see Maddy is all right."

The sirens faded into the distance as Lucio and Pops found Madison sitting motionless on the swing seat, staring into space.

"Heh, Maddy, are you all right?"

Lucio knelt in front of her, looking into her eyes.

"Madison, look into my eyes and take slow deep breathes. Wynne get a glass of whiskey, please. She's in shock."

Wynne rushed into the house and returned moments later with a large tumbler of golden liquid.

"Maddy, sip this slowly. There, look at me."

Madison's eyes began to focus. She looked at Lucio and then at her father who was watching Lucio care for her.

"How could I be so deceived?" Maddy asked.

Her father replied, "Don't blame yourself, Maddy. Colton fooled everyone, me included."

"You have known him a long time, Maddy, and his familiarity blinded you to his ulterior motive." Lucio's words rang true.

"I feel such an idiot. What if he had hurt, Pops? It would have been all my fault."

Wynne placed a hand on her shoulder. "There's no point worrying about the what if's, Maddy. I'm fine, look, really, I am. Thanks in no small part to Lucio here. Your man here has a good right hook."

The two men looked at each other smiling. Madison stretched out her hands and took one of her father's hands and one of Lucio's.

"Thank you both for looking after me. I'm not quite as independent as I thought I was."

"Are you feeling better now, Maddy?"

"Yes, thanks, Pops, although I need to take pain medication my back is singing with pain. Are you sure you are okay?"

"I could do with a sip of that whiskey to settle my nerves a bit, but other than that, I'm good thanks to Lucio."

Madison handed him the glass but only allowed her father one sip. "You don't need to be driving to the sheriff's office under the influence, now do you?"

"Good thinking. I'll go find your medication, then we can all go and make our statements?"

"I can drive you both."

They accepted Lucio's offer.

"I'd better change my clothes if I'm getting into that fancy car of yours. By the way where is it?"

"It's another rental the previous one is having some work done on it, Wynne. It was vandalized again last night and there's no need to change."

"What? Vandals in our little town, I am surprised. What do you mean again? It's happened before?"

"It is the second time it has happened. although I have an idea who did it, Wynne. It is another thing I will report to the Sheriff."

"We are well rid of that scheming bastard, that's for sure, Maddy. You ready?"

She swallowed a couple of tablets and smiled. "Sure, Pops. Ready."

Lucio held open the rear car door for Wynne and the front passenger door for Madison then got into the driver's seat of the car. It was top of the line with leather seats but not as sumptuous as Lucio's own vehicle in Italy.

"You will have to direct me to the Sheriff's office. I only know a few places in the town."

Madison nodded. "Of course, it's on the east side behind our small mall. I'll call out directions."

The ride into town was quiet as the occupants replayed the earlier events. Lucio turned at Madison's instructions until they arrived at the police station. He parked and the trio walked into the brick facade building. They advised the officer at the front desk of their arrival, and a short time later Sheriff Gordon came out of a side door to greet them.

"Come into my office, Wynne. Can you two wait here while I conduct the interview?"

Lucio and Madison nodded and sat watching the deputies coming in and out of the office behind the glass partition, the loud chatter punctuated with the sound of spasmodic ringing telephones. Lucio held Madison's hand, his fingers stroking in a rhythmic motion. *Just having him near makes me happy and my pain is down to a dull ache.*

"Are you feeling all right, Maddy?"

"Yes, thanks, Lucio, my back is aching but manageable. Having you near me helps a lot. Without your intervention, I could be sitting here reporting a very different circumstance. How did you get there so quickly, anyway?"

"When you drove off, I did not feel comfortable leaving you to deal with Colton, so I drove to the ranch's main entrance. I am assuming because Colton did not recognize the car, he did not confront me when I parked up."

"Yes, you are probably right. We have a lot of visitors so it's not unusual to see vehicles coming up the drive."

"It was lucky I saw your father enter Titan's stable, so I headed that way. When I heard raised voices, I crept around the side to find Colton and your father arguing."

"You could have been badly hurt, Lucio."

"I knew I could surprise Colton. His back was to me and when I shouted his name, he turned. That's when I threw the punch."

"A damn fine punch it was as well, Maddy. You needed to see it to see its impact."

They looked up to see Pops standing in the sheriff's office doorway to the side.

"Lucio, the sheriff wants to see you next. I'll sit with Maddy."

When Wynne saw Lucio's anxious look he patted him on the shoulder. "No need to worry, you are not the one in trouble. Your actions saved me from a beating that I'm sure about."

"Would Colton really have hurt you, Pops? I can't believe this is happening."

"If you have seen the look in his eyes, Maddy, you would know. He wasn't the Colton you and I have known all these years, that's for sure. Now while we wait how about some coffee?"

"I think there's a vending machine around the corner. Not sure how good it will be though."

A deputy walking past them shook his head and said, "For your sake, I'd suggest you go to the coffee shop across the road. It'll save your stomach. The stuff in that machine rots the machine every six months or so and they come and change it out."

"Thank you for the warning, deputy. Come on, Maddy, the coffee shop it is."

Chapter Thirty-Eight

Madison put her arm through her father's and they stepped out into the bright sunshine. After ensuring their path was clear, they crossed to the newly opened Coffee Shack and entered the shop. The aroma of fresh ground coffee beans filled their nostrils.

"Now this is a proper coffee shop. Let's see what's on offer, Maddy."

She followed her father to the counter behind which were display shelves of large containers labeled with various coffee bean names. An older woman with silver hair pulled into a loose bun stood at the counter and smiled at them.

"How may I help you, Sir? We have a large range of beans to choose from and we are happy to make up any particular combination you would like."

"Thank you. I love a deep, dark roast myself. The stronger the better but my daughter here isn't a fan of extra strong coffee."

"We can mix separate combinations for you both. Let me go through the stronger tasting beans with you first." The woman peered at Madison's father then gave a wide smile. "Wynne, is that you?"

Her use of his name seemed to surprise him. "I'm sorry, do I know you?"

"It's been a fair time, that's for sure. Ava, Ava Cording in those days."

"Ava! It has been a long while. How are you?"

"I'm getting by, lost my husband seven years ago now. I took this job when the shop opened for the company more than anything. How are you? Do you still have the ranch? How's Maria? Oh, sorry, I'm running my mouth."

"It's fine, Ava. Sorry to hear about your husband, I lost my Maria twelve years ago now, it's been just Madison and me for a long time. Yes, I'm still running the stud ranch. It's in the blood, although my bones tend to ache more nowadays once evening comes. That's not to say I can't work the ranch along with the hands, but I tend to choose my chores."

"I'm so sorry to hear about Maria. She was a good woman. It must have been hard raising a young girl on your own. I certainly know all about the aches and pains, Wynne but keeping busy helps. I can't sit around all day I get too stiff. One of the reasons I took this job."

"To be honest I think my daughter helped me more than I did her, when Maria passed. An eleven year old would keep anyone busy but it was the nights..."

Ava nodded her head in greeting and turned to take down two canisters of coffee beans. "I know all about it, Wynne but I need to be serving you not taking up your time chatting. Maybe, another time? Now let's find you the perfect blend, shall we?"

"I would enjoy spending time talking, Ava. I don't want to get you into trouble so tell me about these beans."

Madison watched in amazement as her father listened, nodded, and smiled as he continued to chat to Ava as she showed him all the different canisters, inviting him to smell the aroma as she took the lid off each one. He had been quite the hermit since her mother passed, never dating or showing any interest but now it was obvious he was at ease with this woman. It warmed Madison's heart to see these old friends catching up on each other's lives. Her eyes widened when she saw the woman's hand touch her father's and he did not pull away. *Could this be a new start for Pops?*

Not wanting to disturb her father's obvious delight in his conversation, Madison left the coffee shop and returned to the police station. She found Lucio sitting in the reception. As she entered the police station, he jumped up worry creasing his brow.

"I had no idea where you were. Is everything all right? Where is your father?"

"Sorry. I didn't think we would be so long. We just popped over the road for a coffee."

"A coffee? Where is the coffee?" Lucio emphasized his statement by looking at her empty hands.

"Well, I came back as Pops was much too interested in catching up on old times with the woman serving and I forgot to grab a coffee. Are we all done here?"

"Yes, Sheriff Gordon said if he needs to talk to you, he will give you a call later but not to worry now. Let's get a coffee then. I would enjoy a robust espresso."

Back in the coffee shop, Madison and Lucio found Wynne and Ava sitting at a red and white checked cloth covered table engrossed in conversation with two cream-coloured mugs with the store's coffee bean logo on the side, in front of them. Ava was still wearing her matching barista uniform, but had taken off the light brown apron. When they entered the shop, Wynne turned, smiled at Madison, and waved them over.

"Ava, this is my daughter, Madison, and this young man is Lucio. The one I told you about. Come and sit with us."

Ava smiled and said, "I'm pleased to meet you both. I will bring coffees for you both. Do you have any preferences? My break is over now."

Ava tied her apron back on as she stood up. Madison looked at her father's face noticing how relaxed and happy it was as he looked up at Ava. *That must have been some conversation.*

"It is lovely to meet you, too, Ava. May I have something smooth with a hint of vanilla?"

"No problem at all, Madison. And, for you, Lucio?"

"I will have an espresso. Thank you, Ava."

Once Ava was behind the counter, Madison turned to her father. "Well, Pops, you seem quite comfortable with Ava. What's the story?"

"We knew each other in high school. Although we never dated, we both wanted to. She is still as cheerful and animated as I remember."

Madison's head tilted to one side as she asked, "So why didn't you date?"

"Either I was with someone, or she was. We just weren't single at the same time, I suppose. Then after high school her family moved away for a while, and we lost touch."

"Ava, seems very nice, Wynne."

"She is a fine woman, Lucio. Although, I have to admit I had not thought about her in a long time. I'd forgotten how engaging she is."

Ava approached the table one mug and one small cup and saucer in hand. "Here we are. Espresso for you, Lucio and a vanilla blend for you, Madison. I would love to stop and chat more but I'm here to work. Hope to see you again, Wynne. I've made you up a blend of South American beans, should be strong enough even for you."

"Thank you, Ava. It has been a great afternoon. How much do I owe you for this?"

"It's on me, Wynne. Enjoy it. Once you have finished that one, we can experiment again."

"That is so kind, Ava, and I will be coming back. See you soon."

Madison watched, surprise on her face as her father took Ava's hand and kissed it. *I had no idea Pops could act this way. Ava has quite an effect on him.*

With a final farewell, the three of them left the coffee shop and walked back to the rental car and Lucio began the drive back to the ranch. Halfway along the main street, Wynne asked him to stop and park.

"I won't be long. I have a small errand to run."

Lucio and Madison watched him walk into the florist. "Well, that's a first."

"Your father is a romantic, Madison. Why are you so surprised?"

"I can honestly say I have never seen my father like this before. I remember him giving my mother flowers on occasion, but I was so young, I was oblivious to that sort of thing. When Ma died, Pops wasn't the same for a long time. He wouldn't have flowers in the house. Just going through the motions, I suppose. Did you see how his eyes sparkled though?"

"He is a man in love, Maddy, that I am certain."

"Oh, I don't think he can be love-struck that fast."

"No? Then are you not *l'amore ha colpito*...how you say? Love-struck."

Madison's blush rose up her throat to her cheeks. She turned to the car window to hide it. "That's a whole other thing, Lucio. Are you?" She turned to look into Lucio's eyes, waiting for him to turn away or change the subject. He didn't break their gaze but grasped her hand and kissed it.

"Your Lucio is *percosso* for his Madison."

"What is *percosso*?"

"Smitten in Italian, my *amore*. You have captured my heart."

She remembered their fateful meeting at the hotdog stand. Her first encounter with Lucio's dark looks and appreciating eyes, how she had felt so feminine in his presence not one of the boys.

His smooth accent sent shivers of delight through her flesh. *If he can make me feel this way with just words...I want him more than ever.* She leaned toward him.

Lips crushed against lips, hearts beat faster and flesh warmed. With a gentle embrace, he held her careful to support her back as they kissed. Her whole body tingled with desire, heat spread through her body. She felt his heart beat in strong rhythmic time as she gasped while he traced his tongue down her neck and along her jawbone. Their heated embrace was interrupted by a sharp rap on the side window opaque with patches of condensation of their heavy breathing. The car door opened to reveal her father looking up and down the street, embarrassed.

"Best we get home, my girl. No need for you to become the latest source of town gossip."

She blushed. "Yes, Pops, sure." Madison shifted in her seat, keeping her head down while her father got into the car. Wynne looked at Lucio, who nodded once his face reddened and started the vehicle.

Chapter Thirty-Nine

The car's inhabitants remained silent, during the journey back to the ranch, each deep in their own thoughts. When Lucio parked in front of the veranda of the ranch house, Wynne turned to his daughter. "I'm going to check on the horses and schedule chores for the ranch hands. I'll be a while. Without Colt I'll be picking up the slack."

Madison didn't miss the quick wink of an eye her father gave Lucio as he got out of the car. *If I needed any approval from Pops, that was it.* She smiled and put her hand on Lucio's shoulder as her father exited the car and shut the door.

"Would you like to come in for a while?"

"Yes, I would like that. I have a feeling your father may be warming to me."

"I would say he likes you rather a lot in light of your actions. Come on in."

He walked ahead of her to the front door and opened it for her to enter. Once inside the hallway, he held Madison's shoulders and placed a gentle kiss on her lips. Her body burned with urgent hot desire. She felt Lucio's unmistakable desire against her hip. The urgency of their lust overtook all other thoughts. Lips tasted and hands explored as emotions intensified. She led Lucio toward the stairs stopping at the first step.

"I can lift you if it will not hurt you, Madison?"

"It would be quicker..."

Strong arms scooped her up. He looked at her face for signs of pain. Madison smiled back and nodded that she was all right.

At the top of the stairs, she pointed toward her bedroom. Clothes were unbuttoned and discarded on the floor. Naked flesh touched and deepened the want and the need for each other. He laid her on the bed, kissing her feet, her legs, her stomach, and her breasts. She cried out.

"Now, Lucio, now!"

He did not make her wait. His muscular arms held him up and above her. She moaned his name as he found her warm wet heat. She gripped his neck, her nails digging into his flesh. There was no hesitation between them just physical excitement. He increased his movements, watching her face. She came once and then again, each time more powerful than the one before. Her body shivered, sweated, and tingled. A rush of physical delight she had never known had her gasping for breath, crying out his name repeatedly. He eased himself downward, kissing her neck and lips. His hot breath on her neck deepened her orgasm as he joined her. His body shuddered as he uttered her name.

Madison lay on her side to face him.

He stroked her face and smiled. "I have wanted to love you for a long time, my *amore*."

She could not hold back the tears and hugged deep into Lucio's chest, letting the tears flow.

"What did I do wrong, Maddy? Please tell me. I thought you wanted this. Did I hurt you?"

She sniffed before answering in a shaky voice. "You have done everything right, Lucio. I am so happy, these tears are happy tears."

His sigh of relief brushed against her cheek. He enclosed her with his powerful arms and kissed the tears from her cheeks. When Madison shivered, he drew the covers up over them.

"I never want to leave here. Let's stay."

"*Bellismo*, indeed, my sweet, Maddy."

They lay together gazing at each other until the back door slammed.

"That will be Pops. I suppose we should go down."

"I would like to keep a trace of respectability in your father's eyes, Madison, so yes, let us go downstairs. Shall I go down first?"

"There's that old fashioned trait. I will have to get used to that. If it makes you more comfortable, you go first."

"Maybe you need to brush your hair and not look so ravished."

"Oh, I like that word. I will come down in a moment or two only if you promise to ravish me later."

"It will be my pleasure."

He dressed, cupped Madison's face, placed a kiss on her nose, and left. She went into her en-suite and looked in the mirror. Her face was glowing and her eyes sparkled. She felt so alive, so happy, so desired. There would be no disguising this from her father.

With her hair brushed and a little powder to reduce her flushed cheeks, she went downstairs to find her father and Lucio sitting in the living room drinking beer and chatting like old friends.

"Am I interrupting?"

"Come on in, Maddy. Lucio has been telling me about his family's business. It has been handed down for generations, just like this ranch."

She sat beside Lucio, took his hand, and squeezed. Lucio gripped her hand back.

"There is tradition in both families, Maddy. We are not so unalike after all."

"Apart from you jet setting back and forth between Canada and Italy. This ranch is it for me."

"Well, actually that is one of the things, Lucio and I were discussing."

"Sorry, you've lost me. What have you been talking about?"

"Lucio, shall I tell her?"

"Of course, Wynne, go ahead."

Madison looked from her father to Lucio and back again, puzzled.

"Lucio just told me he has been searching for a base to centralize his operations over here. I thought he could use the old guesthouse. It will need some fixing up, but it is big enough for what Lucio is thinking of."

"But I thought you already lived here part of the time, Lucio?"

"I have been using my uncle's spare bedroom and motel rooms here and there, but it is not ideal. In Italy, we have the factory building with offices. Would you mind if I rented the guesthouse from you, Wynne?"

"You would be helping me out, Lucio. With a tenant in the building, maintenance problems will be seen sooner, and the income would be useful, too."

"Pops, I'm not sure we can ask for rent."

Lucio pulled his body backwards to look at her. "Madison, of course I will be paying for my tenancy. If I found a place elsewhere, I would be paying. So, why not here? I could employ a permanent member of staff to oversee the Canada business side in my absence."

"It feels awkward, that's all."

"It is a business transaction Maddy it does not affect our relationship in any way."

Madison looked at Lucio and then at her father. Both smiled at her, comfortable with their arrangement.

"I can see I'm out voted. I have to admit it would mean I could see you more, Lucio, and I would feel better having another person near the house when I have to leave Pops."

"I'm more than capable of looking after myself, Maddy. I'm not old and senile just yet!"

She patted her father's hand. "I know that, Pops, but you need the company, too. When I'm on the rodeo circuit, there are only the ranch hands here with you. They may be good for chores around the ranch, but not much at socializing when the workday is done."

"You're showing your soft side there. I have plenty of people around and old Bandit and me like our evenings together in front of the TV."

"It's not the same as having real company, Pops."

"Madison is right, Wynne, living alone is not pleasant. In my travels, I have spent many days and nights alone. Too many, if I am honest."

Lucio's direct look at Madison emphasized the alone. *If I doubted him before, I certainly do not now.* She squeezed his hand.

"I can see I'm going to be the one out voted. We can get into the finer details later on."

She stood. "Well, why don't I fix a late lunch for us all? I don't know about you two but I'm starving. Rental details can be postponed for a while."

Both men were enthusiastic in their agreement and with their beer bottles drained, joined her in the kitchen. She took a pain tablet to ease the dull ache in her lower back, while the men were busy with set tasks.

Madison selected meats and salad from the fridge, her father cut large slices of bread and Lucio laid the table with directions from Madison on where to find the cutlery and crockery. With multi-layered sandwiches plated, and another round of beer, the trio sat to enjoy the meal at the old pine kitchen table.

Half way through, the telephone rang.

"I'll get it. Stay where you are."

"Leave it, Pops, finish your meal."

"It might be the sheriff. I'll get it."

Madison could hear her father talking and soon realized it was not the sheriff.

"Well, hello. It was my pleasure. I hope you liked them. Oh, really, a lucky guess I suppose. How about I come over tomorrow? Yes, ten works for me. Until then, bye."

Wynne answered Madison's querying smile as he entered the kitchen again. "That was Ava. I'm meeting her for coffee tomorrow."

"That's great, Pops. Have a super time. Ava seems like a lovely woman."

"She is, Maddy. I'd forgotten how much I liked her."

Madison saw a twinkle in her father's eyes and was pleased for him.

Wynne turned to Lucio. "Well, shall we get down to business, Lucio? When are you thinking of moving into the guest house?"

"I do not want to inconvenience you, Wynne, what sort of timeline were you thinking of?"

Madison couldn't help a rush of excitement tremble through her body with thoughts of Lucio presence in the guesthouse.

She lowered her head to hide a knowing smile as she cleared the plates. "I'll wash up while you two hash out the details."

As the men talked, Madison washed up the crockery and then made a fresh pot of coffee. By the time, she placed mugs of hot coffee on the kitchen table, Wynne and Lucio had agreed on the rental terms.

Wynne announced, "So, we have some time to clean the place out, Maddy. Lucio will rent from the first of next month."

"I will be helping, Wynne, I don't expect you and Maddy to do it all yourselves."

"That's a done deal." The men shook hands.

Lucio turned to Madison, placing a light kiss on her cheek. "I would love to stay but I have calls to make, so if you will excuse me, I will go back to the motel."

"You can go back to collect your things, Lucio but you are staying here tonight and any night you are over this side of the world. Isn't that right, Maddy?"

Madison's enthusiastic reply made the two men laugh aloud.

"That's settled then. Now I need to do my rounds. See you two later."

"I think your father is happy with our arrangement, Maddy."

"I think so, too and I am more than happy with it as well."

He embraced her, his lips pressed onto hers a feeling of being home enveloped her. Before the kissing developed into more, he stood back, kissed her hand, and turned to leave.

"*Bella*, if I do not go now, I will not want to leave. I will be back in about three hours. Do you need me to bring anything back with me?"

"That sounds so wonderful - you coming back tonight, I mean. Well, how about buying a nice bottle of wine to go with dinner? I will cook steaks tonight."

"I will try to find a good robust red then. Later, my Maddy."

Chapter Forty

S he watched him drive out of the gate, dappled sunlight from building clouds reflecting off the glass. The click of the old dog's nails made her turn around to see him beside her. She gave Bandit's head a gentle pat as the dust trail diminished. She turned and climbed the stairs to her bedroom. The scent of Lucio's cologne hung in the air, making her smile. She made the bed and pulled hangers back and forth in the closet deciding on her outfit for the evening. With it laid out on the bed, she pulled on a pair of jeans and a T-shirt and went to find her father. With Colton gone, she would have to be more involved in the daily practical running of the ranch than ever before.

As she surveyed the lawns, paddocks, and stables she felt at peace. This was home, her home and one she could share with Lucio. Her new happiness opened her eyes, to what repairs were required, how neglected the house's interior was and that with fresh paint the old ranch house would be brought back to life. She felt positive about her future and the ranch's future more than ever. Humming a soft tune, she walked around the stables, and came across her father with the brood mares and Garner.

"How are they all, Pops?"

"All healthy and gaining weight well. I'll have to get Cody over next week for a check up on a couple though. We may have twins."

"Wow, exciting."

"It can be if the birth goes well otherwise not so much. Garner here offered to sleep with the mares nearer their time so he can alert me and Cody once they are in labor."

"That's great, Garner. We can set up a cot in here for you."

"I would appreciate that. It'll be more comfortable than a hay bale that's for sure. My back ached for days the last time."

Wynne squinted at the young man. "What? Wait? When did you sleep on a hay bale?"

"Colton always got me to sleep with the mares when they started their labor. Once I could see the feet I would go and fetch him."

Madison's father's face grew dark as he gritted his teeth. "That bastard, he always let me believe he slept with the mares all night. Good bit of acting that's for sure. All I can do is apologize Garner. We do not expect you to sleep on hay bales. If I had known, I would have taken it up with Colton a long time ago."

"I thought it was all part of the job, Mr. Beauchamp."

"And I suppose, Colton was more than happy to let you think that. I'm going to make it up to you, Garner. How about a raise in pay?"

"That would be great. Thank you, Sir. I have my eye on a beat up truck in town."

"No need to do that, Garner, you are welcome to the ranch truck. I have a new one on order. She may not be the prettiest thing, but she is quite reliable, and it will give you more time to save for a better one."

The young man's eyebrows shot upward. "You are too generous, Mr. Beauchamp."

Wynne motioned the remark away with a flick of his hand. "First orders of the day then, call me Wynne and come with me to look at that truck. We might need to fix her up a bit."

Madison watched in astonishment. Her father had always been a fair man, but this generosity was a revelation. She agreed Garner required compensation for the dreadful way Colton had treated him but a raise and a truck! Maybe Ava's influence was stronger than she had envisaged. Shaking her head in disbelief, Madison began cleaning out the nearest stable while the two men went to view the old ranch truck.

Three hours later with three extra large steaks prepared with marinade in the fridge, Madison bathed and dressed for dinner. A car horn alerted her to Lucio's arrival. She went to the front door to greet him and was surprised to see he was not alone. He opened the passenger door allowing his passenger to step out. Dressed in a floral blouse and ankle length denim skirt, Ava's shoulder length grey hair hung loose on her shoulders. She gave Madison a broad smile.

"I really hope this isn't being too forward, Madison. Lucio assured me it wouldn't be."

"Of course not, Ava. What a lovely surprise. Does Pops know you were coming?"

"Well, that's the surprise. Your man here has a romantic streak, you know."

"I'm just getting to know that, Ava. Come on in. I'll make a pot of coffee."

"I brought a pecan pie for dessert. I can't just turn up empty handed."

"How thoughtful, it smells delicious. I'll put it into the warming drawer."

As they walked into the kitchen, Madison observed Ava looking around. Through another woman's eyes, Madison once again realized how bare and unloved the house had become. *No woman's touch here for a long time. Ma always made it gleam and always had fresh flowers.* She remembered her father hadn't touched the vases for months after her mother passed. The smell of stale water and rotten flower stalks filled her mind. It had been Clancy, who eventually threw them all out, vases and all. Madison had picked wildflowers one day to make her father happy, but instead he'd left her and run upstairs. As he ran, he told her to throw them away or keep them out of his sight. Madison never picked flowers again. Now she could smell a floral scent as Ava approached her looking at her with concern. Memories of her mother flooded her mind.

"Are you all right, dear?"

"So sorry, Ava, I was daydreaming away here. Would you like a cup or a mug of coffee?"

"I would rather have a mug, thank you. Which blend are you using?"

"The one you made for Pops, but I've cut the scoops down so it's not quite so strong. I hope it is all right for you."

"Perfect, dear. Thank you."

Madison handed Lucio a mug. Their fingers connected and a familiar electrical tingle sparked. They sat at the weathered kitchen table.

Ava spoke first. "This is a nice ranch, Madison. I would love to walk around sometime."

"I would be honored to escort you around, Ava. It is a delight to see you here." They all turned to see Wynne standing in the back doorway.

"Hello, Wynne. Lucio came around to the coffee shop as I was finishing my shift and persuaded me to come over for supper. I hope that is okay?"

"More than okay, Ava, give me a few minutes to wash up I'm having trouble getting my nose far enough away from my armpits."

Everyone laughed as Wynne walked through the kitchen and up the stairs. Madison noticed Ava's focused gaze as she watched her father's departing figure. *There's more than an old friendship there. I wonder what the real story is between them.*

While they waited for Wynne, Lucio and Ava helped Madison with the meal preparation. With Madison's help locating things, Ava prepared a salad, and Lucio set the dining table finding the cutlery on the second try and laying out the place mats on the linen tablecloth. Madison placed the steaks into a large cast iron skillet and the meaty aroma filled the kitchen air. She kept an eye on them ensuring they were perfect. The conversation was light and cheerful. Lucio answered Ava's questions about his travels and the factory in Italy and Madison talked about the ranch and her barrel racing. Madison wanted to steer the conversation in other directions at supper. Her father entered the kitchen wearing a fresh shirt and a broad grin.

"Well, this is nice, a full house for a change, Madison. It sure feels good."

Wynne shared a warm smile with his only child. "If I had known you were coming, Ava, I could have bought some wine. It is unfortunate we don't have any."

"Actually, we do, Pops. Lucio was kind enough to bring several bottles."

"Well done. I was worrying about offering Ava a bottle of beer with her meal."

Ava's eyes crinkled with a broad smile. "Beer would have been just fine, Wynne. I'm not prissy. Oh, do you remember Madeleine? Always had her nose up in the air."

"Do I remember her? Of course, I told her once she must have dreadful stinky feet if she had to keep her nose up like that. She didn't think it was funny at all and told the teacher I had pinched her. I got detention. Mean cow."

"You never told me that."

"Think you were away by then. How come your family came back anyway?"

"My father lost his job out there and Ma was so homesick he agreed to come back. I thank her every day for that. I hated it in North Dakota."

"I had no idea you were that far away. It must have been hard with no family or friends."

"My brothers and I were luckier than Ma. At least we went to school and made friends. Left at home all day she complained the neighbors were not friendly and she felt isolated. I'm not sure how true that was but she sure was unhappy while we were there. My father never mentioned moving away again."

Lucio placed an arm around Madison's waist, kissed her cheek and whispered, "I don't think you have to worry about your father being lonely now, Maddy. He and Ava are more than comfortable with each other."

She turned her head, smiled, and whispered back. "Have you always been able to read women's minds?"

"Only when I love them."

Madison gasped. *He said it. He loves me. I don't need to hide my true feelings anymore.*

"I love you, too, Lucio. My heart is so happy it could burst. I have found you and Pops has someone wonderful, too."

"Let us eat, drink, and love together then."

Everyone walked into the dining room, as Madison placed two of the grilled steaks on plates and then cut the third one in half for Ava and herself. Everyone sat down and served themselves salad and bread rolls. Madison could not help smiling at her father. *It's been a long time since I've seen a sparkle like that in your eye, Pops.*

"You have known Ava a long time then, Wynne."

"A very long time, Lucio, we were in senior high together."

"And you were sweethearts?"

"Well, not exactly. We were interested in each other, but our timing was just awful. When Ava was single, I was dating and when I was single, she was dating. We never did get to go out. It was damn frustrating at times, I can tell you."

"For me as well, Wynne. No matter whom we were dating, there were always looks across the playing fields and at the drive-in movie theatre. Then I moved away and thought I would never see you again."

"Although the reason I was at the Sheriff office was not pleasant, I'm sure glad I walked into that coffee shop, Ava."

"It was *destio*, Wynne."

"Would that be destiny, Lucio?"

"Yes, Maddy, destiny. We met because of a hotdog. Maybe not quite so romantic as an expertly blended coffee but love always finds a way."

Ava looked their way. "You see, Maddy. He is a romantic, just like I said."

"He is Ava, and I'm going to enjoy every minute of my life with him."

Glasses raised in a toast to destiny.

"Now shall we sit for a while before the pie?"

"Pie? There's pie?"

She smiled as her father's question. "Yes, Ava was kind enough to bring a homemade pecan pie for dessert."

"Well, I would like to taste a slice right now."

"Shall we see if our guests want pie first, Pops?"

"Sorry, I'm quite out of practice..."

A loud blast preceded a plate on the china cabinet on the rear exploding.

"What the hell was that?" Madison shouted.

"Everybody drop to the floor. That was a bullet." Wynne commanded.

"What are you talking about, Pops? A bullet?"

Lucio grabbed her and pulled her down to the floor while Wynne did the same to Ava. Another wine glass burst into pieces and a hole appeared in the wall.

"Crawl to the stair cupboard, keep as low as you can, Madison, and take care of Ava. Lucio, do you know how to fire a gun?"

"Yes, Wynne, I do, but only for hunting. Who would shoot at us?"

"I can think of only one person. Colton must be out on bail."

Lucio's next remark voiced everyone's thoughts. "Surely, he would not do such a thing, Wynne?"

"Madison and I underestimated him before. Let's not make the same mistake twice. Follow me but keep low."

As the two men maneuvered, Wynne called out, "Do you have your cell phone, Maddy?"

After crawling to the hallway and into the enclosed confines of the stair cupboard, Madison shouted back, "Yes, Pops, I've called Sheriff Gordon already. He is leaving right now and has a car out on the highway that he's diverted this way. Have you any idea where that raging idiot could be?"

"Madison, stay quiet. I reckon he's near the brooding shed, if I'm reading the trajectory of those bullets right. Come this way, Lucio and stay low."

Ava grasped Madison's hand in the dim light of the cupboard. They listened to the two men making their way to the back door.

"Shouldn't we do something, Madison? Who is Colton? I'm petrified something bad will happen."

"The sheriff will be here in no time, Ava. Colton was our foreman, and he was arrested for attacking Pops. We're safe in here for the moment, I'm sure. We have to wait for the police to get here."

"He attacked Wynne, when?" She shook her head, her lips tight. "Never mind explaining it now. We have to help Wynne and Lucio, Madison. We can't stay in here doing nothing. It will make for better odds if nothing else."

"Well, I can go if you are all right to stay here."

Ava's shoulders pulled back. "I'm not staying, Madison. I've shot enough vermin in my time to know I can be of more help out there than in here."

"All right then. We will have to get to Pops' study. His guns are in a locked cupboard, but I know where the key is."

"Would he not have opened it already?"

"No, he has a couple of guns hidden in a lock box by the back door. He would have grabbed them on his way out."

With careful deliberation, Madison opened the stair cupboard door and listened for any sounds. She heard a shuffling noise and a soft whisper she recognized as her father's voice come from the rear of the kitchen.

Staying low, the two women made their way to the study. Crouching behind her father's desk, Madison opened a drawer and retrieved a key. Motioning for Ava to stay put, Madison moved to the corner of the room and stood up flush to the wall. She put the key in the door and twisted it.

A windowpane exploded spraying glass across the top of the desk. The two women looked at each other wide-eyed but stifled their screams.

Madison dropped down to the floor. Ava crouched under the desk. They heard a couple of footsteps on the veranda under the study window and held their breath waiting for them to pass.

Another shot rang out and the desk lamp fell to the wooden floor. Its glass bulb shattered. More shuffling footsteps faded to the rear of the house. Ava pointed to the gun display cupboard and formed her hand into the shape of a handgun then pointed to herself.

Madison crawled over, reached up to the handgun, took it down, grabbed a box of bullets, and slid them across the floor to Ava. Madison took a shotgun and a box of cartridges. Guns loaded the two women exited the study, their backs tight to the wall and then made their way to the rear of the house, crawling on all fours.

With low whispers, they took positions on either side of a large window and peeked out. There was no one in sight. Ava put her finger up to her lips and then pointed it towards a line of trees to her right. Madison whispered.

"Is it Pops and Lucio or that bastard...oh sorry, I shouldn't have said that."

"Under the circumstances I think the language is permissible, Madison. It's your father I can see, but only him."

"Where's Lucio?"

Madison's heart thudded as scenarios rushed into her mind. Had Colton shot Lucio? Was he stalking Pops? *I swear I'll kill Colt if he harms either of them.*

Just as Madison was about to move, Ava lunged and pushed her to the wall. A shadow passed across the windowpanes. Ava cocked her gun and pointed it at the window. A shot rang out. A scream of pain and a thud came from the veranda as the wail of sirens filled the air.

Thundering footsteps echoed through the house and along the veranda. A shout came from just outside the window where Madison crouched looking at Ava in shock.

"Stay down, hands on your head."

"Cuff him, Deputy Cordright. I'll be inside checking on these good people."

Ava placed the handgun on a nearby shelf and took the shotgun from Madison, placing it on the floor. With an arm around Madison, she led her to the kitchen and sat her at the table.

The Sheriff walked in. "We have him in custody. Are you both unharmed?"

"Yes, Greg, we are fine. Madison is in shock, but I can take care of her. Can you please find Wynne and Lucio? They went out earlier to search for that Colton boy."

"Have you any idea which direction they went, Ava?"

"I saw Wynne just west of the study a few moments ago but I have no idea where the other man is. I only hope you find them both uninjured."

Tears streamed down Madison's face. Ava sat beside her and pulled Madison to her. "Madison, don't worry, Greg and his men will find them."

Before exiting the room, the Sheriff turned to say, "I can ask a female deputy to come in, if you like, Ava."

"No, that's all right, I can take care of her."

Madison sniffed back tears and looked at Ava. "How do you know Sheriff Gordon, Ava?"

"He's my sister's boy...well I need to say man, don't I? He was the one who taught me to shoot after my husband passed. I told him I felt unsafe alone on the farm."

"You are full of surprises, Ava. I froze when I saw Colton's shadow."

"My gun training just came in handy. First time I've had to use it on a person though. Until now it's been vermin of another kind I've shot."

Running footsteps alerted the two women to people approaching.

"Madison, oh my *bella* are you all right? I heard a shot and then there were polizia everywhere. I had to identify myself before they let me come in."

Madison rushed to him embracing and kissing him. "I didn't know where you were. I thought he had shot you. I was so scared."

"I was circling the house as Wynne took cover in the trees. We knew Colton was making his way to the rear and wanted to ambush him there. Then we saw him fall. Who shot him? The *polizia*?"

"Well, that was me, Lucio."

Lucio looked at Ava in surprise as Wynne walked in the back door accompanied by Sheriff Gordon. Wynne's wide eyed look showed his concern.

"Is everyone safe and unharmed?"

"Yes, Wynne, we are fine. Are you good?"

Wynne approached Ava, embraced her shoulders, and kissed her on the cheek. "I'm fine Ava, glad we are all unharmed and that maniac is in custody."

The sheriff put his hands on his hips. "Well, I will need statements from all of you and its better we do that now rather than later. I will need you all to sit in separate rooms, however. Can we do that?"

Everyone nodded in agreement. The sheriff called out for three deputies to escort Lucio to the study, Madison to the living room, and Wynne to the dining room while Ava stayed with him in the kitchen. Forty minutes later, with their statements made, they rejoined each other in the kitchen where Ava had made a fresh pot of coffee.

"What will happen now, Sheriff?"

"It was a clear matter of self-defense on Ava's part, Wynne."

Madison watched her father's eyebrows shoot upward. "I'm sorry. I'm not quite with you?"

"Ava is the one that shot him, Wynne."

Wynne turned to Ava. "You shot him? I thought it was one of the deputies."

She gave a slight shake of her head. "He was creeping past the window at the back here and I took my chance."

"You are a woman to take seriously, Ava. I'd better watch myself."

Ava lowered her head, and a small smile crinkled her mouth.

The Sheriff nodded and said, "I will be on my way, if there is nothing else. Colton will have his shoulder wound looked after and then he'll be in jail until his trial. I'll keep you posted."

"Thank you, once again, sheriff, for your quick response."

"We are only doing our job, Wynne. Take care of these women and yourself. Bye Ava, a good piece of shooting that."

"It's all thanks to your great tuition, Greg. Take care."

The sheriff tipped his hat and left the kitchen. They could hear him giving orders to the constables outside as he walked along the veranda. The two couples embraced each other, happy in the growing silence as the police cruisers drove away.

Chapter Forty-One

While Wynne drove Ava home, Madison and Lucio sat in front of a fire in the living room. She felt safe and warm embraced by the man beside her. He held her as tightly as he dared, glad she was safe and unharmed.

"This is a day to remember, in many ways, Madison. Are you feeling better now?"

"Yes, much better, thanks. What do you think of us all now?"

"That you will fight to keep each other safe, as any true family would do. A family I want to be part of, if you will let me."

"Oh, yes, Lucio. I would love that."

"Then I will ask your father for your hand."

"I'm sure he will be happy we are getting married, Lucio, when we tell him."

"It is only right I ask him, Madison. It is the proper way, the Italian way."

"Ava is right, you are a romantic and I am so happy to call you mine."

He kissed her and her whole body responded to him. The heat from the fire added to their passion.

"We need to go upstairs, Lucio, before Pops comes home."

"I am torn between following you to your bedroom and respecting your father's house and asking for your hand before making love to you again."

"Lucio, please, I understand you have traditions, but I want and need you now."

His eyes met hers their chocolate brown deepened as he gazed at her, needing him. "I cannot say no to you, my amore. Lead the way."

She clasped his hand in hers and ascended the stairs with her lover in tow. Madison closed her bedroom door behind them and placed her hands on his chest. She undid each shirt button enjoying the muscular chest exposed with each button. He caressed her face, and ran his fingers through her hair as she slipped his shirt off his body. Before she could unbuckle his belt, he began undoing her shirt buttons and cupped her breasts as he released them from her bra. She gasped and pulled him to the bed pulling him on top of her.

He touched her face, neck, and breasts. As his fingers ran across her skin, tiny electrical tingles excited Madison more. She clasped his face and kissed his eyes, mouth, and cheeks. As he unbuttoned her jeans, she could not contain herself any longer. She tugged at his jeans, her urgency making her fumble and frustrated.

"Maddy, slow down, enjoy the moment."

"Lucio, I have never been this turned on. I need you now."

He kissed her and laid her on her back. He stood up and pulled her jeans off, then stepped out of his own. She relished the warmth and weight of his body on her own. She raised her hips. He slid into her hot wetness. She felt exhilaration like never before. Every nerve in her body reacted to each move he made. Her body was charged and hot, her mind focused on the physical sensations. He began with slow movements at first then increased and pushed deeper. Her orgasm was deep and long, making her cry out.

Silencing her with a long kiss, he listened for the front door to shut. He'd heard Wynne's truck return but realized she had not. He kissed her face and neck as her breathing slowed. He embraced her and pulled the covers over their naked bodies. A door shut downstairs. Madison looked at Lucio.

"Is that Pops? It's after midnight."

"Yes, I heard his truck. Quiet now. Lucio wants to make his woman happy again."

She placed her hands on his chest. "I'm so sorry, I couldn't control myself."

"Don't be sorry. I have pleasure in pleasing you. This time we will go slower. I can wait a long time."

Her hot breath caressed his neck. "Oh, Lucio."

Lips met and they explored each other's bodies - face, neck, arms, stomach, and chest. She caressed his shoulders, kissing his chest as she did. He teased her nipples with his tongue. When he entered her, she echoed his movements bringing them both to orgasm. He whispered her name as he lay beside her.

She laid her head on his broad chest, and listened to his heartbeat slow down to become a rhythmic double beat again.

In the morning light, Madison's hands followed the contours of his ribcage and stopped at a line of scar tissue. He turned to face her.

"How did you get this scar, Lucio?"

"It is a longer story than we have time for now. I need to go and see your father before it gets too late. I promise I will tell you soon."

Madison was curious but also excited. Soon she would be engaged to this incredible handsome and loving man. *Pops will say yes, I'm sure of it.* Lucio dressed, kissed her cheek, and left her bedroom. His footsteps receded as he descended the stairs.

She heard her father's voice and then a door closed. She couldn't sit still as she waited. She re-made the bed and freshened up in the bathroom. She brushed her teeth, smoothed her tussled hair, and sat at her dresser, drumming the fingers of her right hand.

Footsteps sounded on the staircase. She turned to the door and waited for it to open. Lucio opened the door his head hanging down low and unsmiling. She gasped, shaking her head.

"He didn't say no, he wouldn't do that. I'll go and talk to him. Oh, Lucio."

She rushed to him and embraced him. As she clung to him, a chuckle came from his lips.

"My fiery redhead, your father said yes. I wanted to see how you would react if he had said no."

She looked up at him and thumped his arm. "Don't ever do that again, you will have to make up for panicking me."

"And how can I do that, my *bella*?"

"Come over here and I'll show you."

Chapter Forty-Two

Madison was awakened by soft kisses on her neck and a muscular body spooned behind her. She turned to face a familiar face. Her scream ripped at her throat as Colton grinned back at her, eyes glinting with anger and lust. He cupped her breast and pinched one nipple making it hard.

"Colton, stop, please stop, I can't do this. Please."

"You're mine now, Maddy, I'm having you now. You can't go this far and expect a man to stop. A two bit tease wouldn't do that."

"Colton, please, no."

Colton ripped Madison's zipper apart and pulled the denim down. His fingers were inside her before she could struggle free.

"See you do want it, hot and wet for your Colt to fuck."

Madison's screams were cut short as Colton's hand pressed over her mouth and nose. His other hand unzipped his jeans, and he entered her hard and fast.

"Take it, girl. You'll love Colt fucking you."

Madison twisted side-to-side, pummeling at Colton's chest in fury as his hands gripped her neck and squeezed. She began to lose consciousness. *He's going to kill me. Oh, God help me.*

Hands gripped her wrists as she struggled to get free. Then a familiar voice entered her consciousness.

"Madison! Maddy! What is wrong? Look at me, *bella*. You were having a nightmare. What was it? Tell your Lucio."

"Oh, Lucio...I dreamt Colton was...raping me. I felt so helpless, so scared."

"Come into my arms. You are always safe with your Lucio."

A frantic knock sounded at Madison's bedroom door. "Madison, are you all right? What's going on in there?"

"It's all right, Pops. I had a bad dream. I'm fine now. Honestly."

"Gave me quite a shock, may I come in, are you both decent?"

Lucio looked at Madison, with a wild shake of his head he jumped out of the bed and ran to the bathroom.

"You can come in, Pops." She stifled a giggle as her father opened the door and sat on the bed. He took her hand, then looked around the room, frowning. She pointed to the bathroom door and put one finger up to her lips. Wynne nodded.

"Well, I'm glad it was only a bad dream. I'm going to start breakfast, will you be down shortly?"

"Oh, yes in no time at all, I'm starving."

Wynne kissed his daughter and left the room, closing the door behind him a smile on his face.

Madison walked into the bathroom and joined Lucio in the shower. They smoothed foaming shower gel over each other. Standing under the water jets rinsing off each other's bodies their passion increased. He lifted her up. She gripped her legs around his waist. The running water covered their gasps of pleasure. Ecstasy was a word she had not used before but now she understood its meaning. With their desire tempered for the time being they wrapped themselves in towels, and dried their bodies when they heard Wynne calling them down to breakfast.

"You'll need to be hungry. Pops makes a mean breakfast."

"I am hungry but also think I will need all my strength to satisfy you."

He took her hand and kissed it as they walked into the kitchen. The aroma of frying bacon and eggs and hot toast filled the air. The table was set for four. Madison looked around but could not see anyone else.

"Who are we expecting, Pops? There are four place settings."

"Ava's just in the washroom. She'll be here in a moment or two."

Madison looked at her father. A twinkle in his eye confirmed her suspicions. She wasn't the only one in love.

"Good morning, young ones. How are you?"

"Morning, Ava. We are real fine. How are you?"

"Happier than I've been in a long, long time."

Wynne coughed and looked at Ava, who sat down and concentrated on buttering a slice of toast. "Sit down then, I'll bring the plates over."

Once everyone had a plate full of bacon, eggs, tomatoes and hash browns, Wynne brought the pot of coffee over to the table and filled up each mug. "I haven't made it too strong this morning. I'm following orders."

Wynne winked at Ava, who winked back.

"We managed to find a blend that has the richness your father likes without melting a spoon in it. Tell me what you think."

Lucio and Madison sipped the hot liquid. It had a full body and a rich aroma.

Madison sighed. "This is perfect, Ava. It doesn't take my breath away and make my heart race but is rich enough at the same time."

Lucio nodded. "A good bold taste, Ava, I am impressed. What beans did you use? It has a malty flavor."

"You have a good nose, Lucio. It is a mix of beans from Mandehling in Sumatra and there is a sweet malt flavor to it."

Wynne sipped the dark liquid and smacked his lips together. "After all these years, I have a coffee that hits the spot just right, thanks to Ava. I've been mixing them up and never got anything this good."

"I told you, Wynne, the right blend can make all the difference."

Silence fell around the table as everyone enjoyed their meal. Then Lucio coughed and Wynne nodded. Madison looked from one man to the other - *they're up to something. What did Lucio plan with my father last night?*

Ava and Madison both gasped in shock and a wide grin covered Wynne's face as Lucio knelt down in front of Madison.

"Will you marry me?"

Madison's cry of happiness was matched by Ava's thrilled exclamation as her hands went up to her face and Wynne's arm embraced her shoulder.

"I want you to come with me to Italy, Madison. I want you to meet my family, see my home, and to buy your ring. Will you come?"

"Yes, of course. I've never been to Italy. It will be wonderful."

"I am so glad you said yes, after your father gave his approval last night. He was in no doubt you would say yes."

Madison looked across at Wynne and Ava. Wynne was holding Ava's hand. They were smiling at each other.

I'm getting married. I can see Pops is in love with Ava. *How can our lives turn around so much in so little time? Knowing Pops has someone makes me feel much happier about marrying and being away from the ranch.*

Madison embraced her father and saw a small tear on his cheek. She kissed it away, knowing it was a happy tear. Ava held out her arms and gave Madison a hug.

"You will make the most perfect bride, Madison. Don't you think Wynne?"

"I do even though I am biased. I will be honored to walk her down the aisle and give her to this outstanding young man."

Madison turned to Lucio. He looked down unable to speak at his future father-in-law's words. With a gentle touch under his chin, Madison made him look into her eyes. "You are a wonderful man, Lucio. I am the happiest woman in the world at this moment."

"I love you, my Maddy, with all my heart."

Their lips met and then there was only the two of them within its heat and emotion. Madison's father's cough broke the spell, and they turned toward Wynne and Ava who said, "Young love, Wynne, is beautiful to behold. Let's leave these two alone. I would love a tour of the ranch."

"Your wish is my command." Wynne held out his arm and Ava put hers through it. As they walked out of the back door, Ava waved one hand at the young couple. Madison looked up at Lucio.

"It is tempting to stay but maybe we need to go and inspect the guesthouse?"

"Very tempting indeed but I will follow Ava's example. Lead on, Maddy."

The guesthouse was tucked into a secluded corner of the ranch, surrounded with mature trees and the remains of flowerbeds long neglected. As they approached, Lucio asked.

"When was the guesthouse built?"

"It was actually the original ranch house, when my great grandfather came here. As the family grew and the ranch became successful, my grandfather built the larger house. The guesthouse was used by extended family until my father took over. He was the only son, and his sisters did not want to stay and live on the ranch. Neither of my cousins were interested in ranching either, they work in the city so I'm the last of the line."

"We will have to change that, Maddy. I will give you healthy sons. Some will ranch and others will manufacture boots."

She looked at him and laughed. "And exactly how many sons were you thinking of?"

"Four or maybe five - is a good number, don't you think?"

She was about to thump his arm when she saw him grin. "Are you teasing me, Lucio Calligaris?"

"Only a *piccolo*, a little."

"Whew, got me worried there. If you really wanted so many sons and I only manage girls, we could be in serious trouble."

Arms around each other's waists, they laughed together as they entered the guesthouse. The door creaked with lack of use and dust billowed across the floor as fresh air blew into the hallway.

"It's going to need a lot of cleaning and fixing. I don't think I've been in here since high school. It was a super hang out for my cousins and me. We had some great parties in here."

"We can hire a team to clean it, and I will have an inspection done for structural work. Show me around, amore."

She led him through the old house. They peered under dust-sheets at old style furniture as they went. The living room's large bay window looked out over the paddocks. Lucio stood to enjoy the view.

"This will be my office. I will be able to see you working and riding those magnificent beasts from here."

"It is a great view, but you might change your mind when you see it from upstairs. Come."

She took his hand and ascended the stairs. Her hand gathered dust from the banister, so she wiped it on Lucio's shirt.

"Another shirt you are making dirty. Is this a habit of yours I will have to get used to?"

He swept his hand over the railing to place a smudge on her shirt, but she ran up to the landing and disappeared around a corner. She hid behind a bedroom door and waited for him to approach. When his footsteps were level with her, she shouted out. He jumped and turned to face her. He took hold of her and swept her off her feet carrying her into the room.

"Here is your office, Lucio. It is perfect for surveying the stables and paddocks."

He put her down and looked out of the bay window. "This is wonderful. I can see so much more from up here. You are right. The sitting room can be converted into a general office. It is large enough for a couple of desks while I have this room."

"This was my grandparents' room. It is directly above the living room, making it easy to have a bay window up here as well."

"How dusty do you think the bed will be?"

She understood the glint in his eye. *Dust or no dust, I'm not saying no.* Without a word, they removed the dustsheet to find an old quilt on the four-poster bed. Knowing no one would overhear them, Madison and Lucio's expressions of desire filled the room as dust motes floated around them. Sunlight piercing through the window glass.

Later, they patted dust off each other's clothes, discarded on the floor in their haste earlier. Madison pulled her fingers through her hair trying to smooth the auburn curls before putting on a band to restrict them.

"I like your curls, Maddy, why do you tame them so?"

"You seriously like them? I've wanted straight hair my whole life."

"Why be dull? Let them curl and fly in the wind. It is how I dream of you."

"You dream of me?"

Her heart swelled with joy at his admission. She had not wanted to admit that she dreamt of him almost every night. She put her hair band around her wrist, shook her head, and let it fall across her shoulders.

"Beautiful, just beautiful, you distract me from everything."

She stood on tiptoe and placed a light kiss on his mouth. "Before we get distracted again let's check out the rest of the house and make notes of repairs."

"Practical as well as beautiful, I am a lucky man. Lead the way."

He placed his hand on the small of her back and followed her through the rest of the house. There were a few cracked windowpanes and several damp areas with mold that required attention and Madison made mental notes. Once they finished their inspection, she turned to him as they stood in the rosy glow of the living room.

"Are you feeling brave enough to take a ride?"

"As long as I can have the same quiet horse from before I will ride. What was her name again?"

"Mai Curl. I will check to see how she is doing first. We might have to pick another horse for you if she is too heavy with her foal or Cody has restricted riding her."

"Who is Cody?"

"He is our vet. He's great. You will meet him soon, I am sure. He will be around to make sure the foals are born without problems."

The couple walked to the stable closest to the guesthouse and entered the dim building to find Garner brushing Mai Curl.

"How is she doing, Garner?"

"Real good, Miss. Beauchamp, Cody just looked her over. He said we will have to stop riding her in another month though."

"That's good news. I can take her out for a gentle walk then. Where is Cody now?"

"I can saddle her up for you, Miss Madison. Cody is taking a look at Titan."

"If you can saddle her that would be great, I'll have a chat with Cody and then come back. Thanks, Garner. Come with me, Lucio and meet Cody. He is a real character but has a heart of gold."

They could hear a single voice as they walked into Titan's stable. The stallion snorted in reply as they peered into the stall. Cody was standing with one hand on Titan's nose talking to the horse in soft tones.

"There you are, boy, not even a scar to spoil your magnificent coat."

"I'm sure it's due to your care, Cody."

The vet swung around to face them. "Well, hello, Madison. How are you?"

"I'm fine, just fine, Cody. I would like you to meet my fiancé, Lucio."

"Well pleased to meet you, young man and congratulations to you both."

"Thank you. Maddy, has told me you are the best vet around here, Cody. It is a pleasure to meet you."

"You're not from around here, then? What sort of accent is that?"

"It is Italian, but I spend half my time here and half in Italy where my business is based."

"Sounds like a nice life."

Lucion smiled at Madison's face and said, "It is becoming better."

She blushed and turned to the vet. "How is Titan doing, Cody?"

"He is the calmest, most powerful, magnificent horse I know, and he is doing real well. The wound on his leg has healed and I just took out the last stitch. He is good as new. He's also settled down a lot. No more nervous twitches at sudden noises."

Madison stroked the stallion's flank. "That is such good news. It would make breeding difficult if he was spooked at the simplest thing. Do you think we need to keep him quiet for much longer?"

"To be honest, Madison, I think he is all right to meet women friends again. I would make sure there are plenty of ranch hands around the first couple of times just in case, but I don't think there will be a problem. I rattled the door before coming in here and he just turned to look."

"Could I take him out for a ride then?"

"Sure. You know how to handle him almost as well as Colton did. Sorry, it's best not to say that name around here. What's happening with him now?"

"He was charged and is in jail waiting for a court date. We can't believe how he acted, Cody. It came as a complete shock after knowing him so long."

"Stupidity on his part, he could have made a good life here. He was so good with the horses. It's a sad waste of a talent, if you ask me."

"Pops, says he thinks Colton became delusional and somehow snapped when his plan was under threat."

"Well, your father is probably right, Madison, Colton has ruined the rest of his life and for what? Wanting more than was his right when you and Wynne had given him a place here for life. Greed is a powerful thing for some people, that's for sure."

Lucio shook his head before saying, "What's frightening, Cody is the extremes he was prepared to go to for that greed. I thank God I was able to help Wynne on both occasions Colton used violence to take matters into his own hands."

"Yes, I heard you helped out, Lucio. Madison has a protector with her now."

Cody shook Lucio's hand and smiled at Madison. "Well, my work is done here for today. I will come back in three days to check on the mares. If Titan behaves himself when you are out on your ride, there's no reason, as I said, that you can't have him in the breeding shed again next week. See you both and congratulations once again on your engagement."

Lucio's arm circled Madison's waist and his lips found hers, they were lost in each other for a moment. It was a struggle to break their embrace but Madison did so.

"Before this develops let's saddle up Titan and fetch Mai Curl, shall we?"

"If you insist, Maddy, but you cannot escape me for long."

"I don't want to, Lucio."

Chapter
Forty-Three

Lucio watched as Madison saddled the stallion and once again showed him each piece of tack and told him the names and their function. He nodded and repeated the names to ensure he got them right. He relished her excitement and joy in the familiarity of the things around her, simple things that showed him her unpretentious nature, it was engaging and refreshing. So many Italian women his mother tried to introduce him to flaunted their designer labels and demanded only the finer things in life. Not one of them would be as happy as Maddy brushing down a horse's mane or mucking out a stable. He knew in his heart what he saw in Madison was not a charade - what he saw was what he got, and he was in love with that.

Once Titan was ready, Madison put a lead rope on and walked him outside. As they approached the other stable, Garner brought out Mai and handed her reins to Lucio. Madison smiled at Lucio's apparent uneasiness. "She is calm, remember. Let's walk them both to the fence and I'll hold her while you get on."

"All right. How do I make her walk again?"

"Just start walking alongside me and she will follow. Don't tug on the reins, just pick up the slack."

Lucio followed Madison's instructions and smiled when Mai began to walk beside him. When they reached the fence, Madison held the lead rope while he climbed onto Mai's back and took the reins as Madison passed them to him. Then Madison mounted Titan and turned the stallion towards the tree line. Lucio took a couple of deep breaths to remind himself that last time this horse had not thrown him or hurt him but actually tried to help him from falling.

"Let's see if I can show you the woodland without any problems this time, Lucio."

"With all that has happened I forgot all about the track going up to the road. What has been done with it?"

"You'll soon see. Follow me and remember a gentle kick to move Mai forward and pull the reins left or right to steer her."

"Where is the lead rope, Madison? I can wait while you get one."

"Lucio, don't worry. Mai will follow Titan. We can ride side by side."

He swallowed hard before giving her a faint smile. Then nodded and gripped the reins, his Adam's apple bobbing up and down, evidence of the old childhood fear rising.

"Ease up on those reins, Mai will sense your tension. Just relax."

Lucio shook his shoulders and then flashed a broad smile in answer to hers. "Lead on, Maddy."

She kept the pace slow and pointed out the other buildings on the ranch and an old tree house she and her cousins used to play in just as they reached the tree line. He looked to his right to find the track had been cordoned off with a sturdy gate and fencing. The cleared track was blocked with cut tree trunks.

"That will keep out any unwanted visitors."

"Pops got the ranch hands working on it the day after the raid. There is fencing at the other end near the highway as well. And they destroyed the makeshift bridge that was in the dip."

"A thorough man, your father, Madison, I like that."

"I have a feeling you and Pops will get on well. Now follow me up this track, I have something to show you."

Madison pulled Titan's reins to the left and walked him deeper into the woodland. Mai followed with little guidance from Lucio. Birdsong and the fluttering of wings sounded as Madison led them into a small clearing. A stream trickled along one side and the ground grew softer. The sun's rays and heat was dappled under the tree canopy.

"We can dismount here and tie the horses to these trees. They will graze for a while."

She slid off Titan's saddle and grabbed a rolled-up blanket from behind it. She held Mai's harness while Lucio jumped down from the horse's back. With the horses tied with secure knots to a thick branch, she led him to the stream's edge. A single willow bent over, its leaves trailing in the fast running water. Madison shook out the blanket and laid it on the ground then took out a penknife.

"What are you doing, Maddy?"

"Come and see."

He frowned but looked in the direction of her pointing finger. On the tree trunk were two sets of initials inside a heart shape.

"These are my parent's initials. I would love to put ours here too, if you are willing."

"Of course, Maddy, it is a sign of love."

She pressed the knife edge into the tree's bark to begin cutting, but he took the knife away and began carving. Once their initials were completed, he cut into the bark again. She watched and became puzzled when the heart shape she expected was not forming.

"What shape are you making there, Lucio?"

"Wait and see."

As she watched, she began to make out the shape of two cowboy boots. She laughed and hugged his back.

"The boots brought us together, so I thought they needed to be forever beside us."

"A wonderful romantic gesture from my loving Italian, thank you, I'm glad you didn't choose a hotdog though."

"It would not have been my first choice."

They laughed at the idea of a hotdog shaped carving then her face became serious. She kissed him and unbuttoned his shirt, pulling it free of his jeans.

"You surprise me, Maddy, and I love that."

With their clothes discarded, and their naked bodies pressed together on top of the blanket, they found a rhythm in the water cascading over the rocks in the stream. As he pushed inside her, Madison arched her back, gripping her legs around his waist urging him on. He pulsed deep inside her making her orgasm powerful and sweet as she felt his hot breath on her neck. She cried out his name as his final shuddering thrust signaled his orgasm. He embraced her and wrapped the blanket across their cooling bodies, while their breathing slowed. Her fingers traced his ribs one by one and again felt the scar. She looked deeply into his eyes for an answer.

"You are right. You need to know. Let us dress first then I will tell you what you want to know."

They dressed in silence, each deep in their own thoughts. Lucio's shirt hung open exposing his taut chest. Madison could not help but look doubts began to crowd her mind. *Do I need to know?*

"Come, sit with me, Maddy. Closer."

She snuggled into his embrace. Gripping his hand, anxious to know the truth, but at the same time fearing to know it. Tension pulled through her shoulders.

"Madison, I was engaged once before..."

She was on her feet in a second looking down at him. "Why would you keep such a secret from me?"

He caught her hand and pulled her down onto the blanket. "Madison, let me tell you. It is not how you think. Please listen."

He took both of her hands, and turned her to face him. "As I was telling you, I was engaged once before. Our two families had known each other for decades and our parents thought we would make a fine couple. Every celebration, or holiday we were sat together at the dinner table and encouraged to spend time together."

"What was her name?"

"Mariella."

"That is a beautiful name."

"She was a *piuttosto* girl, how you say, pretty on the outside."

"Not on the inside?"

"No, but she hid it well. Always the perfect daughter in front of her parents and my family but once we were engaged her true nature began to come out."

"What did she do?"

"First, she asked for little things. A silk scarf, a necklace, a trinket but soon she was demanding fur coats, expensive trips and a sports car. When I told her those things would have to wait until we were married and settled, she got mad. You have never seen such anger, Maddy. She was wild. I admit I gave in several times just to calm her down but one evening we were walking past a jewelry shop. and she pulled me over to the window. There was a diamond and sapphire necklace displayed. It was a lot of money, and I said I could not buy it. It might be a golden anniversary gift at best. That is when it happened."

"Oh, Lucio, what did she do?"

"I had no idea she carried it in her purse, so I was taken by surprise."

"Carried what? What was it?"

"It was a small dagger, with a blade that flicked out."

"You mean a switch blade? The woman was crazy."

"That night, I realized that, Madison, all too clearly. She plunged the knife into my side and then ran off screaming. My memories of what happen immediately afterwards are dim at best. I was in shock not just because of the injury but that the woman I loved could physically hurt me."

"You are lucky she didn't pierce your heart, Lucio. What happened to her?"

"Several people passing by came to help me. Another called the police. She was arrested, there was a trial and then..."

He bowed his head, swallowing hard. She waited anxiously for him to continue. After several moments, she raised his chin to meet his eyes.

"If you don't want to tell me more, that's okay."

"No, I can tell you. It's just reliving those memories I have not visited them for a long time. During the trial, she was raging, yelling at the judge and me across the courtroom. She lunged at me claiming it was my fault and that she was innocent. Two polizia restrained her. Due to her actions, the judge deemed she required to be sectioned into a psychiatric hospital. She is still there and will remain there for a long time. She has attacked her guards, other inmates and her psychiatrist. She is not the woman I thought I knew."

"Were there any signs she was so unstable?"

"At the time, I was young, totally in love and thought she could do no wrong. I excused her outbursts to a passionate nature and jealousy. It was a long time before I trusted women again. The scar reminds me to be careful."

Madison brushed her fingers across the scared tissue then held his hands and placed a gentle kiss on his cheek. "I may be a redhead, but I would never do such a thing, to you or anyone I love. We have both been ensnared by unstable people and our trust broken, this makes us closer don't you think?"

"Yes, I do. A common thread in our lives and one we have learnt from. I know my love and trust is safe with you, Maddy. I do so love you."

"I love you too, Lucio with all my heart."

A gust of wind tore at the blanket, and blew through the willow leaves as a few raindrops fell making the couple shiver.

"We need to go back, Madison. Come here I will take the grass out of your wonderful hair. Leave it loose for me."

"I can leave it loose some of the time, but when I'm working it is too much of a nuisance to have hanging over my face."

Ava and Wynne were standing by the fence next to the paddocks when they arrived back at the stables. Wynne raised a hand in greeting. Madison waved back.

"Seeing Pops so happy makes me so glad we went into that coffee shop, Lucio."

"It was fate, Madison, like our meeting at the rodeo. Love cannot be ignored it is life, we have to be open to it. Love always finds a way."

CHECK OUT THESE OTHER GREAT READS FROM ROWAN PROSE:

Mandy Eve-Barnett is a multi-genre author writing children's, YA, and adult books. Every story has a basis of love, nature, magic, and mystery. Her passion for writing emerged later in life, and she's making up for lost time. She regularly blogs at www.mandyevebarnett.com, where she encourages and supports the networking of writers and readers alike. Mandy is currently the Secretary of her local writers' group, the Writers Foundation of Strathcona County, and she hosts their monthly Writers Circle meetings. She's past Secretary of the Alberta Authors Cooperative and past President of the Arts & Culture Council of Strathcona County Council.